The Handyman's Habit of Larceny

A NOVEL BY

EVERETT HEATH

Reader House Publishing
The Handyman's Habit of Larceny©
Cover Design: Model T Digital

Everett Heath

Everett was born in Texas. He spent much of his childhood in Europe before returning to the United States. After living in Alaska for some time, Everett now lives in Hawaii.

Chapter 1

Father Roscoe Armstrong bumped his head, crunching his Afro ducking under the visitor's station counter. He readjusted his phone earpiece. At the moment, there was no need to duck and hide because no one was in sight. Not unusual, even for a Sunday. The long, tile hallway of the assisted living center was glinting, empty, and uninviting. He flicked his 'fro back proper and stuffed his pick in his back pants pocket. No mirror around to verify. Father Roscoe remained old school. Sunlight bounced off the fresh waxed floors of the rooms whose doors were open. A good clue determining who was lonely that day—inviting anyone to come pay a visit. And for most, on most days, anyone was invited.

The tall handyman stood in the entry way chuckling, watching Father Roscoe dodge and weave like a boxer sneaking away from the bettors who lost on him. This was not supposed to go down like this at all. Saunders Ravel wore a red retro cowboy shirt with pearl snaps, black jeans, and black half boots.

Looking back to see if Saunders was still waiting, Father Roscoe noticed his legs looked like parentheses stuck together. Roscoe didn't think Ravel looked like any damn handyman.

A bent woman peered out her doorway in her long nightgown, adjusting her permed wig. She watched Father Roscoe bob and weave down the hallway while making a quick sign of the cross to ward off any bad spirits he may have left behind. She turned and noticed Saunders, who smiled and waved. She waved back and disappeared into her room. Smiling, satisfied—she shut her door.

Now Saunders returned to the upholstery store's parking lot across the street. He waited behind the steering wheel, expecting Roscoe's phone call any moment. The upholstery store was closed on Sundays. Saunders had already picked up a few upholstery samples a few days prior. It was just past eleven a.m., and as lunch pangs punched in, he felt the anxiety take over, filling him like a slow drowning—every day for the past God knows how many days, and for a time, how many times over the years. His mind tightened, recalling her sensual excitement stained-glassing his sight. He remembered her offhand, lilting riff on perfume: "One fragrance I love, Pink Fatale Voluspa...can roll it everywhere…cashmere's in it." Now the thought of cashmere in anything other than sweaters and smoking jackets sent Saunders into the trough of the clueless. He knew he had much to catch up on about the lover of Pink Fatale Voluspa. His panic that he may be too late pervaded everyday tasks of late, and extended tasks into unnecessary labor. Stupid actions for no reason. She referred to herself as biblical, although she gave a final scoffing to the Church decades ago. To himself, Saunders referred to her as his soul twister. He had a permanent case of the twists.

Again last night Roscoe had told Saunders outright he was tiring of Saunders moping about. Roscoe thought, *Hells bells, he'd been with Saunders now for how long, two months? This has gotta start going somewhere or he's gonna go even crazier. That boy is in his mid-fifties now and has got to find a world of his own making. He's got to make his world, that's all there's to it.*

Waiting for Roscoe to complete his rescue mission, Saunders's mind dwell time seemed infinite and languishing, leaving him wanting to drive the highways until his thoughts collapsed to a null, and hopefully, nulling the feeling of drowning in distress of his own conjuring.

He recalled expressing God-given thanks the day he arrived in this town. Driving past the sign of any new city's limit for the first time always sparked excitement in Saunders and lent verification to that saying—a new day indeed meant a clean slate—and saved him from drowning. He was all about clean slates and making things new and most definitely not drowning. Prior to arriving he memorized the stats of the new town offered by its Internet site, which proved always to be most telling in what the site did not call attention to. Arriving that day two months ago, cold rain smacked the windshield as the highway was reduced to a wide four-lane surface street with endless street-lighted intersections. The flattest city Saunders could ever remember entering. At the first red light, he jutted his head out the window to determine if his temperature gauge was reading correctly. The temp gauge read forty-three degrees, but his rain-spattered face sensed it was more like thirty-nine degrees. The nationwide Righteous Reverend Delroy James's buoyant sermon had bounced out of the radio, recalled Saunders. The Reverend James's sermon was poke-iron hot, and the resulting impact upon Saunders was the real reason for lowering the window—to feel the sting of cold rain on his smooth-shaven, high-cheeked face. He missed Mass that Sunday, and the Righteous Reverend was always the prime stand-in. At the first stoplight in the new town, raindrops trapped by his eyelashes formed small, soothing pools in his sockets.

Saunders's mind was now back at the upholstery store parking lot, eyes again shut, remembering the pools of rain, pretending not to notice Father Roscoe approaching in a frustrated hurry. Waiting until Roscoe was in earshot, Saunders then sang aloud in a low tone, a silly single, three-note melody:

"Rain, rain, come not near,

Never to mix with my joyful tear

And never, never pool in my beer."

"Do I have to hear your lame, white-ass attempt to sing again?" Roscoe Armstrong jutted his full perspiring face into the open window, breathing heavily and pulling off his priest collar—freeing his bulbous Adam's apple. Ross was his given name, but damn, he decided, it sounded so white. And being past sixty years old, and then some, and by his own reckoning, a black man of complication, he thought it well within his God-given rights to change his first name to Roscoe. Saunders shook his head and reminded himself with assurance that he really didn't miss Mass, not with Father Roscoe hanging around. Never mind the Righteous Reverend Delroy James. Saunders, spiked with a certain impish excitement, now exaggerated his singing like the whitest of white men in the presence of a complicated black man. Then Roscoe gave him the look. Saunders felt the look, stopped singing, and fully opened his eyes.

"Okay, where is she, Chief?"

"She said she didn't recognize me today and turned real scared. Pale-looking kinda scared. Scared me too, so I took off. Let's go." Chief Master Sergeant Roscoe Armstrong (Air Force retired), part-time priest and full-time in love with Magdalena, slumped in the passenger seat, weakly flicked his hand up to get a move on. There was nothing else to say for now. Saunders revved Roscoe's mint condition '74 Ford pickup and returned them to the Scenic View RV Park. *Perfect*, thought Saunders. *We have to do this charade all over again?* How they were going to manage with Magdalena, who was dying, had never been discussed. Saunders decided that was going to change.

Chapter 2

"My early church career was cut short, you see, by the funny grace of God. Hanky-panky with two sisters, can you believe it, was what did it. I thought they were hot at the time. Can't say if that led to a permanent downfall. I didn't consider it no low time though. But the church people gave me hell for it. And out I went, into what they called the 'devil world.' That's what happened to me in the AME. Joined the Air Force instead."

"That's not what I asked Roscoe," said Saunders.

"That's my answer for today. Ask me another time and I may tell you another story. But don't be askin' too soon now."

Inside sat Saunders with big black-framed glasses slipping down his nose, scrunched over the eating table and reviewing his notes on his laptop, legs sprawled out across the sea-foam cushioned bench. No traveling vehicle was big enough for his height, mused Roscoe, sitting across Saunders in a comfortable recliner—the rocking kind, with a squeak in the mechanism just loud enough to have Saunders take notice. Roscoe grinned and rocked. Then the Pomodoro timer went off with a pronounced *ting*. Saunders looked up, electing not to reset the timer. Roscoe pretended to be dozing while grinning. The steady rain created a white noise inside as the gray blanket of clouds moved quickly, impatient to cross the wide, slow-ambling brown river. Soon Roscoe quit pretending and dozed. The squeaking stopped. Georgia O'Keeffe's "Black Iris III" was Saunders's favorite, and a full print was black wood framed and mounted on the only RV wall space without windows or cabinets, just to the left of the rocker where Roscoe snoozed and just behind the passenger seat of his Rolling Haus, as Saunders had come to call his RV. The refrigerator door held a magnetized, enlarged photo of an Ecuadorian river turtle surrounded by brilliant-colored butterflies drinking turtle tears. Why Saunders loved the Black Iris painting, Roscoe understood for some reason. But all Roscoe could do was stare at the butterflies drinking turtle tears and wonder what caused the tears. *What's* in *those tears, and what the hell's goin' on inside Saunders's mind? Good thing I showed up*, thought Roscoe after his first day traveling with Saunders. *Good thing indeed.* At least Saunders had pictures of the fighter jets he flew hanging inside his cramped workspace. Thank God for that. Roscoe kept an eye out for Saunders, making sure he wasn't looking for turtles and butterflies along the river fifty yards behind them. Roscoe watched him run along the river every morning. It did not matter if it was raining or freezing, or freezing rain. Saunders ran every morning. With a damn miner's lamp or some contraption he designed lighting the way. *Man's crazy*, thought Roscoe.

Saunders was not going to ask Roscoe what he did all day dressed as a priest. Roscoe wouldn't tell him if he asked. Tonight, Saunders drove off in his own pickup and left Roscoe watching crummy TV. His current job was servicing kitchens of four Buenos Tacos restaurants owned by three partners, one of whom Saunders flew with in the Air Force while stationed in Germany. Tonight's job: cleaning the kitchen hoods and grease pits of the last of the four. Nasty grease pits at that, thought Saunders. Beyond neglect, though he was getting paid well for this job. The owners' intention being for Saunders to return to service the kitchens every six months—a supposed incentive for taking on the well-paying job in the first place. Over his jeans he wore heavy-duty hip boots. He slipped the goggles over his rainproof hoodie and punched on the portable steamer. *I'll do the easy part before I have to tackle the grease pit. Midnight. I should be done by three or so,* he thought—*if I don't find any surprises nastier than a few rat skeletons.* He hated rats.

The steamer back-splashed against his face, and he occasionally felt a sting from a loosened piece of grit or petrified particle of foodstuff that escaped the sweeper. The steamer hummed white industrial noise, a favorite sound to help blank thoughts swift-streaming across his mind's electronic message board, surrounded by stainless steel. Above him shone hard, naked lights that left him in want of further repose. Stark bright metallic surfaces now steamed shiny, as water droplets slid off the hoods and formed streams of their own, drawn toward the drain hole in the kitchen center. A cleansing. Complete. Until the kitchen fired to life again in a few hours, and the hoods lost their sheen and acquired the cook's signature blend of lard and low-end ground beef, sizzling and hissing upward to collect on whatever surface confronted them. Someone else would have to clean and repaint the ceiling, thought Saunders.

Loosening the nozzle to lessen the sting of water pressure, he turned the steamer on himself, blasting black gunk from his hip boots. A nasty grease pit of a kitchen. The worst of the four. It was just past four a.m. Laying his dripping boots and raincoat over the small red swivel chairs of the fast-food variety, he stood, too tall for the munchkin seats, and sipped stale coffee in darkness, scalding hot from the microwave near the takeout window, as if he were the last Buenos Tacos customer—or the one who never left. The town was coming awake. The rain had stopped as opposing sparse traffic splashed water over each other in the dim rise of twilight.

Saunders merged into the traffic flow, turning on his GPS. The storage rental place was empty, his storage area being in the middle of the middle row. He unloaded his rented cleaning equipment, and proceeded to spread a heavy-duty canvas across the bed of his truck, folding under the excess cloth.

"Continue straight for two miles," said the stoic female voice from his GPS. The darkness abated and the rain stopped as he drove on. Fifteen minutes later he found himself in the upscale neighborhood of town, with large, deep front lawns and oversized houses nesting in tall trees, starting to lose their leaves, far from the street. "You have reached your destination," chimed Ms. Stoic. The house was all but obscured from view, deliberately hidden amongst the trees and a tall wall of evergreen shrubs. Saunders noticed the roof line, a shallow pitch compared to the other homes. A sprawling one-story house compared to the surrounding two-story homes. The straight, short, shrub-lined driveway extended past the left side of the house, leading to a separate two-story garage. It was the first time he had stopped to scout the residence and immediately he concluded the task would take a few attempts. Two lamplights were on in the front rooms. Small floodlights illuminated the garage entrance. The motion detector was set off by a large, thin dog, let outside to do her business. Very well trained, Saunders thought. "Single occupant, female, works in a home studio and travels frequently," he said aloud to himself. *Not that frequently*, he thought wistfully. The other two had been very easy. This one, the last one, to finish the task, was clearly not going to be easy. Saunders had some free time, now that his Buenos Tacos job was finished. He was restless and irritated. He wanted this all to be done with so he could get on with life. Whatever the hell that meant, he thought, shifting into gear and pulling away from the curb. He needed a long run along the river.

Chapter 3

Saunders ranted, "What's your plan after you supposedly rescue Magdalena? You heading off somewhere with her? You *do* know you could very well be accused of kidnapping. Tell me again why I'm helping you with this crazy stunt?" Saunders bent down, clasping his knees, light-headed and winded from his rant—and his run along the river. Sweat rivulets flowed freely from his brow, and the sweat salt stung his eyes. He popped back up erect, waiting for a reply.

Roscoe remained sitting on aluminum steps leading into the RV, sipping his beer as if Saunders was not there. Roscoe lifted his brown beer bottle up to check the quantity remaining. The sky was still mottled gray, but the clouds were drifting noticeably. Maybe the front was finally passing.

"Look here, this ain't no stunt and ain't going to be any kidnapping accusations floatin' around the town. I got a handsome written letter in her very own handwriting with her very own signature on it that we'll leave on her little desk. The letter also states she'll call in a week to let the home know she's all right. It's not like she's skipping out on any payments. They can't be comin' for her money—she's paid up."

Saunders knew it was a bad idea for him to show his face at the home, even if it was only momentary and just inside the entryway. He wasn't going near the place from now on. Handsome letter or not. He'd never seen Magdalena in person. Only a couple of pictures on Roscoe's laptop. Pretty woman, Saunders gave him that.

"You need a beer. Be good for you. Replenish the fluids you sweat outta ya." Roscoe got up, drained the remaining drops of his empty on the wet ground, and went inside the RV.

Saunders was cooling off fast now. Temperature near fifty maybe, he thought. Not quite balmy. He followed Roscoe inside and accepted the cold beer.

"Can't say when I'll try to get her out of that place."

"What'd she tell you when you last talked with her?"

"She doesn't always have her cell phone on. Or when she does she says she forgets to plug it in to charge it," said Roscoe.

"So when was the last time you talked with Magdalena?" Saunders finished his beer in three long pulls.

"Last week."

"She going to remember you next time?"

"Lord, I pray, I hope so."

Saunders tossed his empty in a plastic trash can he kept outside, reserved for the recyclables. A long, hot shower came next. Utilities were cheap at the Scenic View and a ten-minute shower was exactly what he needed now. He stood head down beneath the showerhead, hands up against the wall as if about to be searched for illegal contraband. Lingering doubts pinged his mind about reclaiming the furniture he made, yet sold. He knew it was crazy. Reckless. And if he got caught it would cast a permanent doubt as to his credibility and reliability in any endeavor. But he hadn't been caught yet and he had only one more act of larceny to perform. And then he was returning to Arizona for a good long while.

13

The smell of seasoned grilled pork chops wafted into the bathroom. Roscoe was the cook these days, ever since he joined Saunders. Roscoe would have it no other way. Saunders found cooking to be more of a chore than a pleasure. And it was no small pleasure to have Roscoe around—at least for the cooking. After finishing the pork chops, steamed green beans, and brown rice (Roscoe always made brown gravy), Saunders cleaned up. Little was said during dinner. Saunders was exhausted, and getting back into a day routine would take him about a week. As much as he enjoyed working alone at night, when there was no job to accomplish, he much preferred a normal schedule.

Returning from outside, Roscoe put his phone back in his shirt pocket and announced, "We're now on for Thursday. That gives us tonight and tomorrow night, and the next night to think about the plan." He paused and shook his head, his pacing seeming to help his uncertainty. "Hell, I'm done thinkin' about the plan. It's going to work. It is going to work," said Roscoe, unconvinced he was becoming more confident of his plan.

Saunders wasn't so much concerned with getting Magdalena out of the home as he was with what was going to happen next. *Or*, he thought, *what's the plan if the police are notified and an immediate search gets under way? And somehow my larcenous excursions are somehow revealed?* He said good night to Roscoe and retired into his room in the back of the RV. The one with the king-sized bed. Roscoe slept in the foldout double in the middle of the RV. *I know he's going to want to take my bed when Magdalena joins us*, he thought. Knowing he had to think of some alternative, he let it go any further thoughts until morning. He had no choice. Sleep hit him immediately as the smell of grilled pork chops lingered. He'd awaken hungry.

"Tell me about her, Roscoe." Morning had come and gone, and the long-awaited sun was drying the soggy ground and bringing humidity. Definitely balmy, thought Saunders. *Forget about asking Roscoe how he came to be traveling with me. I'd get elliptical responses and a heavy case of irritation.* And not now, after such an invigorating and cleansing run. Saunders cooled off in an aluminum lawn chair with a white plastic lattice seat and back. Roscoe was dressed in black slacks and a white crew-neck T-shirt. His black priest shirt and collar, plus his black sports coat, were already in his truck. He kept his un-retired, black military low quarters shoes spit-shined and polished.

"You goin' to ask me about her when I'm steppin' out to do some things?" said Roscoe.

"Would you answer me if you weren't going out to do some things?"

"I would—but now ain't the time. Don't wait on me for dinner. I may be late. And I gotta lotta laundry backed up too." Roscoe's flatbed was lined with that tough spray-on, all-weather liner, and he'd customized the whole back end with compartments that could be reached over the top or by flipping down the tailgate. He had built separate accordion doors that were secured with heavy-duty locks. One compartment near the front was completely waterproof.

"My granddaddy was a trombone player from New Orleans. Played in Fate Marable's band up and down the mighty Mississippi—playin' for the white gamblers and their whores. Not sure if it was called jazz back that early, probably was, don't know for sure. Made good money from what I was told. Marable made 'em all learn to read music on sight. He was a tough bastard, so I was told. Marable—and my granddaddy too. He played with Satchmo. Knew him real well. Gotta go." Walking to his truck Roscoe waved his hand over his head.

That was how it had been ever since Roscoe started traveling with Saunders. Never answered the question asked, instead answering a question that seemed to be conjured up in his mind at the time—or perhaps the river they were camped against brought up memories.

Roscoe got in his pickup and revved her up. Great-sounding engine, thought Saunders. Sticking his head out the window, Roscoe yelled, "Remember how a kaleidoscope has all the shiny bits and pieces resting on the bottom of the tube, waiting to be rotated to start the whole explosion of colors and things?" Not waiting for an answer, he said, "You need to grab hold of your kaleidoscope and give it a good back and forth and then take a look inside. And do it again and again. You best not be rotting by this muddy river." He drove on, rolling up his window at the same time.

For some reason Saunders thought that sounded like something a fortune-teller would say. He smiled, thinking that was the first time Roscoe ever answered one of his questions. Then he got the idea to shadow Roscoe today. The town wasn't that large and he figured his truck would be easy to spot, and certainly a black priest in this area would be easy to spot as well. Not waiting to completely cool off, he took a quick shower, got dressed, and left soon after.

Satellite radio was a godsend, thought Saunders as he pulled out of the Scenic View RV Camp. The river was wide, muddy, too shallow in many areas, and not navigable by riverboats, much less canoes. The town did not grow up around river commerce; instead it was the railroad that made the town. Lazy and brown the river always appeared. Those traits Saunders found calming, inducing him into a lazy trance, even when running alongside. He located a Dixieland jazz station. He would have skipped over the station every time had it not been for Roscoe's story about his granddaddy playing trombone with Satchmo. "West End Blues" was the song that caught his ear as he left the river and turned onto the street that led into the middle of the town. Pretty famous song, according to the DJ, who raved about the intro solo—changing jazz forever. To Saunders it sounded like a flurry of notes that ended too quickly, too quick for his novice ears to latch on to a melody. Yet he continued to listen to the station as he viewed the total flatness of the land. No hills, barely a tree outside town, just flatness. The front had passed, leaving hazy blue skies and a prevailing wind, not too cool, just right. He stopped in a doughnut shop known for its coffee. No sartorial display around here other than T-shirts and jeans—worn by men and women, young and old. Fierce pride of their local high school football team was evident by the purple baseball caps. The state university was also a source of pride, well-known for their football team. Farm and railroad people.

It was Monday afternoon. Strolling the sidewalks were older men and women, a few hand in hand. Most walked side by side, the expressions on their faces like strangers, as if by chance they happened to be going the same way, or perhaps to the same store. There were younger women, mostly overweight, in stretch pants of some sort, pushing strollers—and others pulling their kids along by hand; toddlers not quite old enough for preschool. He found St. Patrick's and drove into the church parking lot. Just a few cars were parked near the rectory. Saunders slowly meandered throughout the parking lot of the main grocery store, careful to avoid the shoppers hustling their carts to their cars. He stopped in and picked up some fresh greens mix, baby tomatoes, red and yellow peppers, and a cucumber for a salad. Next stop was the assisted living home. Nowhere could he find Roscoe's pickup. *Maybe he went to another town,* thought Saunders, now starting to feel a bit foolish about his impromptu search. It wasn't that he had little idea of what Roscoe was all about, about what made him tick; it was that Saunders had no idea at all. It had not been difficult having him along these past two months because Saunders knew he was ripe for company, and an interesting yet aloof character like Roscoe was hard to beat. For how long—Saunders didn't speculate, especially since he had not committed to any project after the Buenos Tacos job. Which meant he was getting an impulse to build furniture—his wood shop was calling him to return. Suddenly, the impulse to build conflicted with the impatient urge to collect all the furniture he had sold and re-settle the pieces into his place in Verde Valley. He wanted to be done with the larceny and complete his house.

One shot of espresso was what he needed before he drove back to the RV camp. Looking for street-side parking, he noticed a black man in a full gaping laughter holding the door open for a woman sharing equal laughter exiting the doughnut shop, each with coffee in hand. In his rearview mirror Saunders watched them walk away from him, excitedly talking with their free hands, attempting not to spill their coffees. Roscoe was in his priest attire—complete with his picked-out Afro. The blond woman was in a swirling mid-length dress, wearing a short jean jacket with her sleeves rolled up mid-forearm. Startled by the horn blast behind him, Saunders pulled into a handicap slot, gave an apologetic wave to the irritated man in the black pickup behind him, and turned off the ignition. Stepping onto the curb he noticed the blond woman unlock the main doors to the Walker Performing Arts Theater, where the marquee above them said "Re-opening Very Soon! Keep Watching for the Special Event to be Announced...Soon!" The ornate redbrick building stood out on the block, exuding a sense of swelled pride of some benefactor or benefactors—or perhaps local volunteers working together to resurrect a town's iconic theater of the past, and perhaps further to give a larger sense of pride to those who remained in town, as a remembrance of the times when the piercing whistle announced the arriving trains and generated fresh excitement, not to mention the excitement of catching a glimpse of the exotic, the foreign, and the strangeness of what the trains carried forth.

An old man with a thick, white, furrowed brow paused on the sidewalk in front of Saunders. Small, black, disapproving eyes were distinctly visible. Saunders waved again and started up his truck, noting he did not have a handicap sign dangling from his rearview mirror. Surveying both sides of the street, Saunders could not find an empty parking slot. He pulled out and drove around the block and did not see Roscoe's Ford truck in the rear parking lot of the performance center. As he slowly passed by, Saunders caught a glimpse of a rear entrance door opening. The same blond woman was exiting and approaching the white, imported sport utility vehicle parked nearby. She got in and started to leave. He pulled over and stopped, adjusting his rearview mirror. She pulled out of the parking lot and turned in the opposite direction. Waiting until she was on her way, Saunders made a u-turn and followed her at a paranoid distance. He rolled down his window. He needed fresh air. He watched her accelerate through a yellow light turning red. A grocery store produce truck pulled in front of him, blocking his view as he waited for the light to turn green. Saunders gunned the accelerator and passed the truck but could not see her vehicle. He began a left-to-right visual scan of the parked cars on the street, slowing to search each side street. Leaving town center he decided not to double back. What was he going to do if he found her? *I'd ask her about Roscoe*, he thought. *Ask her what about Roscoe?* He passed the last Buenos Tacos where he had been working. He did not want to do that work anymore, regardless of the steady job and good pay. He didn't need the money. He wasn't ready to think too hard about what he needed.

He now found himself driving to the house where his furniture was residing. He just wanted to focus on retrieving the last pieces and then move on. The day was still as the sun dried up what the rain had delivered the previous days. Startled, he noticed the sport utility vehicle's brake lights coming on and off. It was parked on the street in front the house he'd cased the night before. A medium-sized moving van, backed in, was halfway down the long drive. One burly mover sat in the grass while the other thinner man leaned against the front fender well, finishing a cigarette. Roscoe stopped two houses past the house and looked through his large-sized side view mirror. From their reactions to the woman hurrying out of the SUV with two oversized handbags in the crook of one arm and a white takeout bag in the other hand, they'd been waiting for some time. Saunders watched her apologize profusely, waving the takeout bag wildly about as she delivered her excuse for being late. She gave the takeout bag to the burly man, who with some effort and a wince lifted himself up and, once standing, began rubbing his lower back with both hands. He was not won over at the moment. The woman wasted no time in slipping her free arm around the brawny man, rubbing his arm and dispensing her charm. She seemed tiny against the burly mover. As anxiety took over Saunders, the thin moving man watched the woman attempt to win over his boss. He extinguished his cigarette butt and opened up the moving van doors as the two entered the house through the kitchen door in back. After watching him set up the ramp and roll down the heavy-duty dolly, Saunders pulled away, feeling he was losing another piece of himself. He had sent a text to Roscoe, knowing he'd never reply. Roscoe didn't text and kept his mobile phone off most of the day.

That afternoon, Saunders drove through every neighborhood in the town until his gas gauge blinked red. His legs trembled for the first hour and his heart still felt like an anvil as he pulled in to the Scenic View RV Park. He had no jobs waiting to distract him; none to even develop a plan on, and his wood shop was eight hundred miles away.

****

"She told me all about you, Roscoe, all about you," said Jeanette, whose weary eye flipped to a flirtatious flutter and back in a wink. Her corner smile slid to a smirk as she flirted. Roscoe knew the score. Jeanette was sending mixed signals in order to confuse him, keep him off guard. But she wasn't dealing with an amateur, no sir, thought Roscoe. Just because he never married did not mean he was unaware. In fact, he was very aware, hyper-aware, you might say, of women's behavior with men. *Shoot*, he thought, *once you catch on to their ways, they are no challenge at all. But just because they ain't no challenge don't mean they'll like you necessarily. They gotta see the power in a man, a power that doesn't threaten them but could sure as hell threaten any other man—and that don't mean physical either. Most of it's in the psyche, how you present yourself, how you carry yourself, how you say what you mean to say.*

"You don't say," said Roscoe, unsure she actually had any conversation of the sort with Magdalena.

"I might, and do say," replied Jeanette. She had hips that if swayed against a skinny man could knock him off his stride and cause a knee to buckle. Barely five and a half feet tall and yet she could put on a Kareem Abdul Jabbar height of attitude when she turned it on. *She's got a wide-as-the-Nile smile*, thought Roscoe. *Pretty features. Definitely see Magdalena in her. Definitely.*

"You know she glowed all day long that first day you went to visit her," said Jeanette, now letting down her guard ever so slightly. Jeanette's neutral-colored sofa was accented with pillows that looked as if their slip covers were from scarves one might find in tourist shops; prints of the landmarks and foodstuffs and mountains and ocean beaches each locale was famous for. Roscoe found himself sitting on England and Jamaica pillows. Her modest house was stuffed with furniture. Little tables at each end of the sofa and thick living room chairs, two hutches crammed with porcelain figurines; one of hirsute old men with wide-brimmed hats and suspenders holding up baggy trousers, clustered together laughing and smoking long, thin pipes. Another with dolphins and mermaids swimming about each other as if mutually entranced. Hummel figurines of every kind. Both hutches could hold no more. Her living room reminded him of being stationed in Europe in the late '70s. So many Air Force wives collected all this stuff, officers' wives mostly, and many senior enlisted wives too.

"Nice things you got in your hutches."

"Most are mine—well, not really—half, let's say."

"The other half…?"

"From my mother."

A blend of citrus scents confused Roscoe's nose. A bit too much in the air, he thought. Hiding something maybe. Thick slices of lemon were wedged down in his tall glass of ice water. Nice taste, with the lemon. *May make that a habit in the future, if I can remind myself at restaurants,* he mused, chuckling to himself.

"What's funny?" asked Jeanette.

"Not funny, just smiling 'cause it's nice to be here, visiting." The conversation was not going well.

Although Jeanette appeared none the wiser, she was on to the fact that Roscoe had been probing as subtly as he could muster, trying to determine how strong the emotional ties were between Magdalena and her daughter, long estranged and only recently reconnected. If she still held any ill feelings toward her mother, she hid them very well. So far, Roscoe had been unable to detect any lingering cross feelings, and this complicated his plan. It could put a severe dent in his dream. To make a clean break, no strings of any kind. Just him and Magdalena. No, not a setback, he thought. *Jeanette will appreciate the plan in due time. She'll be grateful. Not a setback. Just some time to take it all in.*

"I plan to stop in to see her later on this afternoon," said Jeanette.

Roscoe raised his brow. "Today you say?"

"After finishing my running around I'll stop in," she said, adding, "I'll tell her all about our nice little visit today. I really do think she likes it there. I thought it was perfect for her."

Roscoe could not have disagreed more. He believed it criminal to lock someone up in a place like that—and call it an assisted living community. He had to control his anger every time he thought of her in that prison. "Wellspring Community." The name itself irritated him. Magdalena was an unwilling participant in the Wellspring Community. Told him so, herself. Her daughter claimed different; claimed her mother loved the place. Roscoe believed he knew the truth. *It'll all work out—for everyone.*

****

Saunders did not want to return to his RV. But then, he could not stand driving around this small town's neighborhoods any longer. There were no blocks or streets or houses that he could connect with. The street names were everyday street names in small-town America: trees, flowers, early founders of the town, railroad themes, and old presidents. Saunders never rode a train in America and could not fathom why anyone would take a train when there were so many roads and highways to explore. The town seemed almost identical to where his wife was from and longed to return after following him around the world during his career in the Air Force. She wanted to return back East to where she was born, visiting her mother on the weekends, get to know her old high school friends and their spouses in person, now that she'd made all the reconnections through the Internet. And that is what she decided to do. He wanted nothing to do with her hometown. She told him, "Then you want nothing to do with me anymore, is that it?" You couldn't argue with that line of reasoning. Three years she'd been living in her hometown. Bought a house with a detached apartment for her mother. Sold her mother's house, downsized her, and moved her mother into the new place. That sealed that deal, thought Saunders, unconsciously heading back to the Scenic View RV Park. His mother-in-law was completely independent, with an active life, involved with the church, and volunteered for almost anything. On-the-go old woman, thought Saunders. He gave her credit for her get-up-and-go spirit. Now his ex-wife was following his ex-mother-in-law's lead. Saunders couldn't stand the East Coast. Never could—even when he was stationed in South Carolina. Not quite ex-wife. No divorce papers had been filed.

Sitting there that afternoon, watching through the side view mirror as the movers dollied the boxes from the house to the van triggered in Saunders every memory of moving from Air Force base to Air Force base. Disassembling their lives room by room, piling up clothes by season onto each bed, agonizing over toys long past their prime and rediscovering never worn clothing and shoes shoved in the dark closet corners, and disgusted with again confronting the accumulation of stuff relegated to remain in cardboard boxes in the garage from the previous move. Later in his career moving served to shed stuff unwanted and seldom used, and the prospect of moving stimulated excited anticipation of the next unknown. On the final move of his Air Force career, he fantasized of not packing anything but his uniforms (because he was not yet ready to let go), blue jeans, T-shirts, and his tools. Leaving everything else in the house behind. The memories crashed his psyche, and raw emotions of every flavor jumbled about his mind as if in a kid's rubber bounce playhouse. He could sum up the experiences as loss and discovery—loss of what took time and effort to discover while at the current station, and the excited and anxious anticipation of the time and effort it always took in discovering the newness each base had to offer.

Despite the mandate of conformity, Air Force bases never were quite the same because the local populace imprinted their way of life, their dreams or lack thereof, their cohesions and disruptions, their temptations and restraints, their ways of conducting themselves and affectations of speech in which they conveyed their conduct, not only upon everything outside the entry gates but also inside the gates. Every moving van transports an interconnected semblance of Jungian memories and a story of lives lived and lives to be reassembled and connected to the next place. His estranged wife was done with reassembling and reconnecting. Saunders was not.

Later that night, Saunders awoke in a full sweat and panic. Forgetting Roscoe's absence, he dressed quickly and drove back to the house. The air was still, the streets were dry, and the back porch light was on. The undaunted glow of the full moon challenged the thick and fast-moving overcast, thwarting the moon's furious attempt to pierce the darkness on the streets. Another front was moving in but nothing moved in this town at three a.m. The air was thick, and creatures and insects lay too still, which evoked some concern—for any noise he made might be heard by anyone as restless as himself, perhaps those roaming about in their dark houses looking for some excuse not to return to bed and lie awake motionless so as not to disturb the other occupant of the bed sleeping soundly, untouched by any distress or worry. He drove past the house, undecided where to park. On the second pass, he slowed and backed in to the long driveway, all the way to the kitchen door entry, turned off the ignition, left his door cracked open to extinguish the overhead cab light, and glanced back to confirm he'd left the tailgate down. With no hesitation, he made his way toward the dining room windows in anxious hope the movers had just started the job and that they had at least another day of packing.

The full moon was relentless and presented him enough light to peer inside without the use of his flashlight. The kitchen looked to be empty. No boxes, nothing on the walls, barren. Some insect was disturbed and let it be known by the intermittent, impatient buzzing, low in frequency but startling in the recognition of just how silent the night was. Saunders crunched undergrowth that seemed to crackle under his weight. He was disturbing the dormant, and frustration mixed with fear quickened his breathing. Sweat formed along his entire brow. His gloved hands grew moist. He saw emptiness inside the house. He turned around the corner, pressing up close to a front window to view what he believed to be the dining room. In the middle of the room was something rectangular and wrapped. Along the walls were what appeared to be chairs, each wrapped for moving. He saw two tall boxes next to the chairs. His heart lightened and the moonlight again broke through a small cloud break, a welcoming light leaking into his life. Saunders retraced his steps back toward the kitchen and without hesitation tested the kitchen door. It was unlocked. He entered and left the kitchen door ajar to see if it would remain open. It did. He slipped off his tennis shoes and once in the dining room he quickly surveyed its contents. He tore through the wrapping and his heart pounded a resounding double thump as he recognized his table. He tightly secured two straps from his backpack to the middle of the table, connecting both with another short strap, lifted the table onto its edge, slung the connecting strap around his shoulder, and carried the tabletop out to his pickup. The bed of his truck was covered in moving blankets. He slid the tabletop into the back of his pickup and returned to the dining room. Adrenaline served as an extra man to lift the large table. Grabbing two chairs at a time, he loaded them into the pickup, on top of the tabletop. He stopped as he realized that there were only seven chairs. The dining room was empty except for the two tall boxes. He dashed into the other large room on the other side of the house. It was also empty. He looked up the dark staircase and hesitated to go up the stairs and check the rest of the house. The eighth chair couldn't be upstairs, he thought. *Why would it?* He returned to the dining room, lifted one of the two tall boxes, which was not heavy, and placed it in the truck. He returned and picked up the last box and managed to wedge it in the front passenger seat. He went back, closed the kitchen door, and put on his tennis shoes. He tied down the chairs with the remaining straps, crept back in his truck, turned on the ignition, and with lights out, slowly drove down the long driveway and turned right onto the street.

Once past the block he turned on his headlights and resumed residential speeds. His heart, however, pounded well above the speed limit, and one thought raced through his cluttered mind a thousand times, at supersonic speed—where was the eighth chair?

Returning to the RV park, he covered the contents of his pickup bed with a brown tarp. There was to be no attempt to sleep. He opened his last bottle of red, a decent French wine from the only wine shop in town, turned on some electronica music—chilled house—checked his cell phone for any messages, and stared at his Georgia O'Keeffe poster of the Black Iris, eliminating the single nonstop question in his mind about the whereabouts of the missing chair and replacing it with why the table and chairs were the only furniture remaining in the house? And why was the kitchen door unlocked?

And then the stupid four-note nonsense tone sounded from his phone. "Going to N.O. C u later. Think it's time for u to split too." His first text from Roscoe. *I'm not sure this counts as a forwarding address,* thought Saunders, smiling and noticing his facial muscles unaccustomed to the stretch.

****

Roscoe didn't consider the request odd. Others might and he didn't care what others thought. He'd been traveling in the Far East using military airlift for the past few months. Retirees being the lowest priority to catch a hop on Air Force transport planes meant having to make sometimes up to two or three treks a day to the airlift terminal to see if he made the manifest. But getting stuck waiting to hop a flight at a base such as Kadena Air Base in Okinawa meant long walks towing his bulky black suitcase on rollers with a full backpack stuck to his sweat-soaked shirt. The air base public bus system was very welcome, but he still had a fair amount of walking back and forth from the visiting quarters to the airlift terminal. Roscoe cursed himself for ignoring his memories of the thick, hot humidity of Okinawa. He would have made this his last visit to the thickly populated island but he had little choice, knowing full well that Kadena AB was a busy military air transport hub offering the best chance to fly out.

He'd arrived from Yokota AB over on Mainland Japan a week ago. He'd been mixing about in Tokyo. He loved Tokyo—in spurts. Tokyo loves blues and jazz. He could fake both on piano. The request from Saunders Revel's father was as timely as finally getting a seat aboard the C-17 going to Hickam AFB, Hawaii. Sweating and stinking from heavy garlic and gin tonics he guzzled at the golf club house bar, he quickly settled in his seat and, once airborne, locked himself in the bathroom to give himself a sink bath and moist towelette wipe over. No amount of mouthwash would suppress the garlic from his breath, but he swirled two hotel room bottles furiously in a vain hope to blunt the smell from the two teriyaki burgers he'd needed the gin tonics to wash down. He went through a box of towelettes and filled the bathroom waste can—sure to make the loadmaster real happy to have him back onboard, he thought. He rinsed and wrung out his V-neck T-shirt before stuffing and zipping it in a big plastic food storage bag, and changed into a clean white T-shirt for the long haul to Hawaii. He bought them in a package of six, wore them once or twice apiece, and then threw them away, buying another six at the next base.

He wouldn't miss the local Okinawans nor their oppressive heat and humidity. He loved to mix with the locals almost anywhere, but there were some exceptions. *The Good Lord knows where I might catch up with Colonel Ravel's son*, thought Roscoe, finally cooling down. *But I'll be in my pickup*, he thought. *If that's what the colonel wants me do to, then fine.* He loved the prospect of hitting the road in his own pickup. Been too long. He thanked the Good Lord for such a quick onset of drowsiness, reclined his seat, pulled up the thin gray blanket one of the load crew handed out, bunched up the cheap little airline pillow, turned on his side, and dropped into a deep sleep.

****

"It's been some time, eh?" Roscoe thought he looked thinner than he'd remembered. Nice guy, he recalled. Quieter than his father. Not quite the sense of humor either. Maybe that'd surface later, but he wasn't holding his breath. Most senses of humor poke out real quick, he thought. Saunders seemed comfortable with Roscoe catching up with him on the road. The Good Lord knew he'd never be in this part of the country had it not been for a damned good reason. And Roscoe had two damned good reasons for being out this far.

Saunders had pleasant memories of Chief Master Sergeant Armstrong, both as a young teenager and as an unvarnished second lieutenant attending the chief's retirement ceremony. As much as he wanted a chief master sergeant like Ross Armstrong backing him up during his own command, that was not to be. The chief who served under him did not have the 360-degree savvy that Armstrong seemed to possess. To measure up to Armstrong was in all likelihood to come up short. And although Roscoe always had a small gut on him, it was overlooked by the absolute crispness of his uniform. The man never even hinted at appearing less than one hundred percent crisp. But he'd let himself go since retirement, thought Saunders—still upright in bearing but lax on how he dressed. Maybe it was because he'd been on the road for ten hours.

"Very good to see you, Chief." Saunders' embrace was firm. A familiar face was welcome, and he knew conversations would be easy because the chief could strike a conversation with a dying match and keep it lit. He wasn't keen on starting them but would warm up and engage after some time, depending on who was in the conversation. Otherwise he would stay silent and courteous and exit when he felt he'd been engaged for the proper courteous amount of time—no more than five minutes. Saunders showed him where to put his luggage, gave him a tour of the RV and where he would sleep, and afterward gave him a tour of the RV park and facilities, should he choose to use the park's lavatories and showers. He then handed Roscoe a Scenic View RV parking card to place on his dashboard.

"Your dad doin' all right these days?"

"Everything's fine down here," Saunders replied, echoing his father's words whenever he called. His father's push-it-up, hard drinking days were long behind him, and he kept himself fit by eating little and walking everywhere.

"He's always telling me about the latest pair of shoes he bought. As if good-fitting shoes were the key to life. Of course he walks as if on a permanent pilgrimage."

"I always knew he was an introspective man. And all that walking about is a dead giveaway. Not sure he'd admit it though. But he is one thinkin' cat, your old man." Roscoe kept adjusting himself on the aluminum lawn chairs Saunders had put him in. He hated those kind of lawn chairs. Reminded him of his youth, in the backyard with all the grown-ups getting completely tore up on Seagram's and 7 Up. And getting loud and sweaty and primitively stupid. This was while the youngsters were still eating and everything. They couldn't wait to start whoopin' it up and callin' each other the damnedest names as they played dominoes. His uncle had what—twenty or thirty of those rickety lawn chairs scattered about the backyard. The plastic mesh shredding on the ends by all the fat asses that crushed them—left by his uncle's friends, who were always too drunk to take them back to their own house.

Roscoe got back up and looked around. *At least the river is wide and lazy, and there's a cottonwood or two and some other tall river trees hugging the banks in little clusters.* Otherwise this RV park would be unbearable to live in long. *There's a damned reason this place and surroundings ain't too populated*, thought Roscoe. Plus the weather—at least New Orleans had some diversions to help you forget the fact that you were at the dirty mouth of the Mississippi River.

"Call me Roscoe now, that's what I answer to these days."

"Okay. Sure you don't want to sit and take it easy? Been a long day for you, I'm sure."

Roscoe rubbed his lower back and stretched. Sitting in those aluminum lawn chairs was exactly what he didn't want to do.

"Sorry, let me get you a beer." Saunders paused and looked back out the screen door. "Or is it Seagram's and Seven? I can get a bottle next time I'm in town."

"Don't bother, thanks. Beer's fine."

Saunders returned with two beers, handed one to Roscoe, and sat down in his chair while Roscoe paced and sipped.

"You gotta hose? My baby needs a real good cleanin'." He gestured over toward his pickup. Saunders got up and showed him one of the RV's storage compartments where he kept his outdoor things and where he stored his lawn chairs.

"Perfect." Roscoe downed his beer in three long pulls.

"Lemme go get a long shower at the public house, get out of these clothes and whatnot."

"You do that and I'll start grilling the chicken."

After retrieving a handled traveling bag, Roscoe turned around and said, "You leave the grillin' to me. Get started on the sides. Roll up a couple of potatoes in foil." Walking to the public house he turned around again. "And if you don't mind, let me prep the grill and stack the charcoal."

Roscoe did not have the ingredients he really needed to make the barbecue sauce that he had in his mind and on his palate, but he made do with ketchup, vinegar, cayenne pepper, black pepper, cumin, paprika, onion, and garlic. He barbecued the chicken in a slow cooker, which he had brought along, predicting Saunders would never think to own one. The grill was for the potatoes. And slow-cooking BBQ left plenty of time for drinking. The crickets carried on as dusk settled upon the wide, slow river.

"Those have to be bullfrogs…hear 'em?" Roscoe was whispering loudly. Insects and bullfrogs were in full-throated competition along the riverbanks. It was late in the season for fireflies but there, in front the two men drinking, was a night show of fluid proportion, illuminating the air in quick pulses of light, as if each pulse illuminated their thoughts about matters serious but made silly, perhaps to ward off any hint of—what? Life's contingency?

"Ain't no worries in the air tonight, Ravel. Y'hear me?" Roscoe was pacing back and forth in full rhythm of the evening's cricket and bullfrog cadences, puffing a long, thin black cigar. "Tonight I'm in the rhythm. I'm in full Pascal rhythm!" His laugh was not that of a cynical clown, but of a craftsman, such as a custom welder, in love with his craft.

Saunders sat on the top step of the side door entryway to his RV, legs sprawled wide, and listened and watched the performance before him: the crickets and bullfrogs in full-throttled high- and low-pitched sound delivery, the fireflies architecting a landscape of light in a dry, still night, and Roscoe, now referring to himself as a black man of complication—in full drunk speak riffing on what it means to be in the full Pascal rhythm. Saunders was at ease and his pressing thoughts were subdued, as if his mind was honoring a white flag of truce with himself. Earlier Roscoe demanded The Stylistics be programmed into the Internet radio station. Saunders had the speakers on loud enough to catch the ear of any bullfrog. The R&B backbeat was the necessary ingredient to the rhythm of the night—just as cayenne and cumin were the backbeat to the BBQ sauce—which, although late in serving due to the slow cooker, was delicious to the last swipe of sauce from the plate. Flicks of charcoal embers scattered above the grill. It was hinting at chilliness, but there was plenty of sensory stimulation to ward off any temptation to shiver.

****

Where to place the money so the owner would find it…? This thought amongst many woke Saunders on a dark, overcast morning that fooled him to sleeping almost past nine a.m. The rain would have awoken him, but the dense cloud layer was holding back delivery, like an anxious and exhausted mother with her firstborn, stubborn to leave the womb. Saunders sprang from bed, his deep sleep rendering him initially unsure of his surroundings. The circumstances were unlike the previous two, where leaving the money was not an issue of concern. The other two homes were occupied. The home here in town was being rented, and now the renter, the owner of the table and chairs, was gone. Leaving the four thousand dollars in an empty house was just short of ludicrous. Perhaps not as ludicrous as stealing the table and chairs and replacing them with four thousand dollars—or maybe it *was* more ludicrous? Saunders's mind accelerated repeated thoughts as his first mug coffee, of a rich and exotic roast, churned his stomach. The ludicrous level of last night's larceny had put him into an irritated morning state. He heard the screen door springs creak open. A flat palm pounded rapid raps on his aluminum RV door.

"Hello? He-llo?" Her midlife twang pierced and startled his thoughts back to the immediacy of the overcast morning.

"Mr. Ravel?" Her taffy-stretched pronunciation of his name caused him to draw a deep slow inhale through his flaring nostrils. His richly caffeinated mind drew attention to the bitterness of taste on his tongue. He popped an ironed white T-shirt off its hanger and put it on, causing the hanger to spring from the closet and onto the floor, and snatched his laid-out black jeans, which were lying on the opposite side of the bed where he slept.

Mrs. Dillingham just wanted to confirm something in her mind, a small thing actually, maybe not worth stopping by to inquire at all. She sensed time was required before a repeated rap on the screen door. But she wanted to stop by because she'd been inclined toward wanting to for some time. Two curious men, a middle-aged white man and an older black man, together, unusual, she knew for certain in her curious mind, unusual more so because she liked them both, for very different reasons. Or…were they really the same reasons? She wasn't sure, but that was okay and fine. Victoria wore tight blue jeans and amply expanded the V in her white V-neck T-shirt. She used to be as slim as a smoker, but quit years ago, and these days her figure tended more toward Mae West than Audrey Hepburn. Thank God she was tall, she always reminded herself. Amazing what tall women can get away with. Her thick brunette hair was pulled somewhat tight and bundled up, secured by an expansive, arced sterling silver clip, a precious gift from her husband, dead now four years.

"Yes?" Saunders had paid in advance, so it must be something else. He kept the grounds clean, emptied the charcoal remains in the designated trash bin, rarely played music too loud (except the one time he and Roscoe partied until eleven p.m.—past quiet hours, yes, but he remembered to turn down the music and assist Roscoe inside because he recognized neither of them had much ability to speak with inside voices). He rarely saw Mrs. Dillingham, maybe a couple of times driving by. Her smile acknowledged her warm feelings. He intuited she was anticipating this encounter.

"So sorry to bother you, Mr. Ravel, honestly."

"No bother. It's okay."

"Victoria." She held out her hand. She backed off the stairs to allow him to step down. His hand was met by a firm, warm grip, not soft, but worn smooth.

"Saunders."

"What an interesting name. Sounds—sounds like a name from another time," she remarked.

He smiled and released her hand. This was a social call.

"Your friend and I were talking the other day and he mentioned you both served in the Air Force. Is that right? Gosh, I'm so sorry for stopping by so early. I really shouldn't have. I do apologize," she said.

"Yes." Saunders was thinking ten minutes ahead of the current conversation.

His mind was also on the furniture in his truck. He glanced over and noticed the tarp appeared not to have shifted or been disturbed. He wished he'd unloaded the furniture into the RV right away.

Victoria sensed this was not going so smooth. *He certainly isn't with it this morning. But he works nights*, she thought, and she felt bad for getting him out of bed. *He clearly looks like he has sleep wrapped all over him.*

Saunders recognized Victoria's regret and put her at ease. "I meant yes, I was in the Air Force." He stood before her with hands clasped behind him and, becoming aware of his superior stance, quickly brought his hands to his sides.

"Well, Mr. Ravel, I just stopped by to let you know, and to remind your friend, about the dance at the VFW tonight, and thought you might want to stop in for a beer. Your friend wanted me to invite you. He told me you aren't working nights anymore?" Victoria's schoolgirl memories rushed back hard. She had not felt this awkward since junior high. High school, however, was a completely different story. Gesturing toward his pickup, she asked, "You getting ready to leave? You look all packed up."

"I am, yes."

"I'm sorry to have bothered you then."

"No, no. It's no bother. I have a new job that I need to get to."

"The VFW get-togethers don't linger on too late. Most of them are 'Nam vets. Four Korean War vets and two left from the Second World War. But a few younger ones have stopped in over the past few years because of Iraq and Afghanistan. My husband was a lifelong member. Good people down there. Just thought you'd like to get out of your RV and meet some of them. But I see you're movin' on," said Victoria. "My husband didn't make it out of Iraq."

Saunders' military instincts were never far from him. Nor his experiences as a commander. He gave a respectful pause and said, "You have my deepest condolences."

"Four years now," she said, standing tall, looking directly into his eyes. She carried emotion within her but not on her face. Victoria's voice stayed strong.

"Both my kids are in the military—can you believe that?" Her smile was pure affection and pride. "Daughter in the Marines. Son too. My daughter Lucy's the oldest. Talked her brother into joining. He of course swears that's not true."

Victoria succeeded in evoking laughter from them both. As usual, she was doing all the talking.

A very nice woman, lonely, thinking I'm lonely too. Very nice gesture, Saunders thought. He was definitely going to text Roscoe and asked him about Victoria. *Appears he's scheming. Where is Roscoe?*

At least she tried, thought Victoria.

"My girlfriend swears your friend Roscoe is a priest. She swears by it. He wears black and a collar and all…"

Their body stances shifted. Victoria's was leaning on her right leg with her left leg bent and hands on hips, Saunders moved to parade rest, hands back behind him. Surprised Roscoe was roaming around in public as a priest and not just dressing up when visiting Magdalena at the assisted living center, but then for a reason he couldn't explain, Saunders was not surprised. Roscoe was full of it, and it made him thankful for knowing him. Everyone needs a crazy person in their life, especially those too cowardly to be crazy.

Saunders lied, saying, "That's news to me. He's a retired chief master sergeant. Of course I don't know if he attended seminary after the Air Force. That's a stretch in my mind." Awakened now and needing a few cups of coffee, Saunders was feeling light, yet not interested in going to the VFW that evening. He wanted to move. But Victoria was a welcome sight this morning. She spiked his curiosity, dormant for some time, and very much missed.

"I'm in serious need of a cup of coffee. Mind if I grab a cup? Like one too?"

"You go right ahead… No thanks. Had mine already this morning. Thanks anyway."

"I'll be right back." His disappointment flashed and disappeared as he entered his RV. "Your friend, where'd she see Roscoe?"

"Well, actually, I saw him too. He entered the theater in town yesterday with my friend. New friend, actually. Sad though, she's leaving too. Anyway…"

"What do you do at the theater?"

Replying in an *aw shucks* way, Victoria said, "Oh, you know, I'm a volunteer. You know, I'm not talented in that way. I just do what needs to be done. Plenty of getting rid of old stuff and rubbish and whatnot. I'm just a worker bee on the theater restoration project. It's kind of fun at times. Boy oh boy, is she super talented."

"Who?"

"Huguette. That's her name. So unusual, especially around here. Most likely anywhere I'd imagine. Sounds so old. Like your name."

"Oh, I didn't mean it like that," she said, touching his arm.

Saunders sipped his hot coffee and smiled. He observed Victoria, so concerned now about offending. She was one to say her mind first and let the consequences flow. She maintained the appearances of embarrassment, though she was not at all embarrassed. He knew she wasn't afraid of much. Except loneliness.

Victoria shivered in anticipation of a wet chill yet to fill the air. Why she wasn't wearing something warmer no longer crossed Saunders' mind.

"Why would he dress as a priest?"

"I have no clue." Saunders wondered if Victoria's friend ever returned to the house to discover her furniture missing.

"Huguette seemed totally at ease with him...like they were old, close friends. Of course, she is the real clingy type. Hugs everyone. Like she's trying to get inside someone, to see what makes them tick. Real, real curious type, too. Guess that's why she's so good at what she does."

He debated whether to ask Victoria any questions about Huguette. No, he decided, no suspicions need be raised.

"She's coming tonight too. It's her last night in town and the mayor will be there to send her off. She's fond of military guys. Sweet-talked half of those who wouldn't even bother to volunteer. She did a fine job overseeing the restoration. She has wonderful ideas. The theater's beautiful."

Saunders slowly finished his cup of coffee to disguise any reaction to what Victoria said. He turned and pitched the last drips onto the grass.

"Thank you very much for the invitation. I can't guarantee I'll make it. Thanks again."

"Okay, then. Well...you're welcome. May see you again, at least before you depart?"

"Maybe."

Saunders nodded and returned quickly to his RV. At dusk, he backed his pickup truck to the RV side entry door. He open the RV door, lowered the tailgate, and removed the binding straps holding down the tarp that covered his table and chairs. No other RVs were parked nearby. It was not the season for RV'ers to be in this part of the country.

Finishing his run, he noticed Victoria's black pickup was gone. Quickly he transferred all the chairs and the table into his RV. They took up most of the limited room inside. To give him some room to move, he placed two of the chairs on the opposite side of his bed, lying on their sides, seats pressed against each other. The chairs reminded him of lovers interlocked in the middle of the bed, their legs extending in opposite directions. Saunders laid the legless table on top of the seat booths of his small dining table. He returned to his pickup, removed and folded the tarp, stored it in an underneath storage compartment next to his lawn chairs, and returned his truck to the concrete slab that was his RV spot's dedicated parking slot. The rest of the day was spent prepping the RV for departure. He was paid what he'd asked, told his friend who was part owner of the Tacos Buenos that he'd think about returning in six months, returned all the rental equipment he'd been using, and gave the keys back to the manager of the rental storage units. He was leaving early in the morning.

For the rest of the day his mind was preoccupied with whether or not to attend the party at the VFW. As the day advanced he debated with himself the risk and rewards of going to the dance. He'd accomplished all the checklist items prior to departure, save for gassing up the RV. His immediate reward was a full of glass of red wine from the opened bottle in the refrigerator. The first sip was a taste test. Satisfied (as he always was) with the taste, his second sip quickly followed the first, finishing a third of the glass. Tonight and tomorrow morning's ablutions were at the public showers. He put on his track pants and jacket, grabbed his bathroom kit and towel, slipped on his rubber shoes, and made the short trek to the showers. Under the moth orbiting an open lightbulb, Saunders leaned under the strong spray of the showerhead, hands against the wall as if being searched, and let the hot spray pulsate against his neck. He wished for Roscoe to return his text he sent him prior to setting off for the showers. He thought about his designs for a tall armoire, its purpose yet unknown. But he was looking forward to sketching the ornate doors and legs that he'd been thinking about. A dark wood. Contemporary, with overt classic influences. He left crafting furniture from reconstituted wood to others. Saunders had a supplier that always came through for him. After Saunders built the koa wood rocking chair he insisted upon, his supplier's prices seemed to be a hell of lot more reasonable. Saunders was waiting for his wood supplier to notify him when to pick up his latest order. Sometimes he waited up to six months.

Entering his RV he noticed his cell phone message alert flashing.

"U R going 2 the VFW. She's not expecting U 2 show. She knows."

He placed his cell phone down on the legless table taking up most of his RV living space. He finally noticed a brown and red designed business card envelope taped to the brown shipping paper wrapping his table. The business card was velvet red with gold-embossed ornamentation along the borders and old-fashioned lettering in gold—Roscoe would have called it a New Orleans whorehouse card. “HS Designs Co.” On the back read, “Huguette Sands, Proprietor.” And below, a phone number and a website address. Saunders did not sell his furniture to this Sands woman. He sold that particular dining room set to an older man looking to surprise his partner, who was evidently very, very picky about house furnishings. The buyer seemed convinced the dining room set would meet his partner’s approval. Convinced Saunders too. His partner must not have approved very highly, thought Saunders, smiling, and he allowed himself for a brief moment to enjoy the sense of pride in knowing that at least the Huguette Sands woman had an eye for unique furniture as he reviewed her business website, noting her design works. She concentrated on restoration projects, according to her website. Theaters, such as the one she just completed in town, restaurants, amphitheaters. Small public commissions in California and Nevada, accenting and ornamenting a park visitor center, and a city hall in an old mining town that had a resurgence when the nearby ski resorts started expanding and curious tourists began to spill over into the town, now filled with cafes and art stores. Her biography was sparse, saying nothing at all about her background, just describing how she became interested in restoration. No picture of her on the website, save that of a sketched profile silhouette of her face. Angular, small nose, distinctive chin, and hair below her shoulders, head arced up in an open laugh.

Slowly, the picture pricked Saunders' deep memories. Then, an instant flash of heat and dizziness overcame him and he exited the website and hurried to his bed to sit down. With little pause, he fell back on his bed and closed his eyes. His heart felt as if his mind had opened the floodgates, as if memories lying still in the bottom of a deep, cavernous lake were rediscovered and violently stirred by an unknown force and now coursing, out of control, throughout his system. But those memories had not always lain so deep and so still. For many years they kept stirring about and creating moments of tumult and angst, followed by the remembrance of fleeting joy that was just as palpable as it was fleeting. And always accompanying the joy was a lingering, soft sting of regret. Fearful that recollection bind him to the past and blind him to the present, Saunders never spoke her name and rarely engaged in any conversation, either with himself or anyone else, of their time together, long ago. But no matter how diligently he persisted in avoiding any memory or mention of her, he knew only too well how deeply she had infused herself inside him. His recurring dreams never let him fully forget. And he always believed himself to be all the better for her infusion than without. Saunders believed she altered his very being, down to the DNA level. And since she did to him what he felt to be impossible for anyone to do to another, he never spoke about it to anyone, for no one would possibly believe him. Or, they would think him crazy.

Seeing her with the two men moving her out of the house had created his first suspicion. Her mix of playfulness and flirtatiousness, the way she arched back and released an infectious laugh, a kind of high, husky laugh as she grabbed the closest arm of any man to make him experience the delight she clearly was having at whatever comment she felt inspired to make. Most men were immediately entranced, the less gifted in looks and talent, the more so. Her charming manipulations were widely known, and only talked about out loud by other women, clearly not in possession of her charm, nor probably ever would be. Men, and many women, just thought of her as completely charming, and were less concerned by her manipulations than by the lack of attention she may decide one day to afford them.

Saunders became a lifelong member of the VFW just before he retired. His operations officer talked him into it. "Yet another great excuse to drink beer," said his Ops O, a fighter pilot who needed no excuse to drink beer. Saunders found himself driving into town, barely cognizant he'd decided to stop by the party. His thoughts were elsewhere and everywhere in between. His son Allan texted him before he left his RV. Just a "how's it going," with the expectation they would talk on the phone sometime soon. Saunders missed his son and sent thanks to the sky that they got along so well.

The cacophony of crickets, frogs, and insects making whirring sounds invaded the evening stillness. A damp chill breezed by as if en route to someplace else. The VFW hall stood alone in a large lot with hundreds of parking spaces, a former bowling alley that became obsolete as fast as video games increased their fidelity and complexity. Not all small towns let their bowling alley die, but this town almost did. The vets thought otherwise. A Vietnam war widow who won the lottery some years back sent the VFW a hefty donation, instructing the members to buy the bowling alley, keep it going, invite the public to play a few days a week, and drink beer, bowl, and bullshit to their hearts' content. Initially the members of VFW 0609 were not in the least enthused about how the donation was to be spent. They all longed for a nice hall, but away from town, an oasis of their own choosing, a place set apart and separated from the rest. Perhaps because that was how many of the Korean and Vietnam vets felt; they were apart from the rest of the world, and they grew to carry that apartness as its own badge of honor, even more distinct from being a veteran in a foreign war. And it may have been the widow's intent not to give many of the old-timers the satisfaction of remaining apart, even with full knowledge her late husband would not approve of her motives—if that was her motive at all.

The bowling alley was in the middle of town, across the street from the newly renovated Walker Performing Arts Theater. The Premiere Lanes sign was the original neon sign. In the lower right corner was the VFW logo and post number. Premiere Lanes was open to the public on Thursdays and Saturdays only. The other days were for the members and their guests. Tonight was Saturday and the parking lot was full. Saunders had to park at the rear of the Walker Theater. It was a particularly crisp, cool evening. The winds had moved on westward, leaving a cloudless sky illuminated by the still full moon that seemed as if its orbit had tightened around Earth. It appeared as if you could drive onto its detailed surface as soon as you reached the horizon.

About a dozen men and women were just outside the bowling alley doors, smoking and laughing with beers in hand. Men in jeans and collared shirts, their sharpest flannel shirt; a few wore western shirts. The women all wore dresses. It was a perfect occasion to dress up, knowing that other than church such occasions were rare. Just past nine o'clock and the party was in full motion as Saunders entered. A few of the smokers took notice of his tall frame, dressed in black jeans and wearing a black sport coat over his crisp white shirt, all trying to recall if they'd ever seen him before. The air conditioner was in a losing battle cooling the place as the loud, excited voices yelling over the country music poured out of the party, into the parking lot, and down the main street of town. It seemed everyone in town was there tonight. Small children ran through the adults in small Conga lines, following their chosen leader for the moment, who was leading them to their next little adventure, if only to escape their parents' attempts to corral them in one spot to keep an easy eye on them. To the right, twenty-five yards away, was the long L-shaped bar and shoe rental counter. Just beyond the bar were four pool tables packed with players, and beyond a row of classic pinball machines lined up against the wall, all flashing and ringing as if in some orchestrated sequence. Every pinball machine was surrounded by intense lookers-on, cheering the person banging away at the steel balls, propelling them into the bumpers that rewarded them with bells and sirens, bright, flashing white lights, and an escalating point tally. Some were so good the counter seemed to be nothing but a blur of unreadable numbers. Music burst from every corner of the building. And everyone of drinking age or close to it had a plastic cup of their favorite libation in hand. To the far left, couples danced on what looked to be two bowling lanes that had their gutters removed and replaced by the maple-pine-maple striped flooring to match the lanes' first twelve feet of maple, followed by pine, and capped off by maple where the pins would sit, which was now the perch of a DJ station, where a young, scruffy-faced man wearing a greasy old baseball cap backward spun the crowd favorites. On the walls and around the entire room, just below the ceiling, full-sized American flags were draped. Saunders guessed at least fifty American flags were on display, with the Nebraska state flag in the middle, against the far wall, over lane number six. The semicircle seats behind every lane were filled as bowling balls tumbled out of players' hands, wiggling their ample-sized butts in self-congratulation for knocking down the pins.

Tonight reminded Saunders of returning from the Middle East after a deployment and being allowed to finally drink beer again. Those return parties started loud and escalated rapidly to dizzy states of rowdy drunkenness since everyone had been without alcohol for six months. Behind his observations of the big party ran a strong undercurrent of intense emotional anticipation. As much as he wanted to see Huguette Sands, to see if she was who he believed her to be, a sense of loneliness invaded him, as if he was transplanted from another time and deposited in a giant room of strangers and human loudness that felt familiar in its vibe but completely foreign in its purpose for such an occasion. As if one really needed an occasion to engage in the longing ritual of connection. Because certainly most, if not all of the townspeople couldn't care less about the renovation of a theater. But Victoria said this party was for Huguette Sands—a temporary town citizen, here to oversee the theater renovation and move on. Huguette had either made an all-encompassing impression on the locals or many in this town were inclined toward social gatherings.

Approaching the bar, Saunders found himself entering the infectious aroma zone of barbecue chicken. Set up along the adjacent wall of the pinball machines was a buffet with Bunsen burners blue-flaming the bellies of what appeared to be an endless line of deep, stainless steel chafers. The wait line was gone but there remained a half dozen or so good-sized men making regular runs back for more, every one of them ignoring the little placards on the table with neat handwritten descriptions of the contents and lifting each chafing lid for a peek inside for themselves. Beautifully barbecued chicken separated out into white meat and dark meat, brown beans with bits of bacon, green beans, corn on the cob, corn bread, baked potatoes, macaroni and cheese, grilled hamburgers and hot dogs, and at the end of the line, vats of sweet iced tea, pink lemonade, and restaurant-sized steel cylinders of coffee. A wide-smiling, short, fat, balding man puffed his red cheeks while carrying a chafing tray of hidden contents. He suddenly stopped in front of Saunders.

“Damn, you’re tall, mister! Eat up, please, plenty of food, God knows. This here’s dessert.” He scurried to the end of the line and swapped the empty chafer for apple strudel. Saunders took his filled plate to an empty seat at the end of the bar and began to dig in. The bartender, busy talking with two other men at the opposite end of the bar, finally noticed Saunders and walked down and said, “If you need a beer, there’re kegs all around this place.” He was a big-gutted man wearing a white V-neck T-shirt and blue jeans. His was not an unfriendly face but neither was it welcoming.

“Any wine?” asked Saunders.

“Red or white.”

“Red please.”

“A glass or half a carafe?”

“Half a carafe will be fine, thanks.”

The bartender pulled up a large bottle of red table wine, a label Saunders nor anyone else would ever recognize, uncorked the already opened bottle, and filled the small carafe. He turned around and grabbed a wineglass from the row and placed it and the carafe in front of Saunders, who had pulled out a ten-dollar bill and placed it on counter.

“Seven fifty.”

“Keep the change. Thanks.”

“Thank you, mister.” Saunders pulled his lifelong VFW membership from his front pocket and placed it in front of the bartender. “No need, mister, I could tell,” said the bartender, and he returned to the end of the bar to continue talking with his friends.

Behind the bar were red, green, and yellow flyers posted, advertising Classic Rock and CW Nite on Saturdays , R&B Nite on Middle Month Thursdays, and Conjunto & Salsa Nite on Last Saturdays. The full-length mirror behind the bar was filled with gold speckles, a remnant from the late sixties and a reminder of the power of nostalgia. Saunders ate slowly, not wanting to move from his seat at the bar. He felt invisible at the moment and preferred it that way. Through the gold-speckled mirror he was able to observe the entire goings-on of the party. Pockets of people huddled together and laughed and talked above the loud classic rock music to create a din of voices over-layering the now country rock medley coming from the speakers. It was a comfortable feeling, the sort of din one could hide within. Saunders lifted his wineglass for his first sip, waiting to finish his meal before working on the half carafe. The slight vinegar odor of the wine elicited a smile from Saunders but did nothing to quell the anxiety he felt swelling in his chest. He finished the first glass without haste and poured another. Other than the two bartender friends at the end of the bar, the stools were empty. Everyone was huddled in their groups or orbiting around the aluminum trash cans containing kegs of beer, passing the tap from one red plastic glass to another, and the memories of doing the same twenty-plus years ago flooded him as Saunders smiled again, recalling one attempt to make homemade wine and getting drunk while trying to figure out how the bacteria entered their batch to cause the vinegar taste, when they were absolutely, drunkenly convinced they were precise and meticulous in their instruction-following. They drank the wine anyway, got further drunk, and the lingering, stabbing headache the next day served as a permanent warning never to attempt making wine again. Thank God he recovered from that experience, thought Saunders, because he loved red wine, which may have been more a testament to his tenacious love for the woman who urged him to try to make homemade wine in the first place.

Saunders had an ideal perch from which to view the entire bowling alley and search for the woman he did not want to engage face-to-face, as much as his swelling desire to brush against her again overwhelmed him, like a song with an entrancing melody that repeats over and over and envelops the listener, who feels like a welcome prisoner in the cocoon of the sweet guitars and steady heartbeat drumming in which the bass weaves its addictive line and binds the song and listener tight—making the song and the listener one. As much as he desired to see her face, he diverted his eyes only toward the men in the crowd, imagining, of the men Saunders observed, which of them she would gravitate toward, which of them she would pull into her orbit and charm, with the addict's hope they would charm her in return. He knew they would not necessarily be the handsome men, but men who sparked her curiosity with their ease of motion in her presence—and how they said what they felt they wanted to say. But there were only faces of strangers, even though they all seemed dimly familiar in their shapes and haircuts and mannerisms. Saunders didn't mind not seeing a familiar face tonight; he believed it helped to leech from his veins the anxiety and unwanted anticipation of seeing her.

Somewhere very nearby—the pop, pop, pop of popcorn, spilt over the seasoned kettle, soon followed by the luring odor of butter salt sprinkled atop. Through the speakers, John Lennon's lone harmonica introduction to the Beatles song "I Should Have Known Better" began and then again Saunders was away in an instant, away from current time, and through the gold-speckled mirror he now watched girls and boys of his late teenage years mix about in an excited concoction of laughter and teasing as gutter balls wiggled down the sides of the lanes. From his remembrance his anguish was extinguished as if by a hidden breath, before its suffering power had any chance to take a deep hold of him, and in a second instant the emptiness of Saunders became filled with a burst of joy that touched his essence and dissipated like frankincense from a priest's thurible. Anyone watching Saunders would see a man transfixed, his mind clearly not of the present moment. It was not Victoria from the RV park's repeated tug at his sleeve, it was The Laugh—the hoarse, warm bursts that never reached the level of a cackle and then trailed off into a wistful sigh that returned Saunders to the VFW party. Still staring into the mirror, he followed her laugh, sending his mind into a spin as he lowered his head and yet strained to look up into the mirror.

Huguette Sands was gliding right behind him with three older vets in ambling tow, corralling her toward the opposite end where the bartender roosted.

"Are you all right?" said Victoria, her shiny hair professionally styled to ensnare, wearing long eyelashes and perfume of strong citrus. She sat in the neighboring stool beside

Saunders, in between Saunders and the opposite end of the bar, and through the mirror Saunders watched Huguette and her escort of loping veterans stop to talk with the bartender and his two friends.

"Mr. Ravel…"

The bartender took notice of Huguette, and one of her escorts said to bring her another glass of red. The bartender left his friends and approached Victoria and Saunders to fetch the bottle and pour a glass.

"Hello, uh, hello. I'm sorry," mumbled Saunders.

"For not remembering my name? Oh, that's okay."

"No, no, I remember your name. It's Victoria." For Saunders, the past and the present slapped against the sides of his brain, causing his mind to go full tilt and dizzy—he was unsure if any number of attempts to reset would return his mind to the way it was before.

"You two need anything from the bar?" The bartender knew Victoria, but neither of them reacted in any way toward one another.

"Manhattan for me, Chambers, please," said Victoria with a tight smile but soft tone.

"Another red wine for you? I'm pourin' one for the lady down there," said Chambers, nodding backward toward Huguette and her new friends.

"Uh, sure…Thanks," said Saunders.

"Yes!" said Victoria, grateful Saunders had remembered her name.

Saunders pulled his money clip out and placed another twenty-dollar bill on the bar. "The Manhattan's on me," he declared.

Victoria's emerald green cocktail dress was not out of place this evening, for most of the women wore wearing dresses.

"You look nice this evening," said Saunders, in a formal tone and soft voice, careful not to trigger any reaction of actual personal attraction, for he was not attracted to Victoria in the slightest, regardless of Huguette's presence fifteen feet away, her face still hidden from him due to her surrounding escorts.

It was no longer a mystery to Saunders who she was. In fact, once he saw her with Father Roscoe walking away from him and toward the renovated theater, he knew. But Saunders chose to float in the dreamy realm of incomplete certainty of her identity, because doing so fully captivated his complete awareness of nothing else but her. And he wanted to remain a captive of the most powerful memories he possessed. These were not static but dynamic memories that had been built upon over the years, carefully constructed. Layer by layer of imagined experiences, a favorite one being in the same sunlit room, sitting on the same lush sea-foam leather sofa within arm's reach, and sharing the same joyous air distilled from the mutual titillation of each other's mere presence. He wanted to roam a skyscraper filled with that air. Or perhaps capture that air in tall blue bottles that for decades were empty and adrift but that returned to land, somehow filled and now resting upon shimmering white sands.

Victoria needed no further evidence other than Saunders' wistful demeanor and his inability to look away from the mirror.

His nod was very slight yet repetitive, answering Victoria's question that would never be asked. Nodding, as if he was immersed in a favorite tune with a rock-steady beat.

Victoria, deflated, joined Saunders's unwavering gaze into the mirror, watching Huguette in full command at the opposite end of the bar. The dour bartender was now no longer. Saunders' complicated smile came on very slowly, giving Mona Lisa a full run for her money. As he watched Huguette, each facial movement of his was the result of unfolding memories—both from the past and the future—experiences lived and wanting to be lived. The mirror now reflected Saunders's skinny teenage years, the awkwardness of boys near girls, the protection of the pack of boys from most anything that was new or different (such as girls), the mutual laughing to cover up the anxiousness of uncertainties of ever knowing what girls really liked about boys.

Then the DJ cut the music, turned up all the lights, and asked for everyone's attention as he began to alternately dim and brighten the lights to the entire bowling alley. Saunders's mirrored remembrances vanished as he watched the corpulent teenagers now present grudgingly pull out one ear bud to give a few moments of attention to Mayor Virginia Cockrell, a stout, bowling ball of a woman possessing a high-pitched chirp, taking the microphone from the DJ and waddling to the center of the dance floor, accompanied by an angular young man in pressed khaki slacks and a salmon polo shirt following behind in deliberate short steps, with something in each hand. She wore a red checkered square dancers skirt, and her calves were thick, down to her feet, her right foot tapping out a cadence long-residing in her quick mind. She wasted no time calling the gaggles of partiers to order.

Huguette and her posse turned their backs to Saunders's gaze and their attention to the mayor. Saunders remained fixed, continuing to watch all through the long mirror, and refocusing every few seconds on Huguette, waiting for her to flick back her hair. Victoria took her Manhattan, thanked Saunders, and walking in front of Huguette gave her a smile of acknowledgment and joined the crowd forming around the dance floor. Huguette reached out and touched Victoria's arm as she passed by.

"All right people…so nice to have such an enthusiastic turnout tonight!" The crowd quieted and then erupted in cheers and whistles. "Thank you, Veterans of Foreign Wars, for hosting this celebration!" Much louder cheers now, and whistles from all corners of the bowling alley, the lights being turned on full, exposing the townspeople in their insulation and causing them to pause momentarily from their entrenched habits. With few exceptions, they were fat and seemingly happy.

"Now where's Huguette…flirting somewhere with the veterans I'm sure!"

Huguette's posse of blue-jeaned and red polo-shirted vets nudged her away from the bar and toward the dance floor. Huguette needed no prodding, swiftly leaving the men, and without hesitation strolled onto the dance floor next to the mayor, creating an unconscious and innocent lampoon in the contrast in body shapes and dress selection. The exchange of thank-yous and gifts of appreciation became a blur of words for Saunders, and he closed his eyes, waiting to hear only her voice, her always playful way of putting sentences together, flattering and teasing at the same time. Her voice always seemed like listening to music; at times frenetic and dancing in her sweet pitch, and in moments of quiet, soft and purring as she trailed off uncompleted thoughts. Then a booming round of applause and whistles as the lights dimmed, the disco ball began its glittering rotations, and the springy guitar intro to Earth, Wind and Fire's "Shining Star" was released from the speakers. And in full Afro, Father Roscoe slid onto the dance floor, whisked Huguette back into the middle of the floor, and both began to dance. There he was, in black priest clothes and collar, bumping and gyrating and waving his arms and snapping fingers high above his sweat shiny face, beaming a smile that could be seen in the next county.

Huguette was in some form of ecstatic soul dancing, head back laughing, then eyes closed, focusing on each second of the rhythm, arching and grinding, also defying her age by decades. The crowd screamed and whistled, as the less inhibited took to the dance floor to join them. No couple came close to matching Father Roscoe and Huguette's intensity. Saunders remained on the bar stool, looking through the mirror at them dancing— transfixed. While Huguette's back was toward Saunders's gaze through the mirror, Roscoe, positioning himself to face Saunders, began waving for him to come onto the dance floor, his eyes wild, mouthing in grossly exaggerated motions: "Get your ass over here now!" Huguette, having willingly succumbed to the tight, funky orbit of "Shining Star," was oblivious to Roscoe's intentions.

Saunders watched Victoria snake her way through the crowd and join in with Roscoe and Huguette, who opened her eyes and gave a ferocious hug to Victoria. Roscoe then turned away toward the DJ table. Saunders stood up to keep a visual on Roscoe, who now had left the center of the dance floor, hurrying through the crowd toward the main entry doors. Roscoe turned back again and began waving his hands above his head—using frantic motioning to Saunders to follow him. Saunders looked over at the dance floor. Victoria and Huguette were dancing together, letting it all hang out, like long-lost soul sisters in a joyful reunion. Saunders turned into the crowd and stepped onto the dance floor, towering over everyone. Victoria saw him approach, her dancing slowing, her eyes never leaving him. Huguette was dancing in eyes-closed, funk ecstasy. He moved back her hair and put his full outstretched hand upon her shoulder, hot and damp from her dancing. Her eyes opened as he turned her to face him.

"My god, I *love* your furniture. Absolutely divine. Heavenly. I want to be your upholsterer."

"Huguette?"

"I *love* that name! Don't you?"

She took his hand from her shoulder and kissed his palm. "Roscoe needs you. Go find him." Saunders embraced her so tight Huguette could not inhale. She didn't care if she could not breathe, returning his embrace in full. Huguette was willing to die at that instant. That would be fine. She had other similar thoughts of dying in moments of ecstasy, for she believed dying in ecstasy was as paramount to living. Saunders released her, her scent of frankincense lingering with him, and pressed through the crowd that thinned as he neared the exit.

"He's got my mother!" screamed a woman behind him. Saunders kept moving toward the door, following Roscoe, whose arm was wrapped around the waist of a woman in a bright flower-printed dress. They were out the door and gone.

"That black man's taking my mother!"

Saunders slowed approaching the door, and arriving at the door, turned around and stopped.

"Get out of my way, asshole!" screamed Jeanette, in full fury, all five feet of her, attempting to push Saunders aside. Slowly, Saunders turned back around, opened the door, and held it open for Jeanette. She ran out into the middle of the parking lot, searching left and right, looking for Roscoe and Magdalena.

"Where'd they go?" she screamed to the small crowd of smokers milling outside. Joining her now was a thick-set man, not much taller than her, breathing too heavily for his age. The smokers were not paying attention to who entered or left the VFW hall. After interrogating a young couple, Jeanette took off in the direction they pointed, her chubby husband in trail, now showing a menacing look, the best he could do at the moment to support his enraged wife.

Saunders was impressed Roscoe and Magdalena had disappeared so quickly, barely having a couple of minutes head start before Jeanette burst out the door. He stood alone in the parking lot staring at the entry door, the smokers having returned to the wide sidewalk surrounding the bowling alley. He waited.

Chapter 4

Roscoe stuck in a new CD he mixed—Sly Stone, Isley Brothers, Jimi Hendrix, Curtis Mayfield—and the Great Al Green. He pressed pause. Magdalena had fallen asleep on his shoulder and he gently laid her head on his lap. She had not moved in two hours, her mild breathing barely noticeable as Roscoe watched the night surrender to dawn. His window was rolled down as he slowed and pulled over off at an interstate rest stop. Roscoe was still too far from home to hear all the migratory birds and smell the water. Living near the river with Saunders confirmed that he needed to head home. It was time to go back. Long overdue. He wouldn't stay long, but he had to go.

Gas and coffee were the first things of this morning and he knew Magda would want a shower and something to eat. For once she had listened to him and packed what he told her to pack. *The woman's damn near impossible*, he thought, looking down on her, curled up on the bench seat, using his lap as a pillow. But it was when she wasn't impossible that he fell for her. And deep did he fall, he thought. In fact, he was still falling. This was no way for a lady to travel, and he had a plan to correct that. As much as he wanted to get off the interstate and hit the small roads, the only way he could make time and distance them from Nebraska was to stay on the interstate at least until east of Dallas.

"Why you stopping?" Magda had been awake for some time but was too relaxed to move. The motor hum was soothing. The mystery of not knowing exactly where she was at the moment was exciting. She did not want to know just yet where Roscoe was going. But it was going to be a good place, yes it was. A better place than where she had been. Her suspicions were accurate about her daughter's true intentions.

"You tired?" She inspected his face like checking for hidden bruises on an apple. "Shoot, Roscoe, I never knew you to be tired once you hit the road. You're a driving fool. It's in your blood, that's what you used to tell me. You remember?"

With deliberateness, Roscoe caressed her hair, as if trying to be an angel's wing brushing over her. "Sure I remember, you sweet, hot thing."

Her piercing laugh of remembrance of what he used to call her burst the silence of the morning as she slowly lifted herself upright, kissing his rough cheek and adjusting herself in the seat. They were both sixty-three and born on the 4th of July. That and their love of Sly Stone and the Great Al Green made them believe they were destined to be lovers forever. Well, a few other things too, he remembered. But dates and numbers and other supposed signs—that's what Magda said just after her astrology days, back when that was all she seemed to talk angrily about. He thought he could dance like Sly Stone too. With a knowing smile, she remembered otherwise. She taught Roscoe to dance within himself and quit trying to dance outside himself. It made him look like a cartoon. Magdalena could swear he was going to hit her that night she told him. He swelled up in fury so tight she thought he'd explode. But he did not. He deflated himself right in front of her eyes. He never said a word. She watched his anger leave his body like released air from a big balloon. But he never collapsed. He bounced back and let her guide him along, saying nothing, only responding to her silent commands, guiding him with her hands and hips. Roscoe then unwrapped her arms from around his neck and held her hands in a firm grip, all serious business gripping his face.

"All right, I can dig that fact...but the fact remains though, girl, I love to dance. And it's you I wanna dance with." Magdalena fell in love with him that day. She was in love with a man who so wanted to be like Sly Stone but had the guts to know he wasn't ever going to be. *Damn,* she thought, *why do men think they have to be someone else to impress a lady? It's up to us to set them straight.*

"I do have to do something with myself, Roscoe. This pickup truck, as glorious as it for you, is not doin' a thing for me right now."

"Read your mind, baby, read your mind. Gotta place for you to get situated." Roscoe was now wondering what that bitch of a daughter Jeanette was up to.

"Thank you. Had no doubt, baby." Magdalena had no doubt at all.

A buzzing sound caught Roscoe's ear. He listened for the location. "You carrying a cell phone set on vibrate?"

She reached down onto the floorboard and lifted up a large purple handbag, stuffed full of her things.

"Who calls you?" asked Roscoe.

"Only one who calls anymore is Jeanette."

"Give me that phone," he said.

"What for?"

"Just give me that phone—please, baby," he said. She tossed him a scowling glance and began the five-minute search for the source of the buzz.

"You got photos on this phone you want to keep?" asked Roscoe.

"I don't use that thing for anything other than to listen to Jeanette tell me things. And I'm supposed to keep it for emergencies."

"I'll get you a new one," he said, taking the long-outdated purple phone from her hand and stuffing it in his front pants pocket. In his pocket it started buzzing again. He pulled back out and flipped the phone open. A message going to voicemail from Jeanette. Roscoe turned the phone to off and returned it to his pocket.

"You know you shouldn't have gone back to town and the VFW hall. I told you everybody would be there last night. Was it really worth it, getting us all uptight and everything, running outta there like we were criminals?"

"I told you I had to go back there to see if my plan had worked. And I believe it did," said Roscoe, feeling very good about himself at the moment.

"What plan you talkin' about, you crazy man? You got Jeanette on to us now. Was that your plan?"

"Never mind that mean bitch." He looked at Magda out of the corner of his eye.

"I see you got your eyebrow raised looking at me," she said. "There is no sense talkin' about her in that way—doesn't do anybody any good except make you feel all sanctimonious."

"Sorry, baby. I'll do better biting my tongue."

"That'll be the day," she said.

He turned and looked at Magda. She gave him the look. It got his attention. Then she broke out in a high cackle laugh. It infected Roscoe right away and both laughed like they needed to expunge a few lingering demons between them. He rolled up his window, started the pickup, and joined the rest of those driving south. He then wondered how many others on the highway were heading to new beginnings or leaving old lives this morning. He felt like they were the only two on the interstate that morning answering their inner urgent call to go somewhere else other than where they'd been.

His plan had worked, he thought, recalling seeing Saunders and Huguette on the dance floor the night before. He liked Saunders. They got on real well. Just like his father. Saunders was different, less overt, and much less over the top than his old man. There was just enough good friction between himself, Saunders's father, and Saunders because they all were firm believers in their own thoughts and decisions, and few could tell them otherwise. And the mutual acknowledgment of that is just how it is in life. But there was something more and Roscoe knew where it came from. Besides, somebody needed to light a fire under Saunders' lanky, bowlegged ass. *His old man had a worry about how Saunders was doing with the separation. Saunders will never be the wiser I checked up on him. Might as well be me. I got the time and the supreme motivation to be around--Magda. Besides, that's what chief master sergeants do.*

Take care of business. Help cleanse the boy of vapidity for God's sake.

Chapter 5

"How did I know you liked nature so much? You like birds, and sitting under a big shade tree! You were all flash and Mr. Late Night back then," said Magda.

"Love birds. Love lookin' for birds, hearing them sing, watching them fish. You know, when the bald eagle rips off the osprey's catch after he does all the dang work. That is one ticked-off bird, that osprey," said Roscoe.

"But I remember you loved your cars, those big engine cars back in the day. All those pictures you bored me with. Had to look at them how many times—lord I can't remember how many times." Roscoe remembered only one time that he ever shared the pictures of him and his brother's cars. Only one time. *And she was so polite and earnest in pretending to be as fascinated with cars as me.* Roscoe's memory remained vivid on this account.

"Roscoe, I do remember why you said you left Louisiana. You said the pine trees went on forever and you felt trapped because you couldn't see anything but the pine trees. You felt closed in, a prisoner." Which was why Roscoe often escaped to the shore of Lake Pontchartrain, growing up in Wharton, less than ten miles from Pontch. At least Wharton was elevated somewhat compared to the surrounding area. Even escaped the terrible flooding from Hurricane Katrina and decades earlier gave Roscoe a chance to see beyond the trees. Traveling on the school bus to football games as part of the high school band. Returning home to Wharton on the small roads, unable to see anything beyond the pine trees. Occasional breaks in the tree line crossing the bridges over swamps and marshes with cypress and hardwood trees acting as overlords in dead, still waters that were actually filled with life. On the road, pervasive blackness, save for the high beams on the bus—the bus driver locked-in focused on the road, scanning for crossing deer and "weavers"—the late Johnny Marable's term for drunk drivers. Since returning from the Korean War, the bus driver's driving record was accident free and he was very proud of that accomplishment. Roscoe stared out in the blackness, unable to sleep on the bouncy, box-spring bench seats. He knew the traffic came in spurts, depending how near or far away they were from the next town. He imagined himself in Paris, playing jazz in small, candlelit underground clubs for whites who fully embraced the American art form and seemed to carry no airs of superiority and hardened illusions of self-righteous dominance over blacks. His father told him his grandfather told him how badly he wished he could have gone to Paris and played jazz with Satch and the other New Orleans cats. That would have been the tops, his grandfather told his father.

The three rivers were a blessing, thought Roscoe, for they also gave him the opportunity to partially visualize his dream. The flowing rivers fed Lake Pontchartrain and, connected by the five-and-a-half-mile Industrial Canal, linked Pontch to the Mississippi River, and she eventually spilt her guts into the Gulf of Mexico—surely one way to escape Wharton, Louisiana.

Now a refreshing breeze flowed around them on the picnic table by the Tchefuncte River in the Riverside Park. He found the closest picnic table, so close to ponds you could cast a line sitting on the bench. In the cool, fresh water Roscoe knew bluegill and perch and bass were all about. Magda sat on the same side as Roscoe, elbows resting on the white tablecloth spread over the table and secured by clips on the ends, her lower legs still wet from the cool waters she had been wading in. He watched her closely to make sure she remained near the shore as she waded and splashed about. Roscoe was a man of detail, and the little things were best not to be forgotten or the big things may not end up mattering near as much as intended. Roscoe loved the summer dresses Magda brought along, showing off her fine-toned legs, with the noticeable varicose veins only starting above her knees. Her legs were nothing but genetic inheritance, she insisted, not being a runner or regular exerciser. Roscoe knew they were a gift from God. *This woman was to have fine legs and He let it be so. So a man like me can take great pleasure in them. Yes sir*, thought Roscoe, *yes sir, indeed.* Arranged on the table was shelled crawfish, jambalaya, coleslaw with more than a hint of jalapeno, smoked brisket, a big jar with half-cut lemons bobbing in sweet iced tea, and a bottle of French red wine that he had been saving for some time. American coots were waddling in an adjacent pool across the just mowed, full green grass field, where two young boys and a girl were chasing a shiny black Labrador who was completely enthralled with his playmates. Their playful screams hindered any attempt by Roscoe to listen for the *thweet, thweet* of golden swamp warblers, or perhaps Blackburnian warblers, although an irritating woodpecker was close by.

He was unsure of what Magda was listening to, sitting still on the picnic bench, looking past the food Roscoe spread out before her, the smell of garlic and Cajun spice released as he removed the lid off the to-go carton and presented it in front of Magda. She smiled and bent her head down to take in the smells, never letting her eyes divert from the children playing with the Labrador. Roscoe was unsure what she was thinking or what went through her mind. Did thoughts of the present occupy her inner attention or did seeing something trigger past memories? He had been reading all he could about her condition so he could best understand how to behave around her. A bluegill burst up, its arching dorsal fin on display as it sucked in tiny bugs skimming the surface. Days spent near the waters around Wharton were a pleasure Roscoe cherished and kept to himself, knowing he would never return to live here. He grew to recognize that experiences and memories are to be cherished, regardless of life's circumstance at the time, especially his early times, when he knew just how little say and influence he had over just about anything. And since that revelation, he made it his focus and directed his drive toward what he could influence and sway in his life. He sat down next to Magda, remained quiet, moving close to feel her body, and looked out over the water, now rippling from a welcome breeze. He wondered what was going through her mind. Then, as if she just noticed the food spread out before them, she searched for the paper plates and plastic utensils, still in their wrapping. Her sense of urgency was as if she had not eaten in days. Roscoe began to get up and assist her and she smacked his hand.

"Sit down and stay there." Magda tore into the stretch wrapping and placed two paper plates on the table. With equal urgency she used her teeth to tear open the utensil packet and pulled out a pair of knives, forks, and spoons. She looked up at Roscoe.

"Did you forget something?" she asked.

"Napkins are in the grocery bag still," said Roscoe. Soon she served two full plates of everything.

"You can pour the iced tea. A lotta ice for me please," she said.

Magda ate like she had not eaten in days, which gave Roscoe great relief because she had refused anything to eat for the last day of the drive. She was too thin, he thought. Maybe she had no taste for the food at her assisted living place, he was unsure, but he was sure that he had no intention of even mentioning that place to her. A memory he actually hoped she would erase from her mind. Magda got up and served herself seconds, greatly pleasing Roscoe. He wondered if the tastes triggered memories for her and if so, were they vivid? And ones to summon up whenever possible and cherish at each summoning? She offered no clue as she concentrated on finishing her jambalaya, once or twice taking long sips from her sweet iced tea. The sunlight was at its high afternoon angle and high cirrus clouds arrived in long, lazy, elliptical spirals. Roscoe repacked the leftovers and shoved them in his cooler, and gathered the used plates and utensils into the grocery bags, looking for a trash bin further away than the one provided for their particular spot. He was getting sleepy from the lunch and driving and wanted to get everything cleaned up and put away before taking a nap.

Leaning over Magdalena, who was still sitting on the picnic bench, Roscoe kissed her cheek. Magda found a face in need of a shave as she caressed his chin. *No matter*, she thought, *it's a nice old chin.*

"I'm down for a little nap. Wake me in an hour, no more than."

"I'm sleepy too." In the afternoon rays and warm breeze, they lay together. Both felt a sense of joy. Magdalena, thinking nothing but the moment, felt secure and loved. For Roscoe, it seemed half a lifetime had been spent waiting to be with her, and as much as he wanted to think about only of the moment, he could not. Pressing matters attempted to weigh on his mind. But joy persisted and sleep came in a near instant as he lay down. The echoed hammering of the woodpecker fell silent—he'd moved on—to be replaced by the call and response *thweet, thweet* of a lovesick pair of golden swamp warblers hidden in the fat leaves of the healthy young magnolia now offering Roscoe and Magdalena comforting shade. The bald eagle curled about them in the afternoon sun, fresh bluegill catch in his majestic claws, recently ripping off an osprey's hard-won success, circling once and then on to his own mate and their two chicks, to wait together with her in excited anticipation for them to break free and fly. The truculent breeze slowed to aged stillness and Magdalena's wading pond became glassy smooth as the perch found cooler waters deeper down.

When Roscoe snapped awake he could not move as he wished. His body was not fully awake and his mind was being stubborn, resisting the clearing of the heavy fog of deep sleep. It was a full minute before Roscoe realized where he was. His disorientation irritated him and stiffness had settled in his neck and right arm from sleeping on his right side on hard ground. His hip ached. The golden swamp warblers were *thweeting* elsewhere in the marshlands. The sun was past its afternoon setting, gliding toward the horizon.

Ignoring aches and stiffness, Roscoe lurched up, now realizing Magdalena was gone. So was his truck. He was not concerned about his Afro being mashed from sleeping. The picnic area was empty save for Roscoe. He brushed himself off, lifted the blanket up from one end, and shook it, causing it to flap and pop as the opposite end snapped, then folded it atop the picnic table, tucked it under his arm, and started walking down the road. His mind's fog of sleep receded and clear thinking returned as he worked to control his initial panic discovering she was gone. *Well, it confirms in my mind that woman can drive a standard with three on the tree,* he thought, chasing other worst-case imaginings from his mind. *But damnit, she shouldn't have gone on by herself.* Roscoe reached a main road—going left was further into the park and more picnic areas, to the right was toward the exit, and with no hesitation he walked toward the exit. As his mind fully cleared, worry entered, and his irritation grew while working to stay focused on where Magda could be, or could have gone. He had not prepared himself to consider Magda might have thoughts of her own regarding her future, or second thoughts about coming with him. After all, she'd convinced him she was ready to go—visiting her for almost two months, relentless in learning as much as she would reveal about her feelings for him, her feelings for her daughter and of relationships long abandoned by either herself or her husband at the time. Of course she loved the idea of Roscoe visiting her as a priest. After getting over the initial shock—she did not recognize him for a few moments, not seeing him in so many years, wearing a priest's collar and picked-out Afro (she thought, *Who wears an Afro these days? Some fool stuck in time? Some fool who's crazy*?).

I had it all laid out in my mind, in my notes I kept, thought Roscoe. *I was right about her, she's the one, she's always been the one.* Despite worry in his mind, he refused to believe he was wrong about her, wrong about his moves to get her to come with him.

"I'm driving…you can navigate. And by the way, where the hell we goin'? I don't mind where we go, but you got to give it up on our true destination. Give it up to me now," said Magda, leaning across the bench seat, talking through the rolled-down passenger window.

He stared at her, motionless and in shock. He never heard the truck approach, his mind was so full of worry and thoughts of where she might be. She surprised and confused him by her coming from the park direction.

"Do I smell the clutch?" said Roscoe.

“What you talkin’ ’bout?”

“The clutch! You know how to drive a standard? I smell the clutch. And your mascara has turned to masc-scary.”

She sat straight up and leaned over to get a close look at herself in the rearview mirror. Licking her finger, Magda attempted to wipe the mascara under her eyes, back and forth between each eye, only to smear it. Abandoning further attempts she cast a cold look upon Roscoe, never letting her eyes stray from his, shoved her foot down on the clutch pedal, exited neutral, and with an aggressive pull shifted down on the gear stick on the steering column and lurched forward, grinding the clutch—on purpose. She was intending to tell Roscoe a more truthful version of her story, but now she was irritated—more with herself than with anyone.

Chapter 6

Anything less than nine feet high was too encroaching, and after a short while Saunders became distracted by the urge to go outdoors and run. He had remodeled his residence with twelve-foot ceilings; with the kitchen and other bedrooms he rarely frequented being nine feet.

Driving his RV was okay, but he only remained in that enclosed capsule for sleeping and ablutions, eating and doing business tasks on his computer outside as much as possible. He relied on the Pomodoro Technique to keep him on task when inside his RV. Complete with a bright, shiny red Pomodoro kitchen timer used by the inventor of the time management technique. Saunders had purchased two spare timers just in case. Using the same kitchen timer as the inventor seemed as important to Saunders as the technique itself. Learning not to wait for the *ting*, as Saunders described it. The timer tinged at twenty-five minutes. Saunders could now not work without the Pomodoro timer—except when he was creating furniture. While in his shop he didn't care because he was oblivious—only the work mattered. Only the wood. Crafting only ceased when he was distracted by hunger or need for sleep. Two mugs of an exotic roast coffee. He relied on his coffee man to supply him with what he thought was the absolute best. Eduardo Hespe was never wrong.

He stood in the doorway of the room where he returned all of his furniture. His larcenous days were done. Save for one chair, he had his creations back. He pulled out the seventh chair and sat down to drink his coffee, thinking about the eighth, but not too much, more speculating about Kristina's motivation to keep the last chair. The rest of the pieces were still covered with white bedsheets. The indoor shutters were all opened as well as the tall windows, everything inside the room anxious for the desert sunrise to appear. Saunders imagined dormant chloroplasts sheltered by the wood now alive, chloroplasts longing for the sensual charge of photosynthesis, as if the wood could somehow beget new life from its dead self. Charged by the rich caffeine, he sprang up and tore off the white sheets covering his creations, dust collected from the time of his last visit spilling into the air, twirling and sparkling in the piercing desert sun, now lifting above the horizon and flooding the room. The room's stagnant air carried the smell of the woods throughout and mixed with the cool outside air of cottonwoods and Arizona brush and hard dirt. Every piece was arranged to form a circle, the sofa and matching overstuffed chairs, the hulking hutch of oak (designed as three pieces that interlocked, for ease of moving—Saunders learned from his military days) that could house the dinner plates of a small Gothic restaurant, the sleek mahogany wine bar and overhang for wineglasses for reds and whites, the low-slung coffee table with its clean lines and bursts of undulating grains within the koa, and bowing to the Danish in shape and contour, high-end teak tables with arching latticework between the legs that could only marry with the sofa and chairs, and the twin magazine racks, elegant slanted shapes of dark, exotic wood, long illegal, refusing to believe hard print magazines would ever become passé or obsolete. All the pieces crying out for attention, desiring to be caressed for hours with only the finest of lemon oil and soaps.

Next to his coffee, lying in front of him on the table, his mobile phone flashed a red light. Only his son and Roscoe ever texted or emailed with any regularity, and as much as he wanted his daughter to stay in regular contact, she did not. And now Saunders was in contact with Kristina—who seemed to love texting and emailing and was very reluctant to talk on the phone. He would have arrived to the Verde Valley six hours earlier if not for the stops he made to deliver full, thoughtful replies to her. She began.

"your furniture is beautiful."

"Thanks very much."

"i had no idea…at all."

"How would you? It's been a lifetime."

"my god that long? sooo hard 2 believe. but I know people. i knew you were a creative mind. but not like this. why did you take your furniture back? did u know it was me?"

"No."

"and if u did?"

"I would not have."

"why not?"

"I don't know."

"what???"

"have u done this before?"

"Done what before?"

"steal furniture. u got larceny listed in your resume? haaaa!!"

"You look fantastic."

"ok changing the subject mr. larceny. if I look so fantastic why didn't u stay?"

"Had to make sure Roscoe was ok."

"sure…"

"Talk to you soon?"

"ummm maybe. bye."

What may have prompted Kristina to text was because Saunders called her as he pulled out of the RV park and left town. It was five in the morning but he figured she would answer regardless of the hour.

"Hi, you've reached Huguette. Leave a message and I won't forget. No promises!" Her recorded reply a reaffirmation of her unwavering attempt to remain insouciant. In their very early years together, her lyrical insouciance was the primal source of an amorous, inseparable twist of desire and frustration. The very essences of bittersweet. He remembered and believed he would always remember that when he eventually did fall in love with her, he felt he was continually falling, as if there was no solid ground beneath him anymore, complete helplessness when he was either alone with her or just alone with his thoughts. Only years into his marriage did his sense of falling abate, but Kristina, now calling herself Huguette, carried over into his dreams for the next fifteen years. An evolving dream, like a TV series that advances a plot line over the course of the series, but certain episodes stall the plot line and stick in one place in time for a spell, then after a while advance again. In Saunders's dreams both he and Kristina advanced in age but never in wisdom, he thought, for there always was a sense of impermanence, always some intangible reality that prevented them from ever actually being together, and never any realization as to why that may be. His dreams were only of the now, and wisdom never grows in the now, but is only realized in the future, after reflection on the accumulation of random happenings that provoke happiness and wonder, and a mind's persistent dwelling on the harsh equality of randomness of loss and tragedy and arranging and processing experiences in an attempt to make some sense of them.

Saunders had resumed his fall again—total free fall—and this time was no different than last time—other than he was aware of the many years that had passed and very hopeful he had accumulated enough wisdom to see him through the rough winds and swirls and helpless tumbling he knew he was in for and, hopefully, land him safe on solid ground. He caught himself trembling in the morning burst of sunrise.

Across a short distance away from where he sat, in front of the expansive, corrugated metal building that served as a garage and wood shop, his RV and pickup waited patiently for a well-deserved wash and wax. Closing and locking all the windows, he surveyed his furniture creations before locking up, leaving the white sheets as they lay on the floor, and made a commitment to return the following evening to give them all the attention they desired, with soothing oils and tender rubbings. He should call his daughter, he thought, knowing Veronica would not call him; she had not in a few months. At least she would answer on occasion, and sometimes they'd carry on for almost an hour, as if their relationship was on the same firm ground as in earlier times. Saunders left a voicemail message for Veronica that he was back in Verde Valley and hoped all was well and he was thinking of her. He then thought of his son Allan and his two-year-old son, whom Saunders had only seen once, at his christening. Allan was off to the races in life and got along with his father. The christening was the last time Saunders saw his wife, reaffirming at that moment that the enmity was never mutual, yet wondering if indifference now was.

Some twenty feet up, mounted under the eaves of the garage and wood shop, six speakers spilled out songs throughout the morning. Saunders set his music player on random song select, turned up the volume, and set about attending to the dirt collected on his RV and pickup, getting lost in the cloudless and still-air day, concentrating on the smallest details of each vehicle, in no hurry to complete his task before him and every once in a while taking a glance up at his speakers, smiling at the disparate songs that segued from Crosby, Stills, Nash & Young to early Miles Davis to LCD Soundsystem, to the myriad thematic variations to Paganini's Caprice No. 24. Thoughts of Kristina now streamed through his mind in steady course. He stood erect with shoulders straight to relieve his tightened upper back muscles, which had become sore due to his extended reach to rid the top of the RV of hardened bird shit. His knees ached from remaining in a crunched position for too long tending to tenacious road tar on the lower wheel wells of his pickup. He then closed his eyes and recalled her face on the VFW dance floor, still radiant in wrinkles around her eyes and mouth, and imagined looking into her deep brown eyes, appearing as if her iris was the consistency of ironwood. Her pupils were filled with her whimsical formulations of episodic playfulness, which Saunders was sure she still took great delight in concocting. She brought all to life by the force of her alluring charm, and *my god,* thought Saunders, *what a master manipulator she probably has become*. But the willing want to be charmed, some badly so, and the mutual benefit of charmer and charmed, both egos billowed by the direct, intimate exchange, serves as a necessary social lubricant. Of that Huguette would never articulate, but would definitely agree, and went about happily fulfilling her role in society. But impish surprises occurred when two charmers were enthralled with each other… And Saunders knew this to be true with regard to Kristina, or Huguette. *The name Huguette is oblique, off-putting in a way*, he thought. He never said her real name back at the VFW Hall. He wondered what her reaction would be now when he called her by her given name.

Saunders rested in his rocking iron deck chair that he kept under the looming cottonwood tree, the desert air quickly cooling the water he sprayed himself with from the hose. He sat and admired his work. He'd become a fastidious cleaner. Then he thought of Roscoe's words to him shortly before they left Nebraska. It was late that night and three empty bottles of red lay upon the grass between their lawn chairs.

"Tell me you got a sense of humor, man. You were sometimes goofy-assed silly and made everybody at ease 'cause you had no problem makin' fun of yourself. You still that way, man? If so, you must be hidin' it deep somewhere inside. You can't lock that kind of thing up and not show it. Not healthy for the mind. Surely not healthy for the soul. You cannot keep within that which always should stay out." A minute of silence that seemed a lifetime followed. Saunders remembered how long it took to reply.

"Thanks, oh wise one. Or is it Soulman Sensei Roscoe?"

"It's Father Roscoe, damnit, just plain old Father Roscoe." And they both fell out of their aluminum chairs, laughing until tears came.

As the afternoon wore on, Saunders dozed off. When he awoke, he was soon alert and he called and left a message for Roscoe. Saunders texted him on his way back to the building where he stored his furniture. He was compelled to return to view his works. Stepping inside, he surveyed them all, arrayed in a circle, as if to close off all externalities, and anyone else for that matter. He felt his pieces no longer were part of a living experience, never having participated in the present—maybe because they had no past to build upon. They appeared to him now as mere things that were readily available—perhaps even to be pulled from a house for constructing a slapdash street barricade against some threatening entity, something he could not admit to being afraid of. He checked his cell phone. No reply from Roscoe. Deeply absorbed in his introspection as to why he stole back his pieces, he gave a solemn look across the room, then sharply closed and locked the door, and marched into his small ranch house. A rush of panic overwhelmed him as he popped open a beer. Lightheaded, he became dizzy and flew out of the kitchen, banging the screen door against its worn rubber stop. He guzzled the beer until empty, and with all his body weight into the throw, shattered the beer bottle into countless shards against the gleaming side of the RV. The scattered brown glass flashed in the lonely desert sun and ignited his memory. The first thing that came to his awakened mind was what a gorgeous day it had become.

Saunders rushed over to examine the half-moon crease caused by the beer bottle in the aluminum siding of the RV. At eye level, he ran his fingers slowly through the crease. It was oriented like a smile. Could have been much worse, he thought, such as the ambiguity of half a parentheses, or of a frown that is in response to a rush to judgment. Saunders drove his RV into the garage and locked everything up—then changed into running clothes. Lacking a purpose of the moment, which made him feel nervous yet buoyant, he sped away in his pickup to a favorite running path along the ambling river. Clocking miles along the river gave him a purpose. And a pleasant excuse to think of Kristina—and Huguette.

Chapter 7

Roscoe's half boots were still too new to take on an unanticipated long walk along a packed gravel roadside. A blister was forming on the top of each pinkie toe, as his swollen feet struggled against the stiff leather. Sweat soaked his undershirt and his handkerchief, which was now around his neck, the way John Wayne wore his in his signature westerns. His pricey cologne now an olfactory memory. Over his right shoulder draped the half-folded blanket and his short-sleeved shirt, sweat-soaked but starting to dry slowly in the breeze that kept threatening to wind up and blow but never did, just teasing him at times, and he cursed when the breeze died away, dashing his hopes again for some relief, giving cause to raise his ire toward Magda, his concern deepening for her whereabouts.

He was two football lengths from the park entrance and had already decided not to ask the young man in the entryway station about whether or not he noticed his pickup truck leaving. No cars were entering, and the last car to pass him from behind was some time ago, as the late afternoon passed on. Life for the birds and animals in the park carried on as every day, but since starting the walk Roscoe had become oblivious to their squawking and rustling about the undergrowth and tall trees. He had hoped to get to his brother's place to at least let him know he was back in Louisiana, but knew better than to stop by unannounced after dark. His brother never answered the phone, and besides, Roscoe was staying off the grid for the time being. No calls, no Internet use, no credit cards. And though he'd taken

Magda's cell phone from her, the thought occurred to him that she may have used one of her credit cards. That would not be a good thing, thought Roscoe, approaching the park entrance, looking for the men's room. He ducked his Afro under the sink and kept his hand pressed down on the push button faucet, sensing great relief as the water seeped through his hair and onto his head. He could have stayed under the faucet for an hour, his head was so hot. Stripping off his undershirt and handkerchief, he rinsed them both and put them back on after wringing them out. The outside water fountain delivered cool water with a metallic taste that Roscoe noticed immediately and immediately ignored as he filled his belly.

Magdalena had never left the park at all. She thought it much wiser to relearn how to drive a stick shift within the confines of the park than venture out and risk forgetting her way back. She was proud of her success yet panicked when she let time slip by and could not find Roscoe. A dread came over her realizing she may have to stop and talk to the ranger at the entryway gate. She slowed to a nearly impossible-to-maintain ten miles per hour as she made her way to the exit, but never popped the clutch; otherwise, Roscoe would have certainly heard. Maybe she should pop the clutch again, she thought. The pickup was almost reading empty.

The headlights flooded Roscoe's cataracts and he was unable to recognize the slow-approaching vehicle. With effort, he grabbed the rail post and lifted himself up from the steps of the visitor's center. His back had become stiff while he sat to massage his sore feet, inspecting the two blisters on his small toes. Recognizing the sound of his truck motor, he quickly sat down, put on his socks, and returned his boots to his sore feet. He stood back up and walked into the middle of the road, now blinded by the headlights. Magdalena came to a stop and shifted into neutral, excited to see Roscoe safe, and nervous in anticipating an angry outburst she knew would be coming her way. She pressed on the emergency brake and got out of the pickup. She kissed his tight lips and squeezed both arms above elbows. He was tense.

"Roscoe, honey, I have to go to the ladies' room *now*. And don't you be mad at me when I come back. I can drive that three on the tree now and won't be poppin' any clutches anymore."

He put the blanket and basket in the back, got into the driver's seat, placing his damp shirt next to him, and noticed he needed to get to a gas station. He wasn't angry with Magda, just very relieved to see her again, as his thoughts turned to getting to his brother's place before it got much later. He could be there in a half an hour if he hurried.

"I knew the tank was getting low, and I didn't want to chance going out to search for gas stations not knowing my way around here."

"We got enough to get to a station."

"I really enjoyed our picnic, Roscoe. I really did. Thank you for putting it all together for us." Magda took Roscoe's hand and squeezed.

"You had been eating like a damn bird, and I knew you'd be hungry," said Roscoe. "Cup of coffee and I'll be just right."

"I know you're tired," said Magda. She let go his hand and gently poked Roscoe's chest.

"You don't know what I know, and I know with a cup of coffee I'll be just right. As long as it ain't no tired fillin' station coffee. McDonald's makes good coffcc, you know. You got cash on you?" he said, adding, "Need you to use cash only for a while, no credit cards, no debit cards."

She said, "Yeah, yeah, cash is king. Right, Mr. Bling? Oh, but you don't wear bling, do you now? Even old-school muthas wore some bling."

Magda's mood lightened his, but Roscoe was tired. Sixty-three was wearing on him much harder than on Magda. Hopefully it would be a short night, he thought, once he swapped out his pickup for the '72 Cutlass 442 W30. Dark maroon and all-white interior. The sexiest car ever made and even his brother Nathan was of like mind, which was rare. "Magda definitely will not be driving the 442," announced Roscoe to no one in particular, as he filled his pickup truck, finding a gas station with a McDonald's next door, where Magda went to buy two coffees.

Before going to get the coffees, she withdrew all her credit cards from her long purse and handed them to Roscoe, saying, "You keep them for me so I don't get tempted to forget what you said." She winked, adding, "I got a few hundred on me. Oughta last me a few days, don't you think?"

"Definitely." This time of the early evening was clear of traffic through Wharton, and once on the north side of the Tchefuncte River and on River Road, traffic was nil. Nathan's place was just north of the Abbey property line, on twenty cleared-out acres, and the other fifty acres dense with pines and oaks and tough underbrush.

"I can drop you off at the hotel and go by Nathan's place by myself. Give you a chance to get all clean and relaxed."

"Are you stopping by there tomorrow then?"

"Nope. Not much to say to Nathan anymore."

"I thought this was your place as well as his?" she said.

"True enough, but truth be told, I paid off the note years ago, and pay the property taxes. I bought all the tools and whatnot for the auto shop. Nathan maintains the place and works on the cars," said Roscoe.

"Will I get to see some of those cool cars of yours?"

"Oh yeah."

"Then I'm comin' along with you tonight. You talked about those cars way back in the day and now I want to see them."

"Then that you will, Miss Lovely." Roscoe was now becoming less worried about arriving after dark than before. Magda by his side gave him great joy, and since he rarely second-guessed himself anymore, he felt he was on the winning side of life at the moment. But there were a few unknowns he had to consider. One unknown was what Magda's daughter Jeanette was going to do now that her mother was gone.

"Miss Lovely, tell me about Jeanette."

Magda looked at Roscoe and then back at the two-lane road, taking a careful slow sip of her coffee. The dusk folded and gave the upper hand to darkness. No lights other than rare opposing headlights.

"You paid her a visit, did you not?" she asked.

"I did."

"And?" she said.

"And, she was pleasant enough, but I'd never want to be married to her," replied Roscoe.

"You never wanted to be married to anyone. Too scared."

Roscoe huffed, "The hell you say…"

"Damn. Missed the turnoff."

He eyed the rearview mirror for anyone behind him, slowed, but not enough for the tires, and made a wide-arced, screeching, 180 degree turn in the middle of the two-lane highway, pinning Magdalena against her door. She composed herself back into her seat and adjusted her hair, as if she wore a wig that had become disrupted. She smiled to herself, knowing she had tweaked Roscoe with her observation, the same one she had told him before years ago—receiving the same huffed-up reaction then, as now. She did not spill her coffee.

Finding the dirt road turnoff, Roscoe accelerated, maneuvering to avoid the deeper ruts. It was not quite total darkness as the horizon still held onto some light, appearing blue with a smearing of gray right above the treetops. He was in no mood to hear Magda's lament about him. But he had given it plenty of thought over the last few years and considered it a psychological victory he'd finally admitted to himself he had been afraid to commit. *But the reasons are more telling*, he thought, as they always are. Roscoe let go of thinking about Jeanette now, and Magdalena had no intention of bringing up her daughter, whose father left Magdalena when Jeanette was twelve, and Jeanette, completely furious and distraught over the separation, sided with her father for God only knows what reason, thought Magdalena, and announced she, too, was leaving with her father, who was caught one hundred percent off-guard and also furious at Jeanette's unwavering decision to go with him rather than her mother. Looking back on all that gut-wrenching strife and the pain from the yoke of guilt; was Magdalena coming back into Jeanette's life now predictable? She wasn't sure, but being predictable did not make it any easier for Magdalena. Now Jeanette was a full-formed women of rage, and the rage directed at her mother for the absolute wrong reasons was kept on low simmer, as if to feed upon it for existence, with no willingness to confront the truths of the matter, because the truths would be just as difficult to bear due to her complete powerlessness to affect the magnitude of self-interest both her parents displayed. No, Magdalena was never in any mood to think of Jeanette, her daughter who might have been the love of her life but would never be, and Jeanette would see fit never to allow it to come to pass even if a cascade of miracles aligned themselves to allow repentance and rectification, for forgiveness could never be an option. Forgiveness was for the weak.

The big light over the cathedral doors to the garage was off. Roscoe could see no other lights on in the modest one-story house one hundred yards off to the left as he slowed and parked his pickup in front of the auto shop. He rolled down the window and heard nothing, save the clicking pop sounds of his engine cooling down and coming to rest.

"Your brother's not home?" said Magda. "You tell him you were coming?"

Roscoe said, "I did indeed. And besides, he can't see all that good at night either. Runs in the family. Does all of his drivin' in daylight these days."

"Just like you should probably too," she said.

"Enough of that now, Magda."

She said, "I'm just sayin'…"

Roscoe cut her off. "Enough. Stay in the pickup. Lock your door and lie down on the seats. Keep quiet."

Roscoe reached into the glove compartment and withdrew a tall flashlight. From underneath his seat he withdrew from a pouch his pistol, a 1911, his favorite. Anger flushed through her as Magda saw the .45 caliber.

"What the hell is *that* for? You think you're Superfly or somethin'?"

"Or somethin'," Roscoe replied, getting out of the truck and tucking the pistol in his waistband. Even at his age, Roscoe knew Nathan still had a habit of idiotic foolishness, regardless of his attempts to hide such facts.

"Yeah, something all right, some kind of fool," Magda shot back. "And I'm not layin' down on the seat. I want to see who's comin'. Give me the keys," she demanded. "You gotta pistol, Superfly, at the least I can drive out of here rather than sit in the truck like some old stupid helpless broad."

After a short stare-down in the dark, Roscoe reached in his pocket, pulled out his keys, and tossed them toward Magda.

"Don't be grinding the clutch…" said Roscoe.

"Um hm…then hurry on back if you're so worried about your damn clutch."

"You know, Magda, lovin' you is a challenge, damn gigantic at times."

"Get on about you and your brother's business," she said. "And you ain't no saint, Mister Roscoe, priest and all… Hmmph."

Damn, thought Roscoe, *she's coming back to life*. He was beginning to really wonder about her, worried that she was maybe getting out of reach. She barely said a word driving down to Louisiana. Now she had some action again in her life. Got herself all fired up at the park and drove off. That was something he had been secretly enjoying since they left the picnic. He smiled to himself and thanked God she was with him now.

The garage doors were unlocked. The padlock was locked in the thick, hinged clasp like always when they were working. Once inside Roscoe knew something was amiss. There were no cars. He went left to find the light switches. Flicking the switches on gave no light. The main fuse box was in front of him and he opened the door to find all the fuses set to "on." Giving his flashlight a wave around, he saw nothing. Quickly he opened both garage doors and went to his truck, waving at Magda.

"Start her up and turn on the lights." Startled, Magda did as instructed.

The headlights confirmed the auto shop was empty. No cars, all their toolboxes gone, all the heavy-duty workbenches cleaned off. Magda was confused at the sight.

"Drive over to the house, stop in front, keep the lights on," he instructed, now beginning to sweat. His heart raced, unhappy with the sudden release of adrenaline, and his chest tightened. Roscoe ignored his heart and broke out into a slow jog toward the house. He had been ignoring his heart for decades. Only until he joined up with Saunders and observed his damn obsessive running did Roscoe begin to think again about his health and condition. He quit smoking thirty-five years ago. That should have been enough time, he reckoned, to help his health.

The faded redbrick house was unlocked and all its contents had been emptied, as if the occupant had sold or died. The house appeared to be awaiting a long overdue renovation and general spiritual uplift. Inside, fear and panic overtook Roscoe. It was never his house, even though he owned it. This was Nathan's place.

From the pickup and within the beams of the headlights, Magda witnessed his shortness of breath flinging open the front door. He slumped onto the front porch top step, clinging to the support beam. She turned off the ignition, leaving the lights on, and dashed to Roscoe.

"I can't help him anymore, Magda." She turned around and went back down and grabbed his flashlight, which had rolled down the three steps. Inside she found Nathan against the far left wall of the empty living room, sitting in a spreading pool of blood, urine—smelling of excrement. His head was angled on his right shoulder, his hands and fingers bludgeoned by emotionless blows from a hammer. His face was grotesque in its distortion from normal; tears streaked and joined blood now softly congealing under his crushed nose and mutilated lips. Magda dry-heaved and then vomited. She spit and wiped her mouth with the back of her hand. As her vision cleared she forced herself to touch his neck for a pulse. She moved her fingers around to ensure she was in the right spot. Waiting, wiping her mouth again of vomit, she detected a pulse in Nathan's neck.

"Nathan!" she shouted. "Nathan!" The stench from his bowel release was suffocating in the empty room, where even the air seemed to have taken an overdue holiday—somewhere far away. She got up and ran to Roscoe.

"Get up, Roscoe. C'mon now, baby…get up now and help me with Nathan. He's alive, baby, and we got to get him some proper attention—*now,* baby." She caressed the sweat off his forehead and kissed him. "Get up, baby…"

Magda maneuvered behind him and slid her arms under his sweaty armpits and attempted to lift Roscoe. He was dead weight and listless. She made another attempt, lurching him forward. Roscoe clutched the support beam with both hands now and slowly stood up.

Her lips touched his ear and she whispered, “We gotta hustle, baby. We gotta hustle… He may die if we don’t get him outta here.”

Slowly Roscoe’s arm muscles tightened as he gripped the porch column. Magda felt his torso tighten and anticipated when he would make his move. As Roscoe’s knees came together and he leaned forward, Magda gave a sharp cry, “Up!” She timed her lifting from under his arms to when he attempted to stand. They both groaned like an Olympian in the initial strain of a dead lift. With Magda’s timely assistance Roscoe succeeded on his first attempt, now holding onto the column to steady himself and await the sensation to faint to pass him by. Magda held him tight around his waist and, using pressure against his belly, guided him toward the front door, and together they crossed the threshold and into the darkness of the living room. In the ten steps to reach Nathan, Roscoe’s head began to clear and his strength increased, yet his chest pain remained, less acute now, dulling somewhat in intensity. Without a word, Magda released Roscoe and went to Nathan’s right side, waiting for Roscoe to position himself on his brother’s left side. They each swung Nathan’s arms around their necks; Magda careful to grab his wrist rather than his mangled fingers. If Nathan had quit smoking, he was sure to be fifty more pounds than he carried, thought Roscoe, suddenly grateful Nathan had not quit yet.

“On three,” commanded Roscoe, weakly. On the third count he yelled, “Up!” Struggling, both Roscoe and Magda used the wall as a brace, leaning back on the wall as they dead-lifted Nathan. Succeeding on their first attempt, they grabbed a breath, tightened their grip around Nathan, and in unison stepped toward the front door, Nathan's bare feet now dragging across the floor, leaving a streaking trail of blood and urine behind them. Wincing in the glare of the pickup headlights, Roscoe now guided them toward the passenger side and instructed Magda to let go and open the door. Roscoe's strength increased as his body released more adrenaline. Magda quickly went around to the driver's side and opened the door and slid inside to help get Nathan situated in the cab. Nathan's unconsciousness cast a pall of calm upon them. Magda squeezed in the passenger side, holding Nathan around his shoulders to keep him leaning on her rather than into Roscoe as he started the truck.

"Is your brother mean?" said Magda, panting and sweating.

Roscoe looked at the faded redbrick house, front door ajar, and put the pickup in reverse. Glancing at Nathan slumped over onto Magda, smelling his stench, Roscoe's eyes caught Magda's, hers almost half lidded in exhaustion.

"You mean like bastard mean?" said Roscoe, finally replying.

"Yes, like a bastard mean," she said.

"I wouldn't say that, but his stubbornness can take all shades of attitude."

"Well, maybe that's good enough then," said Magda.

"Good enough for what?" said Roscoe, slipping into second gear and driving on a different road from the one they arrived on, this dirt road going behind the faded redbrick house and into tree-lined blackness.

"To keep him alive until we get him some help," she replied, looking at Roscoe. Then she turned her head and looked out the front windshield, clutching and releasing Nathan, in hopes for some response in his limp body. Roscoe rolled down the window to get fresh air into the stinking cab. Magda was too exhausted to do anything other than clutch and release Nathan's shoulders.

The gate had never been locked on Roscoe's insistence, and Nathan had kept his promise. Roscoe stopped, put the truck in neutral, and went out to pull open the swing gate. Leaving the gate open, he passed through toward the abbey. *Just past eight o'clock*, thought Roscoe, *all the fellas should still be up and tending about their evening rituals.* Interrupted light now appeared through the trees and soon they were in the clear and the large stone buildings came into view under the lights. Roscoe could not remember the time for evening prayer, but they'd make allowances for him. They had done so a few times before. Leaving his driver door open, he ambled up the stone stairs and let the doorbell ring continuously until he could see more lights appear inside, deep into the tall and embracing foyer. He released the bell and went back to the truck to get Nathan. The door opened and a monk that Roscoe did not recognize appeared in the doorway, backlit against the full white lights of the foyer, illuminating himself to be a short, stubby, bald and full-bearded man, maybe in his late fifties, and not adequate enough to carry Nathan by himself.

"I'm Roscoe Armstrong and my brother Nathan is in a very bad way. I'm your neighbor to the north. Get the Abbot and get some others out here now please."

"But sir!"

Roscoe went back up the stairs, stinking from his sweat and reeking of his brother's excretions. His Afro was in total akimbo.

"I'm no 'sir,' I'm a retired chief master sergeant and I worked for a living. I am in no mood to argue and I can damn well tell you my brother Nathan is likewise in no mood either, so if you would kindly…please…get more help and call Abbot Mercer…now…please."

Magda strained to move Nathan closer toward the edge of her seat, waiting for Roscoe to help her. The moths that swarmed the lights above took no notice on the happenings below, and still air seemed to sharpen the cloudless night. Roscoe could only imagine what the Milky Way looked like tonight. Majestic and awe. That's what it'd look like tonight. He paused as he grabbed hold of his younger brother Nathan, and a welcome and grateful calm coursed through Roscoe, relieving the tightness in his chest and strengthening his grip. Nathan's body was warm, Roscoe noticed, and his mouth gaped now, sucking in air, for his brother's nose no longer functioned as a breathing organ. *He might be coming to*, thought Roscoe. *And when he does the pain may just knock him back out again.*

Abbot Mercer was a tall man with thinning white hair, cropped in a crew cut. He'd grown a goatee since Roscoe had last seen him, and Roscoe's sense of release of anxiety caused his knees to shake as he transferred the weight of his brother onto the shoulders of two monks who accompanied the Abbot.

"Sorry 'bout the night's intrusion, Doc, but it was not a choice I really had. We found Nathan like this not long ago at our place."

Abbot Mercer, Doctor Mercer, the M.D. kind, the surgeon kind, Vietnam veteran back in the early sixties under LBJ's time, whose wife of three years left him because he wasn't the man she wanted him to be, which turned out to be an undisguised blessing for everyone, took charge. Three monks then carried Nathan away, with Abbot Mercer leading the way.

"Get Roscoe and his lady friend to a guest room to clean themselves up. Get him a bottle of bourbon and whatever the lady wishes," barked the Abbot, to no one in particular, but black-robed monks started filling the foyer like ants coming for honey. Roscoe pointed to his truck and told a monk their luggage was in the back, handing him the keys to open the back cab. Another led Roscoe and Magda through the foyer and left toward the guest rooms, neither Roscoe or Magda paying much attention to the photos lining both sides of the hallway, nor the occasional creaking of the dark hardwood floors. They did notice the air-conditioning was set nice and cool. They each were given their own rooms, a single bed with a small bathroom. Magda and Roscoe said nothing to each other as they sat together on Roscoe's bed waiting for the monks to deliver their luggage. The rooms were sparse, a night table and lamp, wooden crucifix over the beds that appeared freshly made. Each had a window and a tiny clothes closet. Magda got up, seeing the monk with her luggage, and followed him to her room.

"I gotta get outta these clothes."

Roscoe said, "Take your time and rest. I'm in and out of the shower and then going to see Nathan and the Abbot. You stay put and lie down."

A monk delivered Roscoe's luggage and bourbon with glass and an ice bucket. Roscoe thanked him and closed his door and filled his glass with ice and bourbon, swished it around a few times, and drained the glass in one tilt of the head. He stripped and piled his soiled clothes on the floor in front of the closet and climbed in the shower and crumpled down onto the floor, letting the hot water soak his Afro and soak his skin. His mind was numb but thoughts were racing. His chest pain, now more dull than sharp, diminished and he now became aware of the soreness in his left arm. The bourbon buzzed his brain. His stress seemed to drain away along with the water.

He awoke to the banging of his door. The shower was delivering lukewarm water over his body, his legs now cramped due to him falling asleep sitting on the shower floor. He could not stand.

"Roscoe!" shouted Magda, entering his room.

"Nathan?"

"Nathan is awake now. The doctor has got him comfortable and under sedation."

"I'm stuck in this damn shower," said Roscoe, too tired and stiff to move.

"Well, I am not coming in there to help your ass outta there. I'll call one of the monks."

Roscoe opened the shower door and with great effort straightened his legs outside of the shower. The cramping became less acute as he massaged his legs and moved them in and out, up and down. Water sprayed out into the bathroom, soaking the tiny white cloth bath mat. He scooted himself over the lip of the shower, got on his hands and knees, and in front of Magda, lifted himself up, and reached in and turned off the shower knob.

"Give me a second here…" he said.

"I'm not leaving until I know you are dressed and all right." She sat on his bed and poured him another glass, much smaller than his first, and made herself one too.

"Recall I've seen you more than a few times in your naturals, baby, although it has been a while now, hasn't it," she said in a soft, warm tone, smiling at him now, now looking away as he attempted to get the short towel around his girth, wider than his much younger days. *But all in all, not bad at all, Roscoe*, she thought, taking a large swig from her bourbon. *Not bad at all, you charming and strange piece of work.* She allowed herself to recall how much she missed him over the years.

"I want to see him," said Roscoe, grabbing some clean underclothes and disappearing with his travel kit into the bathroom.

"He's resting and your Abbot friend ain't gonna let you see him tonight. He's a strong man, your friend. I'm not questioning him, no, not me." She continued to sip her bourbon on his bed, her hair up in a clip and still wet from the shower, now in a long-sleeved, loose cotton green shirt and jeans.

Through the bathroom door she said, "The Abbot wants to see you in his office."

Roscoe opened the door in his white V-neck T-shirt tucked into his BVDs, like his old military days.

"That look is *so* unattractive, Roscoe, tuckin' your V-neck into your shorts," she said, smiling at him. It was like forty something years ago with him--that look of disdain at her observation, more of a put-on disdain than actual disdain, she knew. He kept silent and put on a black pair of chinos and a purple polo shirt, both unacceptably wrinkled from being crammed into his suitcase. She knew he'd never be seen in public looking like he looked now.

In the abbey, she reflected, *I'm in a damn abbey with Roscoe, next to where Roscoe and his brother had their property; now Nathan's been beaten and those who did left him to die, and here we are, in a damn abbey! Drinking bourbon in a monk's room...with Roscoe! All my tarot card reading, all my channeling the "others" outside this world, tellin' people who desperately want to be told anything than what they have already figured out for themselves, but can't stand what they believe to be their truth, all my supposed revelations never would have revealed this moment!* Magda was excited. She had become ebullient. She felt the moment's rush of joy.

Accepting his glass, Roscoe leaned over and kissed Magda, and she responded in kind.

"Go see the man, Roscoe. Tell me all about it in the morning, 'cause I'm so exhausted I may have to crawl back to my room."

"I'll take you there," he insisted, lifting her elbow. She stood and he escorted her to the room next to his and kissed her again.

"You did good, baby," he said.

"I *am* good." A long time had gone by since Magda even had the courage to think she was any good at all. Joy fleeted away, but she knew that was okay, because joy had stopped by and paid her a visit. That was just fine.

Roscoe, empowered from his shower and bourbon in his brain, strode in slow style barefoot on the compassionately worn green hallway carpet toward the Abbot's office, picking his Afro back to bad-ass status along the way. It was an unassuming room for its expansiveness, yet inviting once settled inside. This was going to be a long overdue conversation. He almost felt like it was home. Almost. Roscoe knocked and entered in one motion. "He's all right then?"

Abbot Mercer sat on the black leather sofa adjacent to the large, plain wood desk that took up most of the wall space along with the large rectangular window. He stood and embraced Roscoe, careful not to spill his bourbon. Roscoe returned the embrace and sat in the large leather chair the Abbot motioned him toward.

"He looks worse than he is, and unless he's got a hidden cardiac condition, he's in no danger from his beatings, although a re-visit by those who did this to him would change that certainly. But that's not going to happen now because of you and your friend's timely occasion to visit him," he said, returning to the sofa. He settled in, crossed his blue jeaned legs, and picked up his neat scotch from the side table with the large metal lamp, set on the lowest level, creating an intimate feel in such a large office. His fresh white shirt was unbuttoned and sleeves rolled up to the elbow. His bloodstained shirt had been disposed of.

"Nathan will require follow-up. His fingers were crushed. Getting those fingers to work right again will be a challenge. I straightened his nose to help him breathe, but the nose requires attention too. And he's got a few broken ribs. His knees have been bashed, but astonishingly his patellas are not broken, most likely because whoever did this went for his knees first to immobilize him and then went after the rest of your brother more thoroughly. Our dispensary's first rate, as you know from your younger days, and God has somehow led two additional physicians to our abbey over the past years. That's good news for Nathan, but he'll still require medical attention in his recovery, and I suspect any local hospital is most likely not desirable."

"Now, Roscoe, tell me what you know." The Abbot sipped his scotch and waited.

Sitting still, in the quiet of the warm light of the large lamp, Roscoe's mind attempted to assimilate the facts of the days. The joy of the picnic in the park, the mainly silent but pleasurable drive down from Nebraska with Magda, saving his damn fool brother's life, and getting half drunk with Abbot Mercer, a man he liked very much, and often missed. All this came at a rush to him and he became dizzy. Not wanting to start his reply with a stammer and stutter, he held up his free hand, asking for a time delay in response. The Abbot smiled. Roscoe knew his brother would be all right the moment Roscoe saw Abbot Mercer. *He's a damn stone granite of a man*, thought Roscoe, now flush in a pleasant bourbon haze.

"Still strutting around as the priest brother of Superfly? You are aware of how improbable that scenario is, aren't you? People still fall for that line? Or do most people these days have no idea who Superfly was?"

Roscoe was powerless to raise any of his guards against the impish questions of the Abbot. "*Was*? You mean *is*." Roscoe's tear-inducing laugh could be heard upstairs and through the hallway. His crooked toes cramped he laughed so hard. Now the Abbot's raucous laugh joined Roscoe's and upon hearing both, the occupants in the abbey filled their minds with questions they'd never utter on any other night at least, and quizzical expressions long-forgotten they could form seemed pasted on a few of their faces. Magda was snoring. Their laughing fit lasted until their taste buds sought more bourbon and scotch.

Wiping tears away, Roscoe replied, "If you hadn't got me that fine discount on the priest clothes, I'd have never been tempted."

"I never thought you'd actually go and purchase the clothes, Roscoe."

"Well, that's bullshit, Abbot, 'cause you knew I'd buy those priest clothes."

"I never thought you'd actually wear them and pretend to be a priest."

"Bullshit, Abbot, you knew I would."

"I never thought you'd keep pretending then."

"Bullshit," said Roscoe, now both exchanging genuine and generous smiles. He changed tone. "They took all the cars, all the tools, all the test equipment. The garage is empty. We found Nathan in the house. The house is cleaned out. Nothing inside but Nathan beaten and bleeding against the wall in his own piss and shit."

"Why'd you return? Last I recall you emailed me and said you weren't coming back anytime soon because you were disgusted with Nathan."

"Pissed off is what I wrote, as I recall, Doc." Roscoe always preferred to call William Mercer "Doc."

"And your friend? That's your Magdalena, isn't it? Please tell me you did not woo her back as a priest." The Abbot got up and went over to his desk to retrieve the bottle of scotch. "I always drink more than I should when you're around," he said aloud, barely audible, half intended for Roscoe to overhear, which he did, and he smiled.

"I rescued her from her evil bitch of a daughter, that's what I did, and not as a priest, but as good ol' Roscoe."

"Daughter from…?"

"Husband number two."

"Husband number two," repeated the Abbot. "And you knew him too?"

"Full and complete dumb-ass, but Magda thought he was *the man*," said Roscoe, rolling his eyes and waving his arms in front of him in circular motions. Winking, he said, "I really came back here for an exchange. With Magda with me, the pickup's not enough. I need to get more practical…and anonymous. I came for the 442."

"The 442? Practical…and anonymous? I'll get to the anonymous comment in a moment. How is a voodoo purple Cutlass 442 with all-white interior any more anonymous than your pickup? You going full Superfly, or are you going anonymous?"

It seemed impossible to get anything past the Doc, thought Roscoe, but he'd never give up trying to get to his level, though Roscoe was wise enough to realize he had little idea what "level" Doc Mercer was at.

"The 442's gone, right?"

"No sir, it's not gone, Doc, it damn sure better not be, unless those bastards who beat Nathan know about the storage units. I guess I'll know soon enough when I speak to his lame ass tomorrow. And it's maroon, nothing voodoo about the color."

"Roscoe." Doc Mercer was, in point of fact, Abbot Mercer, Father Mercer, and there came a point when he felt obligated to revert to what he was supposed to be, a man of God, and how he ever became one still was the mystery in

William Mercer's life. Even his ex-wife kept in contact with him. And he was grateful for her contact.

"Sorry, Father."

Abbot Mercer finished his last scotch of the evening. Motioning Roscoe over to the sofa he said softly, "Here's what we're going to do." Roscoe sat by him. In low voices the Abbot talked to Roscoe, and Roscoe acknowledged what was being told to him, with complete respect.

The moment seemed right for Roscoe to ask Abbot Mercer to hear his confession. May not have another opportunity, he thought. Abbot Mercer gave him full absolution, adding that although Roscoe was not Catholic, he was near close enough, perhaps even better than most, and that his personal observation should not go to his head. This was not his first confession to Abbot Mercer, but in Roscoe's mind this one was the one that counted. Roscoe thought his penance to be a helluva lot of prayers to say for what he believed were transgressions on the minor scale… But oh no, not according to Abbot Mercer they weren't. Damn the priests sometimes, thought Roscoe, now touching the wall for support every other barefoot step back to his room. *Damn the priests*, he thought, smiling, as he lay on his back, thinking about Nathan, of all people. He was relieved Nathan was going to recover, and was far less pissed off at him than on most days. Now what to do with him was another matter. Roscoe then thought of Magda. He hoped she thought of him, and with that lingering hope enveloping his weakened heart, Roscoe fell asleep, soon snoring so loud his snoring woke up Magda, who'd been snoring since she'd collapsed on her single bed.

Chapter 8

Magda wondered when the rain would come. The skies had been clear since they left. Bright, beautiful days. *But this is not the desert, not the Caribbean, not a place where the skies are clear more often than not*, she thought, on her knees, leaning on the simple wood headboard, peering through the old white curtains and taking in the grounds of the abbey. A few buildings formed a loose square, with grass in and around the property about a week overdue for cutting. *Not today will anyone be cutting the grass around here*, she thought. She had slept soundly and was hungry, but she'd wait until she could hear stirring about before she'd venture out of her room. She got up from the bed and pressed her ear against the wall. She heard nothing from Roscoe's room. Now she began to feel antsy, the room too small to stay in much longer. The dampness in the air was air-conditioned chilly, and she rummaged through her suitcase, her clothes tossed about from being too tired the night before to properly arrange them, searching for her thin, light blue sweater. Putting it on, she unlocked the door and peeked down the hallway. Seeing a monk at the end of the hall traversing the foyer on his way outside, she figured all of them had to be awake and tending to their daily activities, or whatever it is monks do. The creaking hallway floorboards alerted her to someone behind her. It was another monk. They all seemed to be short, older white men.

"Good morning to you."

"Yes, good morning. Rainy today, I see," said Magda, smiling at the monk, who appeared not shy at all about the presence of a woman in the hallway.

"It is, I'm afraid. But that shouldn't stop you from eating breakfast, should it?"

"I like you already—you're my kind of mind reader," she said, thinking if he only knew what she knew about reading people's minds. The monk laughed in a quiet, polite manner and told her to follow him. She bet she could figure out why every single one of these fellas chose to escape from the world and come here for the rest of their lives. She felt she knew there was a common link to all their stories, things that happened to them that were all similar in many respects, and this place seemed to offer them relief from whatever burdens they thought they felt compelled not to shed. A shame really, she thought, following the monk across the foyer and into the other wing of the three-story building. Entering the dining room, they found only Abbot Mercer and Roscoe at the far table conversing over coffee. The rain was falling heavily now, and you could hear the rain pounding outside on a gray morning, mist wrapping around the looming trees in the not too far-off distance. Abbot Mercer stood up when the monk delivered Magda to their table.

"Abbot William Mercer," he announced, extending his hand. His wide smile and soft tone relaxed Magda, not fond of priests as a general rule. Abbot Mercer and the monk exchanged courteous nods and the monk departed.

"Roscoe tells me you're not too fond of priests as a general rule. But I take it you don't mind if Roscoe mingles in the public eye wearing a priest collar?"

Clasping and holding his hand, the Abbot's fingertips cold compared to the rest of his hand, she replied, "Oh, he does test me at times, that man. But I forgive him in the end."

Still seated, Roscoe's expression went from ebullient to a mocking suspicion, followed by a quick smirk when Magda glanced at him.

"Well, *Mr.* Roscoe Armstrong and his brother Nathan have some catching up to do this morning, and during that time I invite you to join me for breakfast." Roscoe got up and went over to kiss Magda. She turned to receive his kiss on her lips and she squeezed his arm as he wrapped it around her waist.

The Abbot said, "Hope you like scrambled eggs, French toast, and bacon. Because that is what you-know-who ordered for you."

"He did, did he?" Magda allowed the Abbot to seat her. An older man came from the kitchen with water and a coffee cup and placed them in front of Magda, along with a place setting for both her and the Abbot. He offered her coffee and she accepted, only wanting it black.

"I'm very interested in your background. Ross tells me you come from a family of astrologers and channelers, is that correct?"

"True enough, Father, true enough," she said, finding pleasure in the first sip of her coffee. "And I'm very interested in how you know Ross. I do agree with him in that I prefer Roscoe. Suits him much better."

The Abbot said, "I met Ross…Roscoe, through Percy Standing, a writer who lived in Wharton. Quite a character. He's buried here with us. Quite a character." The Abbot could see Magda was very comfortable talking to men, priests or no. She looked relaxed and confident, and he was unable to detect any hint of illness, much less early stages of Alzheimer's, age not having eroded her beauty fully yet.

"Anyway, Nathan kept Percy's car up for him, and Percy got to know Roscoe before he joined the Air Force, and they maintained a friendship until Percy died back in the early nineties—before my time here actually. This I've been told by the Abbot before me, and of course by Roscoe himself, who I got to know through Nathan taking care of our cars here. Both of them know their way around an engine block. And both meticulous when it comes to automobiles. It's very important to both Nathan and Roscoe, regardless how they feel about each other."

Breakfast arrived. Just as advertised. Magda's eyes opened wide. She wasted little time pouring syrup over the French toast, which in her opinion was cooked to perfection. After salt and peppering her scrambled eggs, she lightly covered them with Tabasco sauce. The French toast was delicious. The Abbot smiled as he said grace in a low voice. Magda paused, placing another bite in her mouth, apologized, and resumed eating.

The Abbot said, “Oh, and another thing, I remain a car fanatic myself, being an old gearhead in my early years, actually throughout high school, college, and going through medical school. When you grow up with a father who’s a mechanic, it gets in your blood one way or the other. In fact, Roscoe and I made a swap this morning. I’m relieving him of his 442, and he gets a high-mileage Econoline van that is in great shape still, thanks to Nathan.”

“A what?” said Magda, biting off a piece of her last strip of bacon, wishing she had more on her plate. She was a notoriously slow eater by her own account, and in her early childhood constantly reminded of this by her father, notorious for his impatience with anyone on just about anything. She swore that’s what kept her thin and not the cigarettes. But not this morning. She finished her plate before the Abbot.

“Roscoe’s not gonna like drivin’ around in some old white van. That definitely ain’t Roscoe.”

“Maybe that’s why he initiated the trade.”

“Hmmph. I didn’t know they allowed ex-married priests.”

The Abbot was caught off guard, revealing in haste, “Roscoe tell you I was married?” As the words came forth he remembered Magda’s family trade, confirming his memory by her slight knowing smile as she finished her cup of coffee.

“Ooh la la, Father, that’s what I needed! Thank you, thank you for that delicious breakfast. The French toast was divine,” said Magda, softening her tone into humble gratitude, knowing she got the Abbot to reveal a bit of himself too soon. He'd be a wary one now, she thought.

"Maybe I could invite you back as a guest lecturer? You may not know, but we are a seminary here."

"You make priests outta these guys that come here?"

"Some, yes, others remain as brothers," said Abbot Mercer.

"Why?"

Abbot Mercer said, "Why what? Why do I work to make these men priests, or why have priests at all?"

"We'll start with you first," said Magda.

"I suppose you won't accept the answer that I was called to be a priest, now will you?"

"You suppose correctly, sir." Magda laughed. The older man returned to clear away the rest of the plates and asked if they wanted more coffee. Magda asked for grapefruit juice, now wishing she had a glass with her breakfast.

"This morning I'm asking you to accept just that and leave it at that—and I won't ask about your multiple marriages, plus live-ins, and why you are with Roscoe at this time. Nor will I ask why you are faking that you have early dementia and require assisted living."

Ooh la la, thought Magda, *the man surely has the gift. Of course, God knows he needs it to get the right men hurting or longing enough to drive them to be good priests instead of hiding from themselves. God, please help them all, and you know better than me, oh Lord, they all are surely gonna need it. They do need more women about a place like this,* she concluded. *Just to remind them we are the stronger of the two sexes and you cannot, you cannot live life not knowing about us women. Jesus, what a waste that'd be. For us, and them! Even though there are some asshole, jerk-off, stupid men in this world. I should know; I pick 'em terrible. But not Roscoe, God save me, not Roscoe.*

"You're good," she said.

"Damn right I'm good. And none too terribly humble, either," echoed the Abbot, casting a wide smile across the table. His smile caught her, willingly. "I keep my confessor busy, I never run short of sins."

"Me neither," she confessed. "You know, I might just take you up on that guest lecturer thing you mentioned. You know, down the road sometime." Her smile was genuine, as was her offer.

"I *am* the man to talk to about that." Leaning forward across the table, the Abbot said in a low, confident voice, "And you know as well as I that your road, as well as mine, aren't near as long as they once were. Keep that in your mind. I know I do, every day."

Magda said, "Yes sir, you certainly appear to be the man around here—and I know—and I will." She stood, and because the timing was just right, Magda excused herself, thanked the Abbot in sweet, kind words, and returned to her room. She declined the offer to be escorted because she knew she would give the poor, unsuspecting little monk of a man a full run for his money when she told him his fortune in the two short minutes to walk back to her room. Magda was deeply tempted, but buried the urge. As she shook the Abbot's hand she also kissed his cheek.

Down the hallway to her room, a surge of anxiousness captured her, as if she was late to get a move on to where she needed to go. She realized a rush to get going to wherever Roscoe wanted them to go. Magda didn't have the faintest idea of his plans, and then as she opened her door, thinking about not knowing his plans—not knowing anything anymore it seemed—somehow eased her anxiousness. She grew excited as she closed her door, her eyes drawn to the plain wooden crucifix above the small window. Without hesitation she repacked her suitcase, changed into blue jeans, and when finished sat on her bed, waiting for Roscoe. She smiled, thinking, *How did that man know I was faking losing my faculties? Damn, even Roscoe believes I've got the early beginnings of dementia. And now I feel so bad about that, deceiving the man who'd no more deceive me than anyone. I do love that crazy man.* Magda then composed a most unique contrition on the spot, got up from the bed and genuflected in front of the crucifix, and while kneeling, recited aloud twenty Our Father's for her self-imposed penance, knowing full well God would forgive her—plus He'd forgive her for her temptation to tell Him His fortune.

Now, Roscoe knocked with confidence on Magda's door. Of course she knew it was him. She felt his knock in her heart, which was much stronger than his, she knew that too, no matter how confident his knock.

Chapter 9

Immersed in the rolling booms of Arizona thunder, the booms announcing the advance of a wall of gigantic cumulus clouds, uneven in their respective heights but nonetheless intimidating in their thirty-thousand-feet posture, and in no hurry to advance across the Verde Valley and be done with, the phenomenon known around those parts as monsoon season was here. Saunders sipped wine while shaving in the afternoon, feeling the thunder's rumble in his razor stroke, sensing rare humidity on his fresh shaven skin, and having to tug up his pants, noticing they were sagging against his hips. He wasn't sure who was going to arrive first, or whether Kristina was actually serious about visiting at all. But he knew Roscoe was coming, having finally started communicating again, albeit from a different phone number. Saunders was sure Roscoe would not bother to offer why his phone number had changed. He told Saunders to expect three, and who the third person was, Saunders could only imagine. He put on a collared long-sleeve shirt, rolled up his sleeves to below his elbows, and after locking up, got in his truck for the hour-and-a-half drive to his daughter's house for dinner.

****

"The wine opener's on the counter. Don't pour me a glass just yet; let me make the salad first," called out Veronica to her father, exiting the guest bathroom. Saunders went directly to the counter where he'd placed the two bottles of wine, and uncorked the red, knowing his daughter put the white wine in the fridge to chill. He poured himself a half glass and took in the smells of dinner coming from the kitchen, where Veronica had been busy for the past few hours. The brisket smelled as if prepared in a Texas smokehouse, for indeed it was, Veronica having ordered it from her favorite food store, a high-end market that seemed to have everything you ever wanted, already prepared, just waiting to be heated up to serve. The mashed potatoes and green beans she prepared herself. She loved to cook when she had time, but she never seemed to have any time, except when her father came to dinner.

She was pretty, just a couple of rungs short of beautiful, thought Saunders. And she was fat, which would not have been so bad, he thought, had she not favored her mother's stature. Veronica was one of those happy people, bursting out in smile to match her bustling lifestyle. Saunders sat with one leg straight out on her set of uncomfortable barstools set against the counter and sipped his wine in silence.

"Traffic tolerable on the way down, Dad?" asked Veronica, not looking up while slicing baby tomatoes in half, scooping them up with the large knife and depositing them in conscious fashion throughout the salad bowl.

"Very tolerable," he said, topping off his glass. "Smells fantastic."

"You just can't go wrong with that new market we have here now. I love it so much. Wait'll you taste the brisket. Amazing." Veronica wedged the salad bowl in the already full refrigerator, and removed the white wine bottle and placed in front of her father, who dutifully began the uncorking. She motioned him to follow her to the living room. Veronica had bought a brand-new home just as the housing market bottomed out during the recent recession. The house was much too large for just her, a brand-new neighborhood in Chandler. It would have the new development look and feel for a number of years to come, until the trees grew at least as tall as the two-story, off-white stucco houses that lined the wide streets with high curbs to anticipate flash floods during the monsoon season. With money left over because of the very affordable price of the house, she ordered furniture, carpets, window treatments, and accents out of the same catalog. In fact her home was to be featured in next season's catalog because she invited the company to visit and they were so impressed, they agreed almost as soon as they entered the high-ceiling foyer and took in the view of her open-floor-plan home. As a very tall man, Saunders liked the house because of the cathedral ceilings.

He was not as nervous about telling her as he thought he'd be. He believed that his daughter would soon put a happy spin on the whole thing and that would be that. At least that was what he hoped Veronica would do, having put a happy spin on every disappointment that confronted her or anyone for that matter. *She put one hell of a happy spin on our separation*, he thought, and he was counting on that kind of rationalization for what he was going to tell her over dinner. *Maybe I should have bought four bottles of wine*, he wondered, second thoughts entering his mind as they sat down.

Saunders asked, "Your kids this year—you got a good class?"

"Oh, you know, I have a mixture, a few bright ones, a couple actually scary smart, and a small handful who are just that—a handful," laughed Veronica, gesturing all the while with her hands. She was always animated, as if all conversations of any subject required complete hand motions and arm waving. She wore a big flowered dress to her knees, and her calves were very well shaped, only twice the size they really should be because of her weight. Saunders could never get over the realization that his very pretty daughter would most likely never be a slender woman, and it caused him great pain. He prayed a man may come her way who would be unswayed by her very ample size. Saunders would always wonder if it was because of the separation, regardless if it occurred just as his daughter graduated college. She was heavy in high school, he remembered.

She made her father sit at the head of the table, and after serving them both, she sat down to his right. Saunders held up his wineglass and Veronica followed, creating a soothing chime as they gently touched glasses.

"Fine crystal you have here, my dear," laughed Saunders, always making the same comment every time they toasted. Veronica always returned an earnest giggle. Saunders was famished, having eaten only a banana for breakfast, and knowing his daughter would demand he eat a large portion of whatever she prepared for him.

"Eat up, Dad. You've lost weight, I can tell…something I can't manage to do," she said, attempting to be matter-of-fact, but not quite pulling it off, thought Saunders. "You're either running too much or not eating enough or both. And you *will* be taking home the leftovers this time. Because you know full well, I'll eat it all tomorrow."

"Absolutely fantastic as always, Veronica," he said, already starting to get full. But he was going to clean his plate, and this time and forever more, never complain to her about the portions she served him. "I promise to take all the leftovers home with me this time."

"Good."

"I have to thank you again for helping me get my furniture pieces sold. You know I couldn't have done it without you."

"Dad, you don't have to keep thanking me. I wanted to do it—I've told you I want to start a design business, and I want to feature your furniture, or shall I say, I want to showcase the creations of Pascal Bonaventure." She laughed. Not only did Veronica create the website to advertise his furniture, she used her contacts to spread the word, and in eight months all of his furniture pieces were sold to three customers in three separate states, in accordance with her father's wishes. She was so disappointed he demanded to remain anonymous and use the silly name of Pascal Bonaventure.

"I don't think for a minute either Pascal or Saint Bonaventure would be too pleased about what I'm about to tell you."

"You're not going to stop making furniture for God's sake, are you?"

Saunders refilled his daughter's glass. She was going to need it, he concluded.

"I retrieved all my furniture back from those customers."

Veronica cleaned the last bit of mashed potatoes from her plate with a dinner roll, popping the entire mashed-potato-covered roll into her mouth.

"What does *that* mean?" she replied, asking with her mouth full, now washing it down with a gulp of white wine. She pushed back her chair and stood up, placing her hands firmly down on the white lace-covered table, straddling the place setting, arms locked as if preparing for any attempts to be pushed aside. "What does that mean, Dad?" Her rounded cheeks now flushed pink.

Saunders sat back in his chair. "I mean I committed larceny of a sort."

"And what does 'larceny of a sort' mean? *Exactly*?"

"It means I left each customer an envelope of cash that well compensated them for my furniture."

"You *stole* the furniture from them?" Veronica was in no happy-spinning mood, whatsoever. "You broke into their homes and stole their furniture? It's *their* furniture, Dad, *they* paid for it!" Veronica stood erect, her giant bosom almost preventing her from seeing her plate as she fumbled to get hold of the sides and, upon doing so, stomped into the kitchen, her knife sliding off the plate in the process and clanging on the wood laminate floor.

"Leave that knife right where it is!" she screamed. "I cannot believe what I am hearing from my own father! Go sit in the living room, drink your damn wine, and don't say a word to me. Do I make myself clear?"

In admonished silence Saunders grabbed the red wine bottle and his glass and settled into the extra-large leather La-Z-Boy recliner in front of the large flat-screen TV. He heard her mutter to herself, "Pascal Bonaventure," with full disdain and acid sarcasm.

Veronica made no effort to avoid further clanging as she loaded the dishwasher loudly with plates and utensils. The cupboard doors were shut firmly as pots and pans were bounced back into their appointed places. Stopping in front of the kitchen bar, she leaned in toward the living room and boomed, "And just why did you commit larceny of a sort?" her finger quotes gesture exaggerated for the full irksome effect she fully intended.

Saunders was not ready to answer that question yet because he wanted to be completely sure why he did what he did. The titillation he achieved in succeeding in the thefts was not what he sought. Not in the least. After each larcenous act, he sat alone in the dark of his RV, working himself into a cold sweat attempting to hold back the desire to vomit from the creeping nausea that accompanied hauling his furniture away from the homes he invaded.

"I'm now an accessory to you! My father! My God!" screamed Veronica as she burst from the kitchen and stood before her father, who looked up at his daughter like a teenager trying to come clean to his unthinking stupidity. After discovering the addresses of the two residences, the scouting and executing of the acts were without much thought, his admission finally now flashing through his mind as he returned his daughter's stare. Thank God neither house was alarmed or difficult to break into. Saunders didn't count the third break-in of Kristina's rental. That act of larceny he kept separate from the first two. That act was somehow different, he thought quickly. He was unsure exactly why that act was different, but it was, he decided.

Veronica's expression transformed from the firm face of a scolding teacher to a face of concern for a child, for that is what she viewed her father at that moment, which startled her, and she finished cleaning up after dinner. She was confused and hurt for a confluence of reasons; her father, the rock-solid military man who flew fighter planes and commanded with confidence, a thoughtful and gracious man who was not around near as much as she wanted him to when he was in the military—especially during the tough years in high school where she simply wanted to die of a sudden fatal disease to end her pain of acute loneliness. Veronica was loved by him during what seemed to be the periods that weren't quite when she wanted him, but soon after. No matter, she thought, he was there eventually, *and he made me feel like I was the smartest girl in the world. I knew he meant it with all his heart*, she reflected, now sitting down next to him, as Saunders reached over and topped off his wineglass, waiting for the last few drops of wine to slide down the neck, using any delay possible to respond to his daughter. He knew he could not speak intelligently about his actions at the moment.

What a difference from their last dinner together, when her enthusiastic bursts interrupted every other bite of dinner, when she was talking so fast between forkfuls of lasagna she was sometimes unintelligible in her conveyance of rapid-fire ideas coming to her about how his website layout might best look to attract women, who Veronica was firmly convinced would be the primary site visitors to view her father's wonderful furniture. The warm feeling of remembrance of that dinner now cooled and felt as if it took place fifty years ago—as if perhaps that dinner never took place at all.

"I'm not ready to talk about what I've done. But when I do, I'll talk to you. I promise."

Saunders kissed his daughter's cheek, and she wrapped her arm around him and whispered, "I think you're winging it these days, and you, of all men, are *sooo* not used to winging it. You just can't do illegal things, Dad. Not you. You have to think. You know?"

"I know. That much I know. And 'winging' it is a nice way of telling me I've been reckless. And don't…"

She cut him off. "Of course I'm not going to say anything, because I don't know anything, and I don't want to be involved in anything!" She pushed herself up from the sofa and went to her bathroom to freshen up.

His mobile phone had been buzzing in his pocket off and on for the last twenty minutes. It was Kristina. She was wondering where in the hell he was as she drove around Verde Valley.

Saunders got up and stepped out onto the tiny front porch and called Kristina. She didn't pick up so he left a voicemail asking where she was and to go back to the gas station and quick mart store nearest to his place and call him when she arrived so he could give her directions to his place.

"You leaving now?" asked Veronica, as she stepped outside her front door.

"I am—and thank you for the delicious dinner. Thank you also for not berating me over all this. I'm getting back on track to what I want to do. Just a bit distracted for the moment."

"Distracted? Are you serious, Dad? Your shit is in the street, to quote you!" Veronica never cursed. Her frustration flushed her round cheeks. Saunders hugged Veronica and she slowly succumbed to his fatherly embrace, whispering, "You have a chance to be a successful artisan, Dad; you're a very good furniture maker, so much attention to the little things."

"I'll recover," he said.

As he walked to his car, Veronica called out, "And Dad, do you really need to clean out fast-food kitchens in the middle of the night for a living? I mean, what's with that anyway?"

Saunders opened the pickup door and waved back to her, saying, "Just a favor I promised some old buds. The job is done." He blew her a quick kiss and drove off. "That job is done," he said to himself aloud, his thoughts now attempting to focus on Kristina. Every time he thought of her, his mind would spin. His cell phone vibrated in his shirt pocket. It was an unfamiliar number. The text read, “Inbound soon—1 more with us.”

Saunders texted back, “How soon?” Roscoe didn’t reply. Saunders did not want to call him. He wouldn’t answer anyway. He forgot to take the leftovers.

“Found a bar!! They are sooo nice here! Where r u?” texted Kristina.

“Driving home from my daughter’s house. Be home in 1 hour. Where are you?” replied Saunders.

“Somewhere in Arizona, darlin’!”

Saunders did want to call her, but decided he’d wait until he got closer. He had a feeling he knew which bar Kristina was at. The bikers were sure to keep her occupied, as she was sure to keep their attention, he thought.

His thoughts now shifted to why he stole his furniture back. He wanted to admit to himself the true reason that drove his compulsion to commit larceny—and to what end.

“Your daughter lives here too! I can’t wait to meet her! I bet I’ll love her!” Saunders read Kristina’s text and then turned the phone to silent mode. He had more than enough to square away inside his mind besides dealing with Kristina at the present moment. But of course he knew that she was directly linked to his illegal furniture retrieval, and for the first time he attempted to confront himself and wrestle from his own mind exactly why he had to get back his creations.

Whenever he thought about his actions, he’d go for a run, running as many miles as it took that particular day to clear his mind of any delusional strands of sanguinity when thoughts of Kristina slipped in through the back way. Just like water through cracked concrete, no matter how slight the crack, it is relentless in finding a new space other than standing still—so too Kristina always found a way into Saunders's consciousness. And his dreams? Of course his dreams; Kristina had taken up permanent residence in them ever since they went their separate ways, almost half a lifetime ago. For such a long time Saunders believed his waking mind to be a solid block of concrete, and therefore impenetrable to thoughts of her—after all, he was an old man in his fifties now, he thought, and such musings should no longer be strong enough to find the cracks in his mind. This night, the closest he came to the truth was to acknowledge to himself as he stared into the rearview mirror, squinting to see his own eyes because of the headlights of cars behind him, that he wasn't as blind to the realization that his age had no effect abating his heart's desire, but more worrisome, no effect either on abating his fear that he had been merely in a lapsed state of delusion, only for that delusion to be reawakened. Was this a testament to the human heart or to the reality that delusions remained as powerful a force as ever, until Death discarded the need?

Saunders accelerated, allowing himself a moment of contentment about what he didn't know—or care. His mind now gratefully clearing as the traffic thinned and the city lights became obscured by the scrubby desert hills approaching Verde Valley.

Kristina texted again. She said she was too tired to find Saunders's place in the dark and that maybe she should ask if one of the locals could lead her to his place.

Then a text update. "A party with my new friends! Soon to be at your place!" Reading her last text, contentment vanished and he called her back.

Chapter 10

Nathan Armstrong leaned forward from the backseat and rested his elbows on the top of the front seats of the white van, where Roscoe and Magda were sitting.

Nathan said, "Imagine a cliff, see. Now imagine a rope hangin' down from the edge of the cliff holdin' onto a grand piano. Now—imagine a strong man pullin' that piano up that steep cliff. That's one strong man, see. And he's got one strong pull to get that piano back on top of that cliff. That same strong pull, the very same, is the pull of nicotine on my body, see? That's how strong cigarettes are on me."

Roscoe looked away from the road and watched Magda turn around and give Nathan a shrug and a smile, gently patting his bandaged hands.

"Welcome to the quitters' world, Nathan. It's the same pull for everybody that's addicted to smokes. No different than the rest of us. No different at all," she said, her matter-of-fact tone doing nothing to help him crave nicotine any less. In a huff, Nathan pushed himself back into his seat, folding his arms too quickly and bumping his bandaged hands against each other. Roscoe looked in the rearview mirror and observed Nathan wincing in pain. His lip was healing nicely; some of the swelling was gone. His bandaged nose gave attention to two shiners and his right eye still was bloodshot from the beatings. Nathan refused to keep the ice on his ribs at night, but during the day he relented and wore a heat wrap around his rib cage. It eased the pain, but Nathan was loathe to admit it. He was an outstanding mechanic with a sharp skill in solving tough problems with vintage cars, the muscle cars loved by enthusiasts and collectors. He was also rock-hard stubborn and a fidgety sort, his right knee in constant motion as well as his mind, which scatted in all directions when deprived of certain "mind tamers," as he referred to marijuana and cigarettes. Roscoe thought a saving grace was the fact that his younger brother got so terribly sick on Black Velvet as a high school sophomore, he couldn't stand the smell of alcohol—not even beer. Not such a saving grace was that Nathan loved marijuana because it calmed his knee and his scatting mind. Nathan believed it was in fact a gift from God that he discovered weed because no one could understand how much better he felt not having a restless knee and a racing mind. Rebuilding cars was the first gift from God, thought Nathan, but on many days it most definitely was the fine weed that he scored that achieved the first place ranking. Nathan was built like Satchel Paige; tall, sinewy thin, but possessing fine, long fingers for doing intricate work.

"But it's my fine, up-close vision that makes the difference," he'd say to anyone, although the days were drawing very close to his need for glasses for his up-close work, and looking out the windshield and into the flat distance of New Mexico, his right eye still seeing blurry from the beating, he wondered if his eyes were ever going to be like they were. He was going to have to take some painkillers today, he reckoned, not having any chance to score some muggles before they hustled out of Louisiana under the blanket of fog and night, trading the 442 for the Abbot's white van. Nathan referred to marijuana as "muggles," just like his New Orleans music heroes called it way back in the day. Nathan thought for sure he'd be square with his gambling debts after the hard asses invaded his place and took everything. Surely it must cover it all, he hoped. *God help me, it surely must cover my bad bets. Maybe the beating covered some of my debts too*, looking down at his bandaged hands, afraid to move his fingers any more than the bandages allowed. Roscoe kept telling him his hands were healing nicely, as he tended to them daily. They were ten hours from Arizona to stay with Saunders, who was unwitting to all that Roscoe, Magda, and Nathan would bring.

Chapter 11

Rare is it to find a comparable sound: that unmistakable, uneven pop-pop, low rumble of a V-twin motor on a Harley-Davidson motorcycle. It is the rumble of Made in America. And to Saunders, it sounded tonight as if the air was completely saturated by the V-twin motors of as many as twelve, maybe more, Harleys rumbling like road dragons in heat, closing upon his house, only minutes after he returned from having a disheartening dinner with his daughter. Hearing the sounds brought back a flash memory of the flight line full of jets in idle power, just prior to chocks being pulled from their tires and released to taxi onward.

Lancaster Barton, owner and operator of The Stubborn Mule Bar, led the cycles up to Saunders's front door. Saunders knew Barton, having done some kitchen and lighting work in his bar, and after completing his work stayed and had a beer with Barton a few times. Barton was a retired Army Ranger. Smart guy, a clear leader, and his bark was mainly for show, but you knew he could put a strong man down on the ground before he realized he was no longer standing. Behind Lancaster Barton was Kristina, her ecstatic smile amplifying the aura created by the headlights of the other bikers following. The bikers kept their engines running as Kristina kissed Barton's cheek before slipping off his back seat, adjusting herself and waving to the other bikers behind her.

"Claims she was lost trying to find you, Saunders, and damn if she didn't demand we give her a ride to your place,"

Barton said, just loud enough to be heard over the engines, yet delicate in tone, as if delivering a lost puppy back to its frantic owner. Saunders shook Barton's hand, leaning close to him to reply in private. Lancaster let out a hearty laugh, saying, "I'll take you up on that, Ravel!" Then an imported sport utility vehicle appeared and pulled up next to Lancaster's bike. Lancaster's wife got out of the SUV, gave Kristina a tight embrace, handing her the keys, and took her place behind Lancaster. A quick salute to Saunders and the bikers turned around, leaving only a small wake of dust as they departed into the night.

"I just love that man…and his wife is a precious jewel!" Kristina loved to be enthralled by the act of enthralling strangers, especially the most interesting or the most seemingly unapproachable types. She believed she could enthrall anyone she met.

"Lancaster says he knew you, and after a little chitchat with him and his lovely wife Gina, they offered to give me a ride to your place!" Swirling around in the darkness, punctuated only by the porch light, Kristina declared she loved Saunders's place.

It was almost too much for Saunders. He turned around, and in slow, measured steps up to the porch, sat down in one of the two cast-iron, spring rocker porch chairs, and began to rock. Feeling dizzy, like he was instantly transported to another time, he felt like a stranger on his own land. A lifetime ago does not begin to describe the distance between them, he thought, staring at Kristina as she unloaded two small suitcases from the back of her SUV. The thought of helping her never entered his mind because Saunders could not believe this was real, yet at the same time he did not want these moments to end. He forced his mind to recall the first moments of hearing the Harleys arrive, the moment he recognized that it was Kristina on the back of Lancaster's bike, of her smile and blazing bright eyes, in complete enthrallment. Enthralling Saunders once more, he decided once again he only ever wanted to be enthralled by "Huguette Sands."

The bang of closing the back door of her SUV cleared his head somewhat, and Saunders got up to help her with her bags, both so heavy they seemed to be filled with river stones. She relinquished her bags over to him, saying, "C'mon, you're a big man, you can handle the weight," as she burst out with a sharp laugh. She opened the front door and demanded to know where his dogs were and why weren't they panting and whining to get out and greet her.

"No dogs? I cannot *believe* there are no dogs on this beautiful piece of land! Tell me now, tell me you love dogs!"

"How do you know this is a beautiful piece of land? It's black-coal dark outside," he said, following her into his own home, and then nodding off to the right toward the guest bedroom.

"Because, darlin', I actually found your place straightaway, and not finding you here I had to go someplace else and wait until you came back. And what I saw of the place I simply *adored*. And, I'm very curious about that one building over there," as she turned and pointed toward the building where

Saunders kept his reclaimed furniture. She let him take the lead toward the guest bedroom. As soon as he turned on the bedside lamp, Kristina claimed she loved the room, now wanting to know where the bathroom was. "Oh, I have my very own bathroom too!" She waited for Saunders to face her. Surprised by his quickness as he grabbed her and held her close, she whispered, "Can I just look at you for a while?"

"I do like dogs, but I'm never around here for long stretches of time."

"That's a poor excuse; you have to take them with you then," she whispered.

"Where are your dogs then?"

"A story for another night," she said, clutching Saunders so tight she interrupted his breathing. He felt himself inside someone else's body, because, he thought, there was no possibility of the woman he knew as Kristina ever coming into his life again. In her fifties, she was beautiful as he remembered her that first day on the flight line when he was a second lieutenant and she was a senior airman. Saunders saw her as she looked now, but he also could not fail to see her as a twenty-two-year-old assistant crew chief, distracting every single officer and enlisted man on the flight line.

"Take a hot bath or something and get some sleep. I'll make breakfast in the morning."

He kissed and released her in one quick motion, fearing he'd linger and never want to release her again. She grabbed his arm, and as he moved away her grip slid down to his hand and he squeezed it tight, and he left her alone in the guest room.

The last thing Kristina desired was to go to bed. The bikers gave her a buzz that amplified in the presence of Saunders, as her memories spurred tears.

In unison they said, "Good night."

Saunders left the house and went to the building where he stored his furniture. He unlocked the door and once inside felt his way in the dark to the opposite side of the large room and turned on a lamp on an old metal military surplus desk that he used to store various things such as warranty paperwork and instructions for all his tools and anything else he owned that came with such paperwork. On the top of the desk was a dated portable stereo system, the all-in-one kind with a cassette player, a CD player, and AM/FM. Next to the stereo system was a stack of CDs and a coffeepot, with the filters shoved in one of the top drawers. He clicked the lamp on high and turned around to look at his furniture pieces. Though they were arranged to some degree, as if trying to fit in to belong to a home, they were nothing but furniture arranged in a large room on a concrete floor in an aluminum building designed not to be a home at all. Saunders's recognition of this was what brought him back that night. Then he began to move all the furniture toward the dining table. He worked so as not to make too much noise. After getting all the pieces clustered close to each other, he draped the large canvas tarp back over the entire collection. Saunders turned off the lamp and went to the two windows on the same side as the entrance door and ensured the window coverings were closed. He locked the building and went back inside the house, removed his half boots, and taking them with him, went to his room and showered. Lying awake in bed, his mind charged with the events of the evening. Saunders thought about what he was like as a very young man, whether he was still the same man—or had life experiences changed his outlook, his expectations, and his dreams to such an extent that he was not only different, but now unrecognizable. The thought was absurd, he reflected, knowing he was the same man, and he could never be anything other than what he was, no matter what experiences he found himself in. He'd known some men to quit drinking, and that decision stopped them from self-destructive drunkenness. He also knew one man who, once he stopped drinking, subsequently resorted to a quiet type—who flowed with life's currents rather than swam to the banks to seek out that which was different or untried. In short time he became a sad man, knowing not to die of drink required him to be a go-with-the-flow type, a type he loathed to be, yet he couldn't find that essence within himself to swim against the current without alcohol. *That man remains sober—and sad to this day*, Saunders thought. Turning on his side and staring at the alarm clock in dim amber glow, Saunders believed he may be in the place he disliked the most. That is, Saunders believed he wasn't flowing in the current of life or swimming against the current toward something that he believed he should pursue, that he wanted to pursue. In pursuit of that illusive "thing" that was going to define him.

Saunders felt he swam all right; but he only swam with the current and angled toward the shore, and after eventually coming ashore, sat there—still—watching the current of life flow by—not pursuing a damn thing. Sure, not agreeing to accompany his wife back to her town where she grew up was swimming against the flow, and realizing that he did not think of her as much as he knew he should have maybe was thinking against the flow. And the creative impulse to design and build all the furniture in the building was pursuing something that he sought to reclaim of himself—but now what? Now what? *Well,* thought Saunders, *I did steal the furniture back and that most definitely was against the flow—and a monumental collapse of judgment and definite stupidity.*

And this cycle of thought returned him to that which he refused to think about, and when he was unable to avoid that which he refused to think about, he went running. But not tonight, he told himself, not tonight. *I can run no longer. I will accept what I know and why I chose to swim the path I swam. No matter how ridiculous my decision.*

Now his mind buzzed at the reality of what he wanted for most of his adult life. Already she was changing the way he viewed most things, as if he was not in his own house and amongst his own possessions. The house was his, all right, he thought, but something changed as he got back out of bed and put on his jeans and a white cowboy shirt with wide blue stitching and pearl drop buttons. The theater Kristina restored had given him ideas on what to build next, loud and Baroque ideas that were screaming at him to sketch out.

His bedroom was on the opposite side of the house with a separate entrance to the kitchen. He grabbed the container of coffee and once on the porch slipped on his boots. He walked quickly to his workshop and sat at another old metal military desk, complete with a coffeepot. He didn't need the caffeine yet and instead made himself a pot of decaffeinated coffee and began to sketch, believing Kristina's presence was influencing his will and affecting his design. He allowed himself a small smile that, once formed, turned to a grin and a sharp laugh that he squelched for fear of waking Kristina, unlikely, given he was in his workshop, in another building thirty yards away from the main house. Ten sketches were completed with little thought as to time of early morning, only noticing sunrise had come with stiff winds. Taking a break, Saunders got up and stretched to rid ache from his lower back and shoulders. Through the window next to the door opposite his desk, he looked at a high, overcast, light gray sky with the endless visibility desert dwellers had become so accustomed to—now obscured by kicked-up sand from the winds. He was tired, and thought to himself he could sleep for two hours. But she was present, and though he always wanted her to be continually present, any thought of the occurrence actually coming to pass was never dwelled upon. And no sleep would come until he sat down with Kristina and together they filled in the life particulars that transpired while apart for decades, to see for himself what changes had occurred to the essence of who Saunders believed she was, or if the core of her essence had changed at all.

Saunders returned to his desk and placed the sketches in the top center drawer and turned off the lamp. He was famished from the morning's burst of ideas and from eating little the day before. A large breakfast was on his mind and the smell of bacon crisping and strong coffee percolating would fill the house and perhaps draw Kristina from her slumber. Instead, after closing up his workshop and walking toward the main house, it was Saunders who smelled bacon and the brew of strong coffee accompanied by someone's slightly sharp singing over Sly Johnson's version of "Take Me to the River." Saunders slipped off his boots and tiptoed toward the kitchen. Sliding across the wood floor in orange socks and a daisy yellow sundress, shaking her head as if possessed by the Holy Spirit of R&B, Kristina claimed ownership of the kitchen as she danced from the stove to the refrigerator, grabbing a sip of coffee in between. Saunders noticing she had replaced his digital audio player with her flaming pink player. Hiding in the hallway, he watched her prepare breakfast, whirling dervish style.

"I like Talking Heads's version," he said, announcing himself over the new song—Al Green's "Love and Happiness."

"You would. Sly Johnson's version is the best! Talking Heads's version, I don't know, too anemic. I can't get my body into their version of 'Take Me to the River.' Oh well, shows the difference between us, I guess," she replied in her patented way of ending a sentence with an observation that served as a thinly veiled way of communicating a reason for something not to be.

But Saunders was never fooled by this, as her reply reeled him back to their younger days. It was her way of attempting to protect herself from being led into any circumstance that may be an indication of a willingness to commit. And exposing a difference in opinion or views was Kristina's trademark tagline to communicate why a commitment would not be possible, as if to indicate to any man that everything, *everything* would have to align in some perfect cosmic arrangement before she would even consider a commitment of her heart. It was her way of trying to tell someone that she had feelings, but not to try too hard to form a relationship with her because in fact she was hiding her fear of committing to anyone who offered the slightest chance of disappointment or, worse, failure. She wanted complete control over any relationship so as to shield herself against any slight, any hurt. Her greatest self-lie, Saunders recalled, was her insistence on letting everyone know that she was committed to no one and no way of life other than what she claimed she could choose at any moment. But the facts of her life betrayed her delusion. She changed her name to Huguette in an attempt to become someone other than Kristina. At that moment Saunders became very curious as to her degree of success. So far, from watching her now—in addition to lighting up the VFW hall in Nebraska, nothing seemed to have changed in his two brief encounters with the only woman he ever fully loved, without condition. *She blazes like a star for a while*, he remembered, *and then collapses in exhaustion—most times getting some kind of respiratory infection.*

Kristina separated the egg whites to make a frittata that included spinach, black olives, feta cheese, artichokes, and yellow peppers. She was now tending to the breakfast potatoes, which may have been in danger of too much cayenne had not Al Green's "Love and Tenderness" began to play. Up above her head went Kristina's hand with the cayenne jar as she swirled away from the stove and over to a half-empty Bloody Mary to crunch the remaining stump of the celery stalk bobbing in her glass. Saunders stepped in to take the cayenne from her and she at first resisted. Kristina then relaxed just enough for him to take the spice, and he went over to the covered potatoes and said, "Smells like the perfect amount of cayenne."

"What would you know about cooking?" she said, with a teasing grin.

"Enough to know I love cayenne on hash browns," he replied.

"They're not hash browns, they're breakfast potatoes. They're prepared different."

"I see that," he said, "just as I see that orange socks and a yellow dress with a dash of cayenne pepper on the front is the latest hot fashion trend for cooking breakfast."

She looked down and brushed off the powder.

"Out, out if you're going to be hostile to the chef! And, I demand to be called
Huguette! That other name is not me anymore!" Kristina tilted her nose in the air and waved him off as she checked the frittata in the oven. Saunders was tempted to join her in a Bloody Mary but decided not to partake. He wanted his full faculties with Kristina here. He scooted around her to retrieve the silverware and other accoutrements and set the dining table for two. Her nearness calmed him, always. And Saunders felt he was always going to be just fine with Kristina around, regardless of how much energy she exerted over the most trivial of details.

Maybe that's because to Saunders, Kristina made everything appear as if still—in a kind of suspended continuance, as if there were no subsequent moments because they *were* in the moment that mattered. And she made everything seem unreal, not as if in a dream, but in an existence that was exclusive of the rest of the goings-on in the world. But he was unsure about having this woman "Huguette" around. So far, Saunders only saw the Kristina he knew from the early days.

"In my house and in my kitchen and on my property and in my heart and mind, you are Kristina, and I will call you Kristina." Saunders smiled, remaining unflinching in his tone and in his gaze. She turned to look at him. Her eyes softened, betraying her attempt to be adamant. "I'm going to shave."

"You do that. A Bloody Mary for you this morning?" she asked.

"Not at the moment, thank you."

"Oh, but I made you one!" She opened the refrigerator door and pulled out the drink from the top shelf.

"Kristina, thank you, maybe later, okay?" He excused himself and left her in a pout.

She stared at the drink, wondering whether to drink it herself or return it to the refrigerator, where she knew it would not taste as good later—the other smells in the refrigerator would be quick to invade and spoil the flavor. She didn't mind him calling her by her real name, but was not willing to admit that to him. *Surely not*, she thought, as she decided to drink Saunders's Bloody Mary herself. She returned to her tasks and prepared the plates so as to be ready when he finished shaving.

Then she went and put on some music from one of her favorite bands of the moment, a band that was fond of mandolins, soft beats, and tight harmonies; singers singing songs about themselves dreaming of never having to lose a lover again, as if loss at twenty-two years of age, or however young they certainly were, was the emotional tragedy that already shaped their lives and tainted their future.

If they only knew, thought Saunders. Songs that sounded like old-time songs. But the oldest band member was an over-the-hill twenty-three.

When Saunders returned she placed the plates on the table and went back to get her drink. She was flush from the activity of cooking and the vodka. She gave out a soft sigh of accomplishment as he stood before his chair.

“Smells outta sight,” he said, admiring the presentation of the frittata, potatoes, and bacon, with a garnish of sliced orange and a single strawberry.

“You keep a well-stocked kitchen. I am impressed!” she said, commanding him to sit and eat. She raised her drink to toast and realized Saunders had no glass to join her.

“Ooo, sorry,” she said.

Saunders got up and equally commanded her to stay seated and he got something to drink. He poured himself a glass of tomato juice and stood beside her.

“A toast to the chef, and a toast in gratitude for your presence. Quite the impressive entrance last evening, with the motorcycles and all.”

"I do my best to impress," she said, with an engaging smile. "Now eat before it gets any colder. But wait…before you sit down, get the real toast…in the oven staying warm."

Breakfast was delicious, as it appeared, and they both ate as if not having eaten for some time. The mood was light and Kristina laughed throughout the conversation of catching up with each other, occasionally turning serious and then bouncing back into a lighter spirit as soon as the turn in conversation would offer. They both knew very little about each other's lives over the past many years, only hearing snippets from mutual acquaintances from their days in the Air Force together.

"I was the best crew chief on the flight line and you know it," said Kristina. She was in a very talkative mood when the topics suited her.

"Maybe, but you were also the only chick on the flight line at the time and the only one who could look good in fatigues and boots. Every guy on the flight line had to be snapped back into doing their own jobs because of you. The colonels thought you were such a distraction they talked about pulling you off the line so no knucklehead crew chief would run into a jet with a loader or fire extinguisher," said Saunders. Her fork clinked down on the plate in surprise, which really would surprise no one, especially Saunders.

"Huhh," she said.

"Huhh indeed," he replied.

"Almost everyone there during that time was so nice!"

"Of course they were, Kristina; everyone there during that time was trying to get into your fatigues."

"I really was just a baby back then…innocent, you know." This time Saunders clinked his fork down on the plate and gave her a scoffing look. "Everyone *was* nice! But you, you weren't nice to me."

"Not true," replied Saunders, quickly adding, "I didn't ogle you and follow you around like a lost puppy."

"Why not?" she whined in mock disappointment, followed by her quick trademark laugh as her way of playfully pretending to dismiss the truth that the officers and enlisted men did just what he described—as if to imply the obvious ridiculousness of such an actuality that couldn't possibly be true. But Saunders would have none of it. He never bought into it then and certainly would never buy into it now. They both finished breakfast, but not before Saunders went back for seconds. He was tempted to make a Bloody Mary but held off, instead pouring himself more tomato juice.

"What changed your mind when we went on that training deployment to Savannah? Why did you suddenly decide to talk to me? Why after all that time?"

Without realizing, Saunders slowed his eating, as his mind raced, thinking about those early days.

"No mystery there, Kristina. In fact, you know why because I told you back then."

Pleading in earnest she said, "But I want to hear it again! Tell me! And who are *you* to give me a hard time about calling myself Huguette? You—Mr. Pascal Bonaventure, is it? Whoever *that* is."

"Who's Pascal Bonaventure?" he asked, with no hint of recognition of his online name to advertise his furniture. She made an utterance that sounded like "pshaw," by blowing air out through her pursed lips. It was an ancient utterance, it seemed to Saunders, as if it transcended all ages and languages. She learned it from her mother. He always liked when she did that. How much did she really know about the furniture?

Saunders continued, "I decided to talk with you because for the first time I realized I was the only guy around the flight line not trying to get a line on you. It was just six pilots and what, eight or so crew chiefs and specialists on that deployment? So I said hello to you as you ended your shift. You were sitting on the curb, tired and sweaty, and your hands were black from the tire change you just finished. I know because I watched you change that main gear tire."

"You said hi to me for the first time!" Kristina was drinking her second Bloody Mary very slowly.

"I sat down on the curb next to you, as you recall."

"I was shocked," she said, gazing at him as if it were the first time she laid eyes on him. She had an overt way of looking at a man in such a way to let him know she was interested, and then only to claim later that she just happened to be interested in what he was saying at the time, not necessarily him in particular. Kristina was a master of the flirt and never minded that more often than not it got her into situations where a man perceived exactly what she intended to convey. She was just playing them, making sure she still could catch an eye and swell an attraction.

She learned this when she was five years old; catching her father's eye was everything to her.

She said, "We talked until two a.m.…about everything. You had a lot to say about everything besides the Air Force and jets and the like. You talked about music and literature and the beauty in wood, and the beauty in small things," she recalled, not looking directly at Saunders, but off to the side of him, back those years ago, recalling more than a memory, recalling when she believed her life changed.

"I did ramble on and on that night. I also remember calling you a flirt of the highest order."

"Yes, you did. And I recall punching you in the chest."

"Yes, you did. That's when I learned you were a wee bit thin-skinned," said Saunders, laughing.

"And that's when I first called you an asshole out loud," said Kristina, not remembering the moment to be nearly as funny as Saunders, but remembering that she may have gone too far calling an officer an asshole when she was a mere senior airman. Kristina looked down and shook her head in a soft manner, emotions flowing through her and over her, never wanting to admit to herself much less anyone else that the feelings she had for him were unchanged, as if the decades in between living separate lives with no interaction at all never existed.

"Breakfast was grand," he said, getting up. He asked if she was finished and she nodded, her head still bowed down.

"I'll clean up," he said. "I didn't know if you were listening because I was a lieutenant and you were a respectful airman." But he knew, or at least he thought he knew, that maybe he wasn't just another of her flirtatious conquests.

As Saunders passed her with their plates heading to the kitchen, Kristina lifted her head and gave a tired sigh. She said, "I'm going to change the music. I need something with a hard beat—and some very strong coffee. I want you to show me your world, and where your two children are now. A son and daughter, right?"

"Right."

"And I want to know all about your lovely wife. She has to be lovely, I'm sure, because I can't see you with anyone other than a smashing beauty," said Kristina, wanting to size up whomever Saunders ended up with over the past decades.

"And I'll ask the same about your children. And I know who you married."

Pouting, she said, "And you didn't come to our wedding…"

Saunders ignored her and set about to clean the kitchen. As his mind settled into remembrance, he rinsed the dishes, placing them into the dishwasher, and began to scrub the pans, unaware for some time that no music was playing. He devoured a slice of bacon and placed the rest in the refrigerator. He then began to make a pot of strong coffee and called out to Kristina. When she didn't respond, he went to the living room and found her curled up on the thick leather sofa, sound asleep, and her light snoring sounded more like a soft, rumbled purr. He sat down on the rug in front of her and studied her in great detail, making a wistful note of every wrinkle around her eyes, knowing they were well earned because he had heard she spent much time outdoors and living on the back side of the clock. She remained as beautiful to Saunders as he remembered her so many years ago, and then remembered what Faulkner wrote—something about the past. He wrote the past was never dead. And the past was never past. Saunders always felt that was true, and sitting cross-legged there in front of Kristina, he knew it to be indeed factual. Saunders added to Faulkner's observation—remembrance does not merely recall an experience from memory; it serves as the life blood of keeping what has been lived very much alive and in the moment, and infuses the very thoughts and behavior of the current moment and moments to come.

He then placed under his head a sofa pillow next to Kristina's orange-socked feet, and fell into a fast sleep on the floor. Soon after Saunders fell asleep, Kristina stirred, one sleepy eye opening with fierce reluctance—attempting to catch a glimpse of something familiar around her to thwart her sense of disorientation. Seeing nothing familiar within her limited view, her eye lowered and she saw Saunders asleep on the floor. She slipped off the sofa and placed her pillow up close to Saunders's chest and settled in as close to him as she could dare, without waking him. Believing she succeeded, she felt her mind still and anxieties she never would admit to anyone release the clutch of her heart and she fell asleep again, having no care or worry about her complete sense of disorientation. She lusted for this kind of experiential disorientation, almost as much as she was now lusting for Saunders, reawakening a desire she thought she had long ago successfully abandoned. She was content this time in knowing that no matter how much she attempted to delude herself that Saunders was just an experience a long time ago that had no lasting impact on her whatsoever, the truth was the exact opposite. She awoke when Saunders shifted to his side and wrapped his arm around her. Her mind became as charged as her body, and she grew restless in attempting to lie still.

Chapter 12

The rest of the morning Saunders tended to washing vehicles, including Kristina's, who finally quit protesting about not bothering with her SUV, remaining in the house to do her laundry, which she was overdue attending to. Her mood had turned foul after the nap; Saunders had spurned her morning advances. Adding to her foul mood was Saunders not allowing her to see what was inside the building where he kept his furniture. She knew the pieces that he stole from her had to be in there. *He is so maddening*, she thought, finding a momentary spike of self-satisfaction that he was *definitely not* the man for her back then and most likely now (and she repeatedly announced to herself she wanted never to marry again), but soon after became deflated knowing she hadn't picked the right man to marry either, and after decades with her husband Robert she finally gathered the wherewithal to leave him. But she allowed herself an adequate measure of comfort knowing she had beautiful children whom she adored.

Kristina sat on the sofa with her laptop, going through her mail and returning correspondence with all the friends she had collected over the many years. For Kristina, the personal encounter was an absolute requirement to establish any further relationship, professional or otherwise, and she often counted a chance encounter with a stranger in an airport or bar or on the street as the beginning of a new friendship. So many times in her conversations she would start off talking excitedly about the "new friend" she'd just met—while crossing the street no less.

If it wasn't for the gusty winds kicking up the dust, she thought, she'd have strung all her brassieres up to dry on the porch, but instead she found a ball of twine in a kitchen drawer and strung them up across the kitchen, between opposite cabinets, ignoring the prospect they may smell like the just-cooked bacon. And why Saunders was washing their vehicles in this wind was maddening too, she thought—the dust would collect on them anyway. Saunders didn't want to talk about his wife, where she was, if they were fully separated or divorced or whatever they were. And he certainly became angry when Kristina brought up the fact they'd had sex before and it was not that big of a deal. Kristina thought, *it obviously is a big deal to him for some reason. And that reason must be because he and his wife have not agreed to see other people. He is being like an old-school female*. And as she hung up her last brassiere she said out loud, "I'm certainly over that way of thinking." As if the roles were now reversed between men and women regarding sex. *How peculiar he thinks that way,* she thought. Never mind that there were no personal photos of any kind hanging on any wall in his little place. Kristina had divorced girlfriends who kept the family pictures present around the house, complete with ex-husband, and those who did not. She herself opted not to keep photos around her place.

She checked every room in the house, especially Saunders's room, who had seen fit to make his bed in the morning. She peeked out the front window to check on the maddening man who washed vehicles in gusty winds in the desert, noticing both vehicles were now gone. Staring in disbelief, she then saw Saunders appear from the big building where his workshop was located—the other part of the building being a large garage where he parked both his truck and her SUV next to his RV. That man liked his buildings, she thought. Now Saunders began to run, waving to her as he passed the house. *How did he know I was watching him? Maddening!* Down the road he ran in a quick pace, she noticed. He never was a runner back then, she thought, and she returned to her laptop and began to search the Internet for everything and nothing; whatever grabbed her attention she followed, now fuming because her clothes may be taking too long to dry. She wanted to run too—away from this mistake of an encounter. But she loved the intimate conversation they had, laying on the living room rug. He told her he had always loved her and no matter how off-kilter she believed him to be, he said he loved her—no one else but her. Easy to say when you're twenty-one, thought Kristina, and perhaps easy to say in your mid-fifties too, having not lived with that person all those years. But he was convincingly adamant, she thought. She believed him now, just as she believed him back then. Saunders told her not a waking hour went by that he didn't think of her at some moment in that hour, *and that is beautiful!*

Kristina's mind had not ceased thinking of Saunders since she saw him at the VFW hall. All her dreams about the new future she was going to embark on were now being reconstructed in her mind to include the possibility of Saunders back in her life. *Maybe I can see him now and again, whenever the moments allow. Enjoy each other and then move along. Ah, that would be nice, wouldn't it?*

It was an unpleasant day to run. The gray-brown sky gave no indication when the winds would die down as Saunders held a fast pace, knowing he'd tire soon and shorten his total distance, which was fine for today, not only because of the wind but because a worry planted itself in his head that Kristina may find the key to the garage and then drive off in a complete huff. But the bigger worry was if she lifted the tarp up to see what was underneath in the storage building. He was not ready to talk to her about the motivation for creating the furniture, much less the motivation for larceny to reclaim the furniture.

Saunders talked to himself while running, in spurts as his endurance would allow. Sometimes a sentence was too long and he had to take breaks in between to breathe in more air in order to continue the dialogue. Most times his mind raced through the sentence, but he broke up the sentence in fragments to keep his breathing rhythm regular. He had said what he needed to say to Kristina. His professed love of the highest order. And no other person ever pulled him away from himself but Kristina. Saunders believed Kristina changed the way he viewed everything, as if she not only amplified what he took in but reoriented his reception of listening and seeing. And that he continued to believe this into his later years was all the more reason to believe. Saunders went on aloud about why she affected him so and remained grateful no one heard him describe the effect she had on him, because people would think him, at best, off-kilter. He told himself it was not obsession but a passion to experience in the moment and in continuance, breath by succeeding breath, passing through day or night. It was experiencing how her mind seemed to work, her reactions to a face, a hard-beat dance song, her being mesmerized by the blurring of a high-speed train passing and once passed, thrilled at the apparent stillness of life in place after passage. She believed street performers possessed the courage of saints and revered them so. Kristina perceived light, sound, and smells as textures to be felt by touch. She wanted to touch that which could not be experienced by touch. And although she never expressed this to Saunders in any direct way that he could comprehend, this is what Saunders perceived how Kristina lived in the world. And how she came the closest to accomplishing what could not be accomplished was by designing rooms with fabrics of all textures, leathers of all grades, walls and other room surfaces painted or stained or woven or even branded in colors—all to serve the interpretation of the dynamic or subdued nature and purpose of the room, large or small, a kitchen or an amphitheater. And she listened to music of every flavor while doing so, as if music guided her touch to manipulate textures and achieve what she sought to bring forth.

None of this she articulated to Saunders, for she couldn't care less to speak about what she did or why she did things. But Saunders spent a great deal of time thinking about what she did and why she did things. It was vital he knew the best that he could. Because knowing also meant he knew himself that much better—perhaps completing the picture of himself. And Saunders's wife? Never had she inspired any contemplation close to how Saunders contemplated the life of Kristina. *Maybe*, thought Saunders, *maybe wives and husbands are not supposed to inspire this depth of contemplation of such a fierce and compelling force of attraction.* It certainly wasn't lust, he mused. Then again, he thought, not sexual lust alone—but almost as a less-than-primary attraction—a lust to know himself and, finding a woman who influenced him in total, a lust to know why. *Maybe I know myself as well as can be known. And there arrives a moment of realization that the habit of self-regard is actually satisfying the desire of self-adoration through a complex disguise of denial and deceit—where the courage to search for oneself is actually an act of cowardice—the cowardice to engage and act beyond oneself. Have I reached that moment of realization?* He was sprinting now down the final stretch of road leading to his compound, fearing Kristina had left.

Leaping up the porch steps Saunders opened the front door and stood at full rest to better sense if she was still present. A wind gust assisted the slamming of the door, the bang echoing in the house. He walked to the kitchen, where he found Kristina feeling her brassieres strung across the kitchen to see if they were dry. Amongst the lacy black were an orange and a chartreuse bra, making the pink and cherry red ones seem so ordinary.

"I'd have been gone by now if these damn things weren't still damp," she said with her back to Saunders, her full attention on her brassieres.

"What is this? Circus clown bra washing day?"

Kristina stepped back to take them all in view, very much wanting to get angry, but failing.

"How dare you insult my bra collection! Circus clowns would kill to have these!" And she burst out laughing, turning around to see Saunders sweaty, dust clinging to his running shoes and lower legs.

"And where is my sweet little SUV?"

"Washed and parked in the garage."

"I didn't ask for you to clean it."

"True, your SUV asked me on its own, so I obliged. I'm going to shower."

"Then what?" she asked.

"Then we'll talk some more."

"I'm done talking to you," she said.

"Would you like a full tour of my compound?"

"Oh, it's your *compound*, is it? I've seen enough, thanks," she said. His furniture she was dying to see, but having Saunders know this would limit her control, and Kristina was very much about control. She was almost all about control.

"Let me give you a quick tour then," he said, approaching Kristina, now leaning close, threatening to kiss her.

"Go shower," she commanded, pushing him away in resignation to her desire to stay. As he showered she pulled off all her brassieres from the line—they had been dry for some time. After taking down the line and wrapping the twine back onto the spool, she went to her guest room and placed her things on the unmade bed, staring at them, her mind filled with memories of Saunders, and she found herself thinking about the day they could no longer see each other. She no longer cried thinking about that day. But, at that moment, she wanted to cry. She believed she had much to cry about. *All right, a quick visit around his place and then I'm off.* Kristina always attempted to command herself to do something, or behave in a way that demonstrated self-control, because she knew what self-control conveyed to some and what abandoning self-control conveyed to others. And as much as she loved to be with the others who gave up self-control, she knew it came at considerable cost, and what reminded her of the cost were the wistfully beautiful, lonely melody lines from Chet Baker's trumpet. And on the crushing headache mornings vomiting awake after a bohemian night, feeling used and spent, and needing further reminding, she remembered her brother Caldon. He would have given Chet a run for his money, but Caldon never made it past twenty-six. That's when Kristina learned the term "suicide by cop."

"Hey," whispered Saunders, now so close that Kristina could feel the heat from his shower. A new morning never smelled so fresh, she thought, and she just wanted to be curled up in his left shirt pocket so she could stay in the trance of his heartbeat. She leaned into him and let his chest keep her upright. She reached around for his arms and wrapped them around her.

Chapter 13

"He's one of those types, isn't he?" Magda was very much looking for a break from Nathan. Three days traveling with him was three days too many, where barely an hour was necessary to complete the picture of Nathan in her mind. Magda sat on the end of one of the queen beds in the hotel room, hands pressed down on the mattress as she rocked back and forth, preoccupied. On the first day of the trip to Arizona, Magda tried to be cordial and attentive to Nathan when he spoke up, but by lunch the first day she was done with conversing with Roscoe's brother—for everyone's sake, she figured.

"Which type you talkin' about, Madga?" Roscoe was lying on the other bed, clicking through TV stations, settling on a sports station, looking for game highlights. He still enjoyed following college and pro football, having long given up on pro basketball. And during this trip he'd been giving thoughts to getting back into following pro baseball. He was a rabid baseball fan back in his youth.

Magda now moved from the end of the bed to the side of the bed that faced Roscoe. "The type that believes everyone's against him, the world's not fair to him, and how everything and everybody needs to get realigned in thoughts and deeds to suit his notions of how it all shall be in the world.

"Were you ever like that, Roscoe?" Magda stopped rocking forward and backward, waiting for a reply.

Roscoe punched the mute button on the TV remote. *She doesn't remember? I thought surely she'd remember.* Roscoe remembered. How he and his brother fed on each other's grievances and slights, actual and perceived, whipping themselves up into a self-righteous frenzy that seemed so expected of them back in those days. It was their right to be swaddled in indignation and anger.

And remembering, it seemed that all it took for Roscoe back then was to have Magda deliver a scathing rant on why she was not going to be with a man who was just that very type. Roscoe remembered he became so angry he wanted to slap Magda and scream unspeakable things to her and kick her out of his apartment. But he did not. Instead he sat down in a chair and listened in silence as Magda delivered her ultimatum to him. He didn't kick her out of the apartment that evening; she marched out in righteous anger toward him. He slept maybe twenty minutes that night, and when he finally emerged from a long, hot shower in the early morning, he sat naked on a dining chair and drank a cup of coffee and smoked a cigarette in silence, vowing to never be that type of man Magda despised so much. She gave him the reason to change the way he would forever think and therefore behave. Roscoe believed she was God's gift to him and yet, here he was in his mid-sixties and never married to her. And he knew why he never married anyone else, just as he knew why he never married Magda.

"If I was like that, it wasn't for very long, Magda baby," Roscoe said, smiling at her, searching for any indications of her remembrance of the past.

She stood up and straightened herself, and went out to get some fresh air on their miniature balcony, saying, "I most certainly do know I made the cut that drained that kind of poison out of your system a long, long time ago."

"That you did, baby, that you did." Roscoe turned off the mute and was inflicted with a spike of joy. She turned back and blew him a kiss, saying, "You welcome, baby." He watched her close the sliding door and sit in the metal chair, putting her feet up on the railing.

Never seek joy, because you never find it, he thought. *Joy finds me, and be grateful on those occasions, Roscoe, because joy dashes in and never lingers. Joy resets my bearings and brings momentary clarity in the quest for meaning. And that woman is the only one who ever reset my bearings—permanent like*—and soon Roscoe was snoring.

The loud double door bang woke Roscoe, who for a moment was disoriented. Magda was still on the balcony staring out and away as the second double rap on the door occurred.

"When we goin' to eat?" demanded Nathan, in his new tank top T-shirt that Roscoe purchased for him, along with the black khaki trousers and new tan leather work boots Nathan favored. His small gut seemed to jut out rather than droop. The swelling in his face had come down but his eyes were still bloodshot. He had removed the bandages from his right hand, revealing the splints on his thumb, index, middle, and ring finger. His left hand was cut up but escaped broken bones according to Abbot Mercer, proclaiming a minor miracle, seeing how viciously Nathan was beaten. From the time they left Louisiana Nathan had refused any help tending to himself.

Roscoe still couldn't figure out how he could zip up and down his trousers.

Nathan's beard was coming out salt and pepper and his nose was no longer protected by the firm nasal bandage applied by the Abbot. He still looked like a recovering wreck of a spent, bare-knuckle fighter. Roscoe motioned him into the room. Once he got Magda's attention, he then pretended to eat from an invisible plate. She noticed Nathan in the room, paused, and then shrugged her shoulders. Roscoe pointed at Nathan and indicated he was hungry. She flashed both hands with fingers extended.

"Okay, ten minutes and we'll grab some supper somewhere," said Roscoe.

"She don't like me much," said Nathan.

"She don't believe everything you've been sayin' on this trip," said Roscoe.

Nathan knew better than to pretend to be offended. Long gone were the days his older brother believed in his stories. *Or, maybe, let me believe he believed in my bullshit,* he thought.

"They say my debts are squared up, I'm tellin' you," said Nathan. Roscoe had paid for almost all the expensive tools and machinery, and he let Nathan put all the cars in his name. Long ago he bought out Nathan's share of the property at Nathan's insistence, and all that money was gone.

"Then why did they beat you so damn bad then, if you're all squared up?" said Roscoe.

"I dunno, teach me a lesson, I guess."

"And what lesson is that, Nathan?"

"Pay my debts on time."

"That's it? That's the lesson you think they were tryin' to get across to you?"

"What else could it be?"

Roscoe stared at him in silence.

"Maybe, now just maybe they were tryin' to do you a favor," said Roscoe, in a further moment of clarity. *Maybe*, thought Roscoe, *maybe his beating will make him want to change, make him man enough to change, to change into being a man that will work to control himself rather than stay unleashed and angry.*

"Those kind of dudes ain't doin' nobody any favors unless they get paid, and they get paid to beat on a man."

"How 'bout you start *thinkin'* about it as an opportunity then?" said Roscoe.

Nathan glared sideways at his older brother and shook his head. "An opportunity? To do exactly what?"

"To quit behaving like an angry boy that thinks the world has done him wrong, and move on," said Magda through the small opening of the sliding glass door. She had been listening to their conversation from the beginning. She entered the room and walked up to Nathan, looking up and staring at him eye to eye.

"Let's say for a quick second that I believe what Roscoe says—that you got a real good way with cars, from top to bottom, inside and out. I'm sure you can be successful out west. You know all them rich white dudes out there are in love with those old cars with big engines. Gotta be plenty of demand for your skills."

Nathan raised up both his hands in front of Magda's face. He then looked at Roscoe. "With these? I'm goin' back to my room. Bang on my door when it's time to go," he said.

"He smells like cigarettes," said Magda as she went into the bathroom to freshen up. "Did you break down and get him a pack?"

"Soon he'll be whining again about needing some weed to get high and relieve the pain and stop his knee from twitchin'," said Roscoe, popping out his Afro and then putting on his shirt.

"You better not let him score any weed, Roscoe."

"Twenty bucks won't get him much—and I warned him—if he so much as attempts to get some weed, I'll leave his ass in the middle of nowhere."

"Hmph," grunted Magda, and finished touching up her makeup.

"He *is* in pain, baby, you know that," said Roscoe.

Magda turned off the bathroom light. She kissed Roscoe softly on his cheek. He held her against him. She put her ear against his chest to listen to his heartbeat. She wasn't sure what to listen for.

"I'm all right, baby—heart's still tickin' away," he said softly.

"We're getting you checked out ASAP when we hit Arizona, you hear me?"

"Yeah, baby," whispered Roscoe.

Soon they left their room and Roscoe banged on Nathan's door. Nathan wore a collared shirt, but it was unbuttoned in front and on the sleeves. Roscoe motioned to him to button it up and tuck it in. Nathan complied as instructed. His mood did not appear to be sullen, as Magda had predicted. She promised herself she'd pay attention to Nathan, taking subtle measures to let him know she cared about him. She knew that was what Roscoe was hoping for.

Nathan said, "Seriously, what's with the Afro? You gotta shiny bald spot back there, man." Nathan kept his head shaved.

"Keepin' up with appearances, brother, gots to keep up with appearances."

This was their last night on the road. Tomorrow afternoon they would be in Arizona.

That morning, before their van left the hotel parking lot, Nathan whined about wanting to score some weed. He was in pain and his knee would not stop twitching. His mind had scatted the night before, as he lay awake in his hotel bed for three hours, and when he awoke his worry about the men who beat him had returned.

Driving through Tucson, what had passed for conversation had now ceased. Magda was entrenched in her disgust, listening to Roscoe and Nathan argue about Nathan's gambling and when learning that all the expensive tools and equipment and machinery the debt collectors hauled away totaled up to one hundred thousand dollars, not including the value of their restored cars. When Roscoe forced Nathan to admit that he may still may owe another fifty thousand dollars to fully pay his debts, Magda released her rage. Roscoe had to exit the highway and stop by the roadside until she could be calmed down. Roscoe made sure Magda was looking at him when he clutched his chest. Only then did she stop screaming at the both of them.

Magda then directed her scream at Nathan. "You! You sit back there and keep your mouth shut, do you hear me? Not one word from you! At all! You fuckin' loser of a brother! And, my God, if I find out it is you that's been makin' Roscoe's heart go bad I swear to the Almighty that I will put you down on the ground and you'll never get up!" It was then she produced Roscoe's pistol from under the seat and pointed it at Nathan. The smell of urine soon hit them. Nathan's lips turned pale.

"I am not going another yard until this no-load brother of yours apologizes to you. Then and only then will you drive to the next rest stop so he can change his pants."

"The apology won't mean a thing, baby," said Roscoe, exhausted. "He's been apologizing to me for twenty-five years. And put that damn pistol in the glove compartment."

She leaned forward and placed the barrel between Nathan's eyes. In a deliberate manner, her voice low and shaking, Magda said, "Not until this worthless motherfucker apologizes—and fucking means it."

"Jesus Lord," cried Nathan, and he apologized to Roscoe once more. Magda removed the pistol from Nathan's forehead and returned it to her purse. Roscoe motioned to her to return it to the glove compartment. Her nose flared as she pursed her lips. In a slow and deliberate fashion she engaged the safety and returned the pistol, and then sat still as a statue staring out the front window.

Roscoe said, "Over these years, neither of you have helped my heart—but it ain't all y'all's fault, I guess."

He started up the van and drove ten miles to the next rest stop. The high overcast sky was clearing and the sun was back to heating everything within its reach. To Nathan, the ten-mile drive in urine-soaked trousers, drenching in the fear of dying by Magda's hand seemed an eternity in the lowest rung of hell. Even more traumatic than the savage beating he received back in Louisiana. Because he knew the debt collectors weren't going to kill him—because they said so. They were going to return and get the remainder of what Nathan owed them. And Nathan knew leaving Louisiana wasn't going to stop them from getting what their boss man claimed was still owed to him.

Magda flipped on the radio and searched the stations for nothing in particular other than silence. Nothing playing on the radio satisfied her. She cursed and clicked it off. Nathan welcomed hearing only the steady sound of the van's engine humming. Within a few minutes he realized he wasn't seething with anger over Magda's putting the pistol to his head. Any other time in his life, including up until now, he'd have been fighting to control his rage. But the rage didn't surge through him like he'd expected it to. His mind did not start racing and no thoughts formed in an instant, casting blame on someone else for being wronged. His knee did not bounce up and down as if his nerves were short-circuited. He felt he was encased in a river mud cast of shame. Never in his life had he ever permitted shame to surface, his anger more than sufficing to disguise and assist in burying any hint of shame from surfacing to the point of recognition. He scooted sideways on the backseat bench to sit directly behind Magda so as to avoid any eye contact with her and to observe his brother.

Roscoe's forlorn expression matched the weariness his body appeared to convey in his slumping position, his forearms resting on the steering wheel. Nathan thought his brother's head would bow down at any moment and Nathan wanted to reach out and help Roscoe hold his head up to keep his eyes on the road. For the first time in his life Nathan was worried about Roscoe. He didn't look well at all. Nathan wanted very much to do something for Roscoe, to help him in any way he could, but his feeling of powerlessness was as powerful as his strongest desire to gamble, as strong as his undefeatable urge to get high. To be unburdened by the humiliating gravity of compulsion and fear was what drove Nathan to seek what was impossible to achieve. Nathan reached out and grasped Roscoe's shoulder and squeezed until the tears in his eyes revealed the pain in his fingers.

Again Nathan said, "I'm so terribly sorry, Roscoe. And I ask your forgiveness please." Before Magda could scoff and attempt to further shame Nathan with a litany of damning profanity she had already formed in her mind, she watched Roscoe place his left hand over the top of Nathan's bandages and gently pat his beat-up hand. Nathan then slumped back in the seat, overcome by the exhaustion of guilt released. He soon dozed off. Magda held back and returned to her statuesque pose, glaring straight ahead through her squinting eyes.

Chapter 14

"How many times do I have to say this? You're not ready for me in your life again," said Kristina, window down and behind the wheel of her vehicle, shiny clean from Saunders's earlier efforts that day. The desert sunset was burnt orange sky laced with slithering high white clouds. The rough wind had cleared and the evening was pleasant. After the gorgeousness of the setting sun, darkness came in haste. Saunders leaned against her door, the same position he had been in for almost an hour, neither of them wanting to separate, but in Kristina's mind, the issue was settled. Or almost. The "almost" being as much her not wanting to leave because Saunders's subtle, entrancing insistence she stay awhile longer was whittling down her resistance. Rarely in Kristina's mind was anything ever *fully* settled. She always left an escape route. She had convinced herself early on that an escape route was where the fun and excitement lay. But with Saunders, she knew leaving an escape route was very dangerous to her heart.

Saunders will never know the impact upon me when the colonel ordered us to cease contact, thought Kristina, because admitting that would expose her claim to be invulnerable. She fought hard to convince anyone that everything was of the moment and therefore relative, and since everything was relative, any in-depth meaning or impact upon her was never life altering, much less worth an uncertain trail of lingering, mixed memories. What Kristina failed to observe was that no one with any shred of perception believed her.

Saunders was stalling, trying to keep her from departing before Roscoe arrived, which according to Roscoe's cryptic phone message the day prior was to be at any time now. Kristina claimed she much preferred driving at night to avoid traffic, except if an awesome vista called for traveling during the day. In their shared silence, with Saunders's elbow resting on the driver's side windowsill and Kristina's hand resting on his forearm, they both listened for what Saunders described to her as the desert ensemble, comprised of the steady frequency of crickets, along with the cooing doves alternating with the hoo-hoo-hooing of some sort of desert-dwelling owl. They were not disappointed, for the ensemble was in full swing as the orange glow of the sun dimmed behind the hills.

"Beautiful," she said, squeezing his arm. "I *am* going now."

Saunders could stall no longer without making her more uncomfortable. He leaned in and they shared a long kiss. "Keep me posted, Huguette, you know, on your happenings and whereabouts."

Kristina smiled at him for remembering to call her by her new name. "I will," she said, starting up her vehicle. She shifted into drive and slowly drove away from the compound.

He watched her drive away for a few moments and decided he did not want to watch her fade from view, so he turned and went inside the house. He never showed her the furniture. Saunders wasn't ready for what may have followed after he removed the tarp; perhaps the great unveiling would prove to be his great folly. He maintained a firm notion, however, that Huguette, or Kristina preferably, because that was who he remembered, would return at least once more to accept the specific invitation to view all the furniture in full. To view his folly, in full. That suited Saunders just fine.

Attempting to take his mind off Kristina, the woman who always had been inside his head, Saunders picked up his cell phone on the kitchen counter to check for any message from Roscoe. Then he heard a vehicle maneuvering to a stop out front. In the desert darkness Saunders determined it was not Kristina's SUV, but a van. The inside overhead light illuminated as the driver opened the door. Saunders turned on the porch light and waited just outside his front door.

"Finally made it," said Roscoe as he walked slowly around the front of the van and opened Magda's door. Roscoe called out for Nathan to join them. Magda wrapped her arm around Roscoe as they waited for Nathan to emerge. He was as tall as Roscoe had described, thought Saunders, but taller than he imagined he might be. The three stood together in descending height, all looking weary. Saunders stepped down from the porch and introduced himself to Magda first and then Nathan. He gave Roscoe a fast hug and invited them inside, pointing out the guest bathroom off to the left. Magda returned to the van and grabbed her arm bag, then excused herself. Saunders now saw Nathan in full light, noting his stature to be near his, and then the swollen face and nose, realizing now why Nathan did not volunteer to accept his handshake offer.

"Hungry, or thirsty?" asked Saunders, stepping into the kitchen to retrieve a bottle of red wine.

"You got soda pop?" said Nathan.

"He won't touch the stuff," answered Roscoe, nodding toward the wine bottle in Saunders's hand.

He removed two wineglasses from the cupboard. Lifting the wine bottle toward Roscoe, Saunders asked, "Magda too?"

"Never can tell about her. Have to wait until she tells you."

"Sorry, Nathan, no soda pop, but I have different flavored sports drinks in the fridge."

"You got orange?"

"I believe I do. Help yourself. If you need ice it's in the freezer, and the glasses are up here," said Saunders, motioning to the same cupboard where the wineglasses were stored.

"You know, we passed Huguette Sands leavin' your place a moment ago. No surprise, I guess, to see her here. We chatted for a moment while up the road. She seemed happy to see me, and sad to be leavin'. Glad I could introduce her to Magda. Even Nathan. Couldn't convince her to turn around. Thought I could, but she seemed to be wantin' to get goin'. Helluva time to be driving. Black as Africa out here in the desert at night."

"Worse," said Nathan, carefully looking at the orange sports drink he held in his hand.

"How would you know? You never left Louisiana in your life," said Roscoe.

"Been to Texas and Mississippi," replied Nathan, twisting off the plastic cap and taking a large gulp. After swallowing, he again inspected the orange sports drink, and gave Saunders an impersonal nod of approval. "And now I've been to Arizona," he added.

Roscoe accepted the glass of wine and leaned against the kitchen counter. Magda returned and although she looked tired, Saunders noted there were plenty of hints remaining that sold him on Roscoe's claim she was the hottest woman in the Air Force back in their day. She certainly kept herself trim, Saunders noted with firm approval.

"I do stand corrected," said Roscoe to Nathan, acknowledging his worldly travel experience, in much less of a snide tone as Roscoe would normally deliver to his brother.

"You gotta beer, handsome?" Magda had reservoirs of charm, Saunders guessed.

"I do," Saunders said, going to the fridge and inspecting his selection. He kept the lightest beer on the market for those days he worked up a long sweat in the workshop, more so he wouldn't get too much of a buzz while working with the saws. But he kept German beers too, Pilsners being his favorite from his time stationed in Germany.

"Anything imported will do me good," said Magda, smiling as she entered the kitchen and gave Roscoe a peck on the cheek.

"Never seen her drink a beer," said Roscoe, smiling in appreciation of Magda's never-ending ability to surprise him.

"Just watch," said Magda as she swigged two full gulps and let out a satisfied "Ah, nice and cold." She didn't care what kind of beer it was; she was thirsty and tired of drinking iced tea the whole trip.

For some time they lingered in the kitchen, only some small talk about the length of the road trip and change in weather going west—no one seemed to be in any hurry to move—and no one noticed Huguette—until she greeted everyone with a wide smile and an outburst of "Hi!"

She had returned, bearing an armful of plastic bags of apples and grapes, cheeses, Italian meats and sausage, crackers, and assorted nuts—which Saunders thought to be the most appropriate food item for those assembled in his kitchen. Of course the food was appropriate, because Saunders had purchased the food and Kristina had taken it from the big refrigerator in the RV garage. Saunders emptied his wineglass and just stared at her.

"Clearly, dear man, you need another glass," said Kristina as she whisked past him and started searching for cutting boards and serving trays. "Okay, since I'm here, I'll have one too," she said as she laid the cutting board to be used for the cheeses and meats.

"Now that woman looks like a full-throttle bottle of energy to me," whispered Magda to Roscoe as they both watched Kristina prepare the food.

"I have no doubt about that, baby, no doubt a'tall," Roscoe replied for everyone to hear, remembering those days when he used to describe Magda in exactly those words.

Backing out of the kitchen, Nathan sipped his orange drink while still watching Kristina flit about the kitchen. He then recalled the first day Roscoe introduced him to Magda. Nathan was a senior in high school. And only because of the unending patience of the principal, Mr. Gauthier, was Nathan allowed to graduate. He was making good money back then hot-rodding cars, and the more days he skipped out of school, the more he got paid.

Kristina was now paying attention to Nathan because she knew he was the challenge for her. She aimed to win anyone over with whom she crossed paths. It was part of the engine that drove her, to have a stranger be interested enough to be captivated so that their guards were lowered ever so much to reveal who they really were. That was Kristina's way of thinking—ever since she became aware that people paid attention to her. As if remembering something she had to attend to, Kristina stopped laying out the meats and cheese on the tray, grabbed her wineglass, and approached Nathan.

"Hi! You're Roscoe's brother, yes?"

Nathan backed up further into the living room.

"My God, you poor man! You must be in pain!" She attempted to touch and caress his forearm.

Nathan stiffened and pulled away. "I'm all right."

"I'm Huguette."

"Nathan. Thought I heard you called Kristina. Huguette your last name?" Nathan was unimpressed but doing his damnedest not to be an asshole.

Laughing, she nodded over to Saunders. "He still calls me by my old name. He can be obstinate, that man."

Nathan wasn't sure what "obstinate" meant, but he figured it was a polite white woman's way of calling him an asshole.

"Nice to meet you. Do people call you Nate? I like Nate."

"They try, but I tell 'em that ain't my name."

"Nice to meet you, Nathan—I like Nathan best too—and I do wish you a very speedy healing! Were you in a car crash?"

"Yeah, somethin' like that."

"You must be starving after being on the road all day," said Kristina, walking back to the kitchen. She brushed by Saunders and grabbed the meat and cheese platter that Saunders had finished assembling.

"Oh, thank you—whoever finished this tray," she said to the trio in the kitchen, and taking an appetizer plate from the stack on the countertop, she returned to Nathan and offered him first dibs. Nathan was sitting on the edge of the sofa and waved off Kristina.

"Ain't hungry."

"Oh stop it, you must be starving! Help yourself and take all you want. Saunders bought enough to feed a basketball team." She leaned over and placed the tray in front of Nathan.

"I said I ain't hungry." Nathan refused to look at her.

"All right then, when you change your mind this will be on the counter," said Kristina, returning to the kitchen and offering the others to help themselves.

Magda wasted no time and prepared herself a full plate. Saunders glanced over at Nathan sitting on the edge of the sofa, staring at his orange drink. Up until then it was just kitchen small talk about the road trip between Roscoe and Magda—and

Saunders listened. But Saunders had many questions in his mind and told himself to wait until Roscoe started supplying answers.

Roscoe looked worn out as he leaned against the kitchen counter, his frailty demanding he do so. He noticed Saunders looking at Nathan.

Kristina either didn't notice how tired all the new arrivals were or considered their weariness to be a challenge for her to liven their spirits and get them engaged in conversation and laughs. Kristina loved nothing more than having everyone laughing, no matter what, especially when she generated or spurred the laughter. The road weary were indeed a challenge to be transformed into the life of some spontaneous party.

"Leave him be. Nathan won't talk to women, especially a white woman, and most particularly a pretty white woman. *Disdain* would be the proper word, I do believe—much disdain," said Roscoe, and he poured a small amount into his almost empty wineglass and swigged the wine in one gulp. "I'm beat to all get-out. Suggest me and Nathan sleep in your RV and put Magda in the house for the night."

"There's a bathroom with a shower out in the garage," said Saunders.

"Where's all your furniture?" asked Roscoe, his whisper not soft enough.

"Yes, Saunders, where *is* all your furniture?" asked Kristina, now facing Saunders, and frowning as if to acknowledge her failure to get a party started.

"Catch you all in the mornin'. I'm off to get me a long sleep," said Roscoe, and he moved over to Magda, whispered in her ear, and then kissed her welcoming cheek. She smiled with a mouthful of cheese and cracker and caressed Roscoe's arm as he went to inform Nathan that they were going to sleep in the RV. Nathan said nothing, finished off his orange drink, and left the empty on the sofa table, following his older brother out of the house. Nathan grabbed his bag out of their van and waited until Roscoe delivered Magda's bags to the guest room where Kristina had slept the night before. Kristina's frown disappeared and her eyes lit up watching Saunders direct Roscoe and Magda to the guest room.

"I pray I look as good as her when I get her age," whispered Kristina to Roscoe before he left for the RV.

"In her day, she was so fine-lookin' nobody could get any damn work done. Plus, she's a damn genius. I think they call it emotional intelligence. Got it from her mother's side, she claims—they're all fortune-tellers and channelers on that side of the family. Made good money at it too, Magda told me, but after a while she thought it was wrong for it to be so easy to get money from someone who so badly wanted to believe in something.. She felt sorry for them. Her own mother kicked her out of the family for turning her back on their profession—or so they called it. So she enlisted in the Air Force—of all the silly things for a woman to do."

"Natal astrology?" asked a wide-eyed Kristina upon hearing that Magda was a channeler.

"Oh, yeah, that too."

"Not so silly, Roscoe. I enlisted in the Air Force too. Then became an officer."

“Don’t tell me,” said Roscoe. “Don’t tell me you met that tall galoot Saunders in the Air Force.”

“Okay, I won’t,” said Kristina, with a tearing gleam and a Mona Lisa smile. “How well do you know him?” Kristina followed him out of the house and toward the garage where the RV was parked.

“Know his father real well. Served with him. Knew Saunders as a teenager for a spell. Didn’t get to know him until a few months back when we were up in Nebraska.”

“I can’t figure it out. How’d you two hook up?” she asked.

“His dad told me where he was, and the coincidence was just too strong for me not to go find him and drop in. He was staying not more than ten miles from where Madga was, so it was nothing at all for me to stop in and say hello. Cleaning out all those fast-food kitchens in the middle of the night. Got paid real well for the work, but good God, man, that’s shit work for someone of his type.”

“I will apologize for my brother. He’s never tolerated any real kindness—and white women don’t rank too high on his list of likes.” Roscoe put down his bag and gave Kristina a tight squeeze and kissed her on the cheek, saying good night.

“And for certain he cannot—or shall I say will not—tolerate a black man close associating with a white man, and so much less a white woman,” said Roscoe, adding, “If God has a way of crackin’ open his kind, with that kind of attitude, and changin’ their minds, He sure ain’t revealin’ it in any obvious way a man like me can figure.”

"Learnin' how not to be afraid in life requires some way of reaching inside himself to show the strength he's got hidden away that he needs to fight—to fight the fear. I thank the good Lord I think I found it for myself way back when."

"My brother Nathan—now that man has not found a way to fight the fear yet. And I've never given up on him; Lord knows I have wanted to. Many, many times." Roscoe then motioned for Nathan, who was waiting by their van, to follow him inside the garage. Kristina said good night to Nathan, passing him while on her way back to the house. Nathan's unintelligible reply was a nasty slur, said more to himself than to Kristina.

On the sofa sat Magda, and Kristina came into the living room and joined her. Saunders delivered Magda's suitcase to the guest room. He then put Kristina's bags in his room, but had no intention of sleeping with her. He decided on the sofa. He joined the women in the living room, sitting in the lone easy chair across from them. It was the first time Saunders had been in Magda's presence for any length of time. She was a former beauty, just as Roscoe described—and proudly so. The two women were chatting away when they finally acknowledged Saunders had returned. *No time wasted between these two*, thought Saunders, now realizing he was very tired. He began going over the options for the rest of the evening. *Do I suggest they both go to one of the bedrooms and continue their conversation, or, do I just say good night and go to my room and when they decide to call it an evening and retire, I then get up and go sleep on the sofa—only to infuriate Kristina further?*

Kristina then asked Saunders in a teenage flirtatious way if he would be so kind to pour them both small glasses of wine. He obliged with a sigh of relief. Returning and handing them their glasses, for which they both thanked him with much enthusiasm, he announced, “Ladies, I’m off to bed. We’ll have a grand luncheon tomorrow, I promise you.” Touching his lips to Kristina’s ear he whispered, “Love, don’t go ballistic on me when I tell you that you will sleep in my bed and I am sleeping on the sofa.”

She tilted her head and bumped his lips, as if to make him move away, all the while still smiling and talking to Magda about her absolute fascination with astrology. It was the exact opposite of what she wanted to hear from Saunders. He kissed her cheek and said good night to them both and went to his room. Within her frustration Kristina found the wherewithal to grab his arm and squeeze it tightly before he left. He stopped and lifted her hand and kissed her knuckles. She pushed him away with renewed affection. Magda caught the entire interplay between them and smiled to herself.

“Is it just nostalgic sentiment?” Kristina woke Saunders up, repeating the question in a whisper. Saunders had fallen into a deep sleep soon after he lay down on his bed, fearful to undress and sleep under the sheet lest he’d be unable to leave when she eventually came in and lay down. He stirred awake, disoriented. Kristina moved over and onto Saunders’s chest as he rolled on his back.

"That's my mother for you. Telling me all this is just nostalgic sentiment and it will pass as do all nostalgic feelings," whispered Kristina.

Still fighting off the drug of sleep, Saunders struggled to process what she was saying—something her mother said, he thought.

Kristina placed both hands on his cheeks and shook him. "I'm sure she's right, you know, my mother. She's always right." She looked at Saunders, waiting for his eyes to focus on her. "She's right, isn't she, Saunders? Of course she's right, yes, for sure she's right." Kristina rolled off his chest and lay on her back beside him.

Saunders was now fully awake—and irritated by the accusation. Now he rolled over and laid his head upon her. He whispered to her what he'd been waiting to tell her for half a lifetime. Tears came quickly for Kristina as she listened. Saunders expressed his sentiments as if time did not exist, as if it was merely a pause between seeing one another. His low voice carried low anger not directed toward Kristina's mother, whose assertions he rejected like a trial lawyer scoffing at the prosecution's lame attempt to convince a jury of evidence that was not only not evidence, but a distraction from the truth. The truth in this case, Saunders told Kristina, was that old people fear being gripped by nostalgic sentiment because their life has been already lived. And what remained was only nostalgic sentiment, which was hollow, brittle, and of no lasting value because it yielded no satisfaction of accomplishment, only failure.

Punching his chest she said, "Don't speak about my mother that way."

"You know I'm not speaking about your mother. I'm telling you that's what I think people think at our parents' age. My father intellectualizes the argument by dismissing nostalgic sentiment as childish and not worthy of men to dwell upon. The past stays the past, he tells me. And of course I don't believe that for an instant because I believe there is no such thing as the past—all of our life experiences are always with us, and memories are as much of the present as me kissing you at this moment." He kissed her, wanted nothing more than to kiss Kristina until their lips blistered.

She welcomed his weight upon her equally as his lips. "Please stay," she said.

"I want nothing more than to never leave," said Saunders. "Let's get some sleep, at least, because we're going to have a grand lunch tomorrow. Plenty of beer, wine, and barbeque, and God knows we have some characters here now." He whispered what he always whispered to her the moment he knew he loved her. Rarely did Kristina ever give up on a demand of hers not met, but she did. He shut the door, carrying to the sofa his pillow and extra blanket from the foot of his bed.

Chapter 15

Saunders opened his bedroom door without making noise. Kristina was buried in the sheets, with only a small tuft of her hair showing. He could not begin any day without a shave, especially on Saturdays and Sundays. He retrieved some clean clothes from his chest of drawers and went into the bathroom to complete his morning ablutions.

"You are up too damn early, handsome man," said Kristina from underneath the sheets.

"I'm going to Mass. Be back in an hour. You need anything?" said Saunders.

"Do I *need* anything? Yes, I do *need* something, and I certainly won't be able to get it at Mass." Her resigned wit was something Saunders had actually forgotten about. She rarely expressed herself in such a way, but it was her way of showing deference to him.

"Shall I come along?" she asked, as if attending Mass was something to do to pass the time. But she did not mean it that way.

"When's the last time you attended Mass?" asked Saunders.

"Every time I visit my mother, who demands I go, and further, she demands I go to confession—which I will not do… ever," said Kristina. "And what difference does it make when I attended Mass? I raised my children Catholic and I attended enough Masses for a lifetime. Taught Catechism too, so there," she said as she popped her tousle-haired head out from the sheets, holding them just below her nose, like the World War II graffiti caption "Kilroy was here."

"I'd love for you to join me," he said. "Leaving in five minutes."

"Ten? And you do know that today is Saturday, not Sunday?"

"I do, thank you. I go to early Saturday morning Mass instead of Sundays. Now, get out of bed now. Coffee will be waiting," said Saunders, shutting the bedroom door. He heard her yell "Coffee, yay!"

One moment she's leaving with no expectations to keep in touch, much less see each other, and then she's back like a boomerang, he thought, noting this was her modus operandi these days. Whir in, fly out, perhaps return again, more than likely not, but you never know. Her way of reinforcing the illusion of being free. He'd accept any length of time here in Arizona she was capable of giving. The morning was still, and the cloudless sky was showing off its beautiful desert blue luster, as if to imitate a peacock's vanity in full iridescent plumage attracting the most desirable pea hen, but instead attracting the shimmering morning moon, which seemed to pause in awe of the sky's transcendent blueness, while arising in full innocence, now just above the horizon.

Saunders had continual difficulty understanding the young associate pastor from Panama, but Saturday morning Mass was celebrated in swift fashion in the new church building, staying true to the Mission style, and without families, who generally attend on Sundays. This gave Saunders a head start to get things done in town before the traditional affairs of Saturdays got under way. Kristina, in her lovely daisy yellow summer dress, appeared not to have a care in the world and had little problem understanding the Panamanian priest, yet she chose not to listen to his homily at all because all homilies bored her to distraction, and the newly renovated church proved to be plenty of distraction for her. She used the homily time to take in every design detail, approving most times the design decisions made. Certainly her approval would be considered a devotion to God, she thought, and He would then look down at her with soothing mercy. She needed soothing.

Saunders also used the homily time to let his thoughts wander. His daughter Veronica thought he was daffy to attend Saturday morning Mass, she being still a churchgoer and dedicated organist for noon Sunday Mass back in Phoenix. Saunders texted her the night before and was hoping her irritation with him had passed so she would come out for the luncheon. His text message left him confident she could create no flimsy excuse not to attend. Letting her know that Kristina, from his past, was here was all she needed to know. He predicted his daughter's after-luncheon report back to his estranged wife would no doubt be slanted toward the salacious side once Veronica observed a mere few minutes of Kristina in full. And to date, Saunders had made no effort to seek another woman because no other women were interesting enough for him to be bothered, occasional episodes of loneliness be damned.

Veronica and her mother had a running bet as to when Saunders would find another woman, his estranged wife convinced she was dumped in order for Saunders to find someone younger. Saunders learned very quickly that nothing he said would be persuasive enough to ever change his wife's mind. Saunders told his wife he married her for his lust and her looks. She screamed in reply that she married him because she loved him more than anything. Saunders told her he grew to love her, but he never loved her more than anything. She was never the center of his life. At no time during their courtship and marriage did he ever *fall* in love with her. And the absence of wrenching loss convinced Saunders that what he told his estranged wife was truthful. It was the sometimes stabbing pain of knowing he had perforated his wife's sole focus for living her life, and no distance existed he could run to rid himself of that knowledge. And no amount of alcohol cured anything, he, of course, knew, because his body and mind only tolerated so much, and he thanked God for that condition, whatever the diagnosis would be labeled. But most days and most nights were free of this particular pain, and he worked every hour of the day to live within that hour and the next, and only those two hours. He never succeeded in making a habit of living within the hour and the next, for the hours to follow were on his mind because he loved to take action to achieve the plans he made. Saunders was never a meticulous planner, nor ever found pleasure in constructing the actual plan. He only planned in sufficient detail so that he could determine what actions to take at that moment.

Kneeling next to Kristina after returning from Holy Communion, Saunders was struck by the remembrance of how he fell in love with Kristina, and the fact he could not love her any more than he did resurrected the frightening realization of his feelings for her. Saunders thanked God he had found a woman to love with such ferocity, and though Kristina was never his wife he thanked God all the same. To think of all the actions he undertook all these years to divert his ferocity for Kristina into other endeavors, never could he divert the ferocity of his love for her to his wife. He knew, many moments before he married her, that she would never receive the same ferociousness of love he felt toward Kristina because the total allure never presented itself at any time. And whether that fact was a self-fulfilling prophecy or not did not matter to Saunders. It was for him a truth that caused him to comport himself in certain manners of thought and social orientation with all women, that is, to approach them as if they could possibly ignite the first ferocity created by Kristina, and to see whether another woman could evoke the extreme paradoxical satisfaction that he received from loving Kristina in a life apart, and even extract from the paradox the same fleeting moments of a kind of ineffable joy.

That day Kristina and Saunders renewed the same question they used to ponder, the what-would-have-happened-if-we-got-married question. With total conviction they were being mutually rational in their thinking, both elevated the question out of the nostalgic swamp of sentimentality. Both wanted to be with each other—back then—and now. And neither could help asking themselves if they were in a willing, uncontrolled state of emotion. Kristina believed she now plotted her life on such a premise. Saunders knew he was always tempted by nostalgia, but never close to cloying. They were now together, attending Mass of all things, making small decisions on what to buy at the market, gassing up the truck, engaged in the intertwining conversations of a man and woman living out daily existence—engaged in trivialities that life was constructed around. It was the newness of someone you had not been with, but in Saunders and Kristina's case it was the startling remembrance of the familiarity with one another that in itself was new. And because it was the present, the thought of nostalgia was not on their minds. What was on their minds was the fear of repeating decisions in the past that led to each of their permanent stains of regret, each different in its psychological pattern and effect, as it would be for a woman and a man, stains not as vivid in their respective brightness as in the past, but now a new vividness of a different age, startling in its visibility, and influential in creating a habit of seeming permanent distraction.

The drive back to Saunders's place included caffeinated bursts from Kristina reacting to sights along the roads, names of stores, any building that stood apart from the strip mall conformities, color of attire that seemed to her out of place, many more white people around than she imagined, and names of restaurants other than the chains that infected the townscapes throughout the country.

"No clown-colored brassiere stores nearby, I'm sad to say," said Saunders. To him, Kristina's laugh was an audible elixir, especially the sound she made pursing her lips as if to attempt to contain the inevitable, and then the outburst once released would recede into a high to low lyrical sigh.

For a reason he never cared to ponder, Saunders had a habit of checking his rearview as he turned off the main road toward his place. In his tire dust he could make out Veronica's own white pickup, having just turned onto the dirt road that led to her father's place. He knew she'd come and knew she would want to be in the mix of things, getting the grand luncheon ready. A flush of embarrassment overcame Saunders as he became aware once again of his daughter's obesity.

"Look at that," said Kristina, pointing ahead.

"I do believe Roscoe would say that that qualifies as a genuine sur-prise," said Saunders, watching Magda appear to direct Nathan how to lay a tablecloth over the long tables that had been brought out from his garage for the luncheon. They were working together to set up the table and chairs under the weary pair of tall cottonwoods. Roscoe was not with them, and Saunders noticed his absence.

"And speaking of...surprises, my daughter Veronica is behind us."

Kristina straightened up and looked in the rearview mirror, checking her sparse makeup and adjusting her hair, and trying to catch a glimpse of Veronica, whom Kristina knew nothing about because that damned frustrating man kept no pictures around his house.

"Oh Saunders!" said Kristina as she rushed out of the car to meet Veronica.

Saunders's embarrassment retreated into his low mental regions, somewhere near the I-don't-give-a shit region, which brought on relief to a father who loved his daughter. He watched their introduction to each other, Kristina giving his daughter a hug she never expected, and for an instant grew irritated at Kristina's brashness, but not long after he noticed Veronica smile her genuine smile and laugh at some silly remark Kristina made. Saunders stayed in his pickup as he watched Magda and Nathan stop their activities to check out the scene. Nathan wasted little time getting back to the business of setting out folding chairs around the table. Magda stopped directing Nathan around and went to meet Veronica. Soon all three were lightly chatting away in gaiety. Saunders finally got out of his truck and approached Nathan.

"Where's Roscoe?" he asked.

"Inside your place on the sofa, watchin' TV, I suppose," said Nathan.

"How's he doing?"

"Not well, I don't think. But he's not sayin' much to me today—and he ain't sayin' much to her neither," said Nathan, nodding toward Magda, now helping Veronica with things she brought for the day. Kristina began unloading the items she and Saunders bought that
morning.

"Can you work a barbecue grill?" asked Saunders.

"I cooked for myself my whole life with no help from nobody. Damn straight I can work a grill," said Nathan, almost registering a smile, but his old habit tweaked his lips into an irritated tightness.

"Then how about you lighten the fuck up, Nathan, and consider getting my grill ready for some ribs and chicken…please," said Saunders, standing near eye to eye with Nathan, not a muscle wavering in his face. "It's on the side porch from the kitchen. Whatever else you need is in the garage or in the kitchen. I'm going to check on your brother."

"I'm not sure he likes you much," said Nathan.

"And I'm positive you don't know shit about him and me," replied Saunders, and he left Nathan to go see Roscoe, thinking to himself he thought Nathan would reply differently to his request to help him get the grill ready for today. "Your face looks a hell of a lot better than yesterday," he said, with his back turned to Nathan, walking to his house. Nathan almost said thanks aloud, but said nothing and walked around the house to the right to check out the grill.

The three ladies were in high chat mode. Their nervousness in meeting each other had abated and they mutually assigned and divided their labor to make the grand luncheon just that—grand.

Roscoe was dozing on the sofa, arms crossed over his chest. The screen door creak stirred him and he peeked at Saunders walking into the living room.

"Nathan pointed out to me that you don't care for me very much," said Saunders, now sitting on the chair adjacent to the sofa.

Roscoe pulled on his chin. "Well, that's sorta true. When I met you again a few months back after only knowing you as a teenager and then as a lieutenant before your father retired, I wasn't so sure I was going to take a liking to you. But I was comparing you to your old man, a man who I grew to respect and even like. I wasn't in the habit of making friends with officers, no sir, not at all. But we got on—your father and me—got on real well. And when I met you I wasn't so sure I'd get on with you the same way. But that wasn't fair, judging you like you were your father. So yes, back then I told Nathan I didn't much care for you, but I haven't had the time to tell him different."

"How you feeling? You're looking tired," said Saunders, asking if he wanted something to drink.

Roscoe shook his head. "I am tired—and it's about time I told you what happened to Nathan."

"And while you're at it, tell me about you and Magdalena too. I knew only what you told me in Nebraska, which was next to nothing. The whole bit about rescuing her from that assisted living place—if rescuing is the correct term."

"Course it's the correct term. That woman was being beset upon by that she-wolf daughter of hers," said Roscoe, getting himself agitated, but too tired to sit up.

Saunders went into the kitchen to get a tall glass of water for him. Nathan was on the kitchen porch uncovering the grill and giving it a thorough inspection.

After the first careful sip of water, the story of Nathan unfolded. As Roscoe told his brother's story he gradually went from lying down to sitting up on the edge of the sofa.

"Of course I had no earthly idea Nathan was in that deep with the riverboat casino, and it was pure damn happenstance Magda and I came in that night; otherwise, he'd mighta died soon after—maybe a couple days after, who knows. The Abbot tended to him and as soon as we could move him we took off outta Louisiana. I'm worried about the Abbot too, you know, but he insisted we go and I made sure not to tell him a damn thing about where we were headin'—which was always going to be your place here. But I couldn't tell anybody or make any phone calls except on a few throwaway cell phones I picked up. Paid cash all the way from Louisiana. What's that noise?" he asked, accepting the second glass of water from Saunders.

"Nathan's scraping the grill, getting ready for the big afternoon lunch. We bought enough food to feed a small village," said Saunders. "And Nathan has volunteered to cook the steaks and chicken—and I thought I heard him grumble about having to cook for a bunch of white folks and a Puerto Rican woman—but I couldn't swear to it."

"Do we need to take you to a doctor?" asked Saunders, suspecting that Roscoe no sooner would go see a doctor than shave his Afro.

Roscoe waved him off, not saying a word. Getting up from the sofa very slowly, he went and put his empty water glass in the sink. Leaning against the kitchen counter, he watched Nathan prep the grill.

“When my brother’s on a task, he’s money in the bank. Except for gambling. But otherwise, when he can focus on a mechanical project, he can’t be beat. You’d be amazed at his patience when trouble shooting a problem with our cars. As if you’re watching another man in his likeness doing the work.”

Then all the women came into the house at once, immersed in laughter and talking in excited voices. After Kristina and Magda hugged and checked how Roscoe was faring, Kristina kicked the two men out of the kitchen and out of the house and commanded them to go find something useful to do before lunch. While passing, Saunders gave his daughter a glancing peck on her cheek that she accepted with a brow of mock disappointment, then smiled and waved at her father as he and Roscoe went outside. The tables and chairs were awaiting their occupants under the cottonwoods, offering shelter from the sun as it approached its reserved noon position in the blue desert sky. A little too warm for Saunders, he thought, but the ice-cold beer would make up for the temperature. A month or two later and it would be like eating in furnace heat. Saunders returned from the garage with a cooler of ice-cold bottles of imported pilsner beer. Roscoe returned from the RV in the garage showered and dressed in priest black, in full white collar. His Afro never looked so primped and fine and at first, his gleaming Afro distracted from his weariness, which was less obvious, but ever present in his movement. It was then that they told each other about the women who altered their lives forever, and they toasted over their third beer that both women were here today, both knowing that such an occurrence was the rarest of rarities.

The women finally came forth, as if in procession, and filled the table with jalapeno spiced creamy potato salad, rich coleslaw from a secret recipe from Magda's father's side, sweet, luscious, buttered corn on the cob, garlic French bread, and a platter of grapes, sliced strawberries, and perfect cantaloupe. With a surprising sense of dramatic timing, Nathan arrived last with steaks and chicken breasts. Saunders placed two chilled bottles of Sauvignon Blanc in front of the ladies and added another six-pack of pilsner in the cooler between him and Roscoe. In front of Nathan's place setting sat a tall bottle of cold orange soda, a smile now forming on a face that had long forgotten those muscle movements. Kristina discovered through Magda about Nathan's Bob Marley desire for a quality joint, and when Nathan was in full grilling mode, with wafts of fine grilling steak and chicken enveloping the kitchen porch, Kristina and Nathan shared the fastest smoked doobie on record—by their own accounts.

Veronica was in a bright green dress of designs by late Matisse, or so the designs reminded her father, ever the amateur lover of painting and sculpture. It was painters and sculptors who he chose to be influenced by when he created furniture. Kristina gave Saunders an A+ when he whispered in her ear to confirm his daughter's dress print reminded him of Matisse. Her ear lingered near his lips to also hear the soft admonishment of sharing a joint with Nathan, who was attempting to kick marijuana—and nicotine—the combined abstinence too difficult for mere humans. On that observation both Saunders and Kristina agreed in confidence. Sitting at one end of the table was

Saunders; at the opposite end was Father Roscoe. Now Veronica was the only one not aware of Roscoe's habit to don the priest's uniform of black and white collar, and after glancing at everyone—attempting to seek any kind of reaction and finding none whatsoever—settled into her seat next to her father, with Magda sitting next to Roscoe, and Kristina and Nathan sitting in the middle, opposite each other.

Kristina persuaded Nathan to change into a collared shirt after his stint at the grill, which he obliged in too eager of a fashion, but the promise of an after-lunch joint was too good to pass up. Magda and Kristina also wore bright-colored dresses, as if all the women were in sync. Magda was radiant, thought Roscoe, and Kristina looked pretty too, but her marijuana glaze seemed to diminish her natural ebullience and tame her aggressive charm.

Father Roscoe tapped his knife against his ice-cold bottle of beer saying, "All right now, I ask you all to bow your heads and let's get a little prayer goin' on."

"Amen, amen!" said Kristina with a stoner's giggle. Father Roscoe looked at Kristina and smiled, and Kristina shut up and bowed down her head, but not before stealing a glance at Saunders, as if seeking forgiveness for her interruption.

"Kristina told me all about you two; how you met, how you fell madly in love with her, and she with you, and how you were split apart," whispered Veronica to her father. "I don't know why I feel like I have to say I'm sorry for what happened back then. But you know, Dad, I'm not sure about her, not sure how she's keeping it all together—she seems like she's trying to juggle chaos, as if that's what life's about. But I can't help but like her, Dad. And she says *madly*—a lot."

On her hand he rested his and waited for the prayer. Roscoe waited until Veronica was finished whispering to Saunders and began.

"Oh Lord, thank you for this fine feast laid out before us, prepared by these fine ladies amongst us. Thank you for gettin' us through some tough times and havin' to deal with some real tough mothers out there in the world, yes sir, some real hard heads with rock-hard hearts out there in the world." Nathan kept quiet and kept his head down, knowing his brother was staring down at him at that moment. Father Roscoe continued.

"Now most people haven't a clue as to who our father was, and now I'm talkin' about Nathan's and my father. He was a good man and did his damned best to keep us on the right track. And he was a kind man, a fact some people seem to find rare about us maybe, but that was a fact and even Nathan here will be forced to swallow his goddamn pride and admit as much one day. And I bring him up because tomorrow's his birthday, and I want to let you know about Ernest Armstrong, our father, God give him peace, because we sure did not, no sir, we did not.

"Now war, it seems, is such a permanent habit of man as is breathing, but that don't mean you can't break that habit by putting in its place another habit. And the only habit I learned—a habit that is so damn hard to learn, but once you do, it changes you—is gratitude. I learned it from my father and after he died, much too young—but Lord knows maybe not— and I learned it another time from Percy Standing, a man who made his livin' writing essays and such who I met at the abbey near our home, and is buried at the abbey. My father introduced me to Percy Standing a long time ago. And the toughest thing about life, Percy Standing told me, was substituting a bad habit for one at least not half as bad, and then substituting that habit for one not half as bad as that other one, so that you try to end up not being a total and complete ass of a man." Now looking directly at Saunders, he continued, "And I will tell you, I learned it again another time from serving with your father. Okay, then, enough of that.

"Now I don't pretend to know a damn thing about how women think other than the fact, and I thank God for sure, that some of the best women do indeed like men, and only those women and the Good Lord knows why they do. That's their secret and I'm fine with keepin' secrets because I don't want to know everything about everything—I prefer a lotta mystery and happenstance myself. And finally—now raise your glasses and bottles, everybody—now I'm convertin' this prayer into a toast, and I toast to the ones we love who are dead and gone, and those goin' soon after...here, here...and a toast to all of you sitting around here today enjoyin' Lieutenant Colonel Saunders Ravel's fine hospitality and willingness to harbor some of us who are lying low for a while from some real tough assholes. Amen."

Everyone stood up and clinked their wineglasses, beer, and soda glasses together.

Magda leaned over to Roscoe and said, "I've heard worse ramblings from you, Roscoe Armstrong. But I almost pulled on your trousers to sit you down."

"I love you too, baby," said Roscoe. "Now will you hand me that platter of steaks before the flies take them away?"

"I think your friend Saunders is a bit taken aback about what you said about his old man. I also think he's the only one around this table that don't know what kind of trouble Nathan has got himself into. I told his daughter and Kristina all about it because I knew I should. And you should tell your friend Saunders about it too, and I mean soon—today," said Magda, handing Roscoe the meat platter and sliding a chicken breast onto her plate.

"Already done that, baby, already done that," said Roscoe. Magda kissed his cheek.

Kristina poured more wine into her glass and continued her animated conversation across the table with Nathan—about cars. She told him her father owned a car repair shop for most of his life and she loved nothing more than hanging around the garage with the three mechanics her father employed for twenty-five years—all of them Korean War vets—and she loved watching them troubleshoot and fix engines. Nathan became confident and technical in explaining how he approached a challenging car problem, and Kristina appeared fascinated. And when Nathan finally told her about his real love of car restoration—especially the old muscle cars—Kristina swooned.

"A fellow restoration addict like myself," she exclaimed out loud, silencing the conversations of Saunders and Veronica, and Roscoe and Magda's. Conversations then resumed, with Saunders explaining to a very attentive daughter his version of what happened between him and Kristina.

"I wanted to marry her, but she was enlisted and I was an officer, and fraternization between the two was a serious offense, particularly when we had a wing commander who not only disliked the fact women were in the Air Force but took it upon himself to punish any offenders to the maximum extent because he believed women were ruinous to unit cohesion."

"Kristina told me you offered to resign your commission, but that was not possible because you had a commitment to fulfill," said Veronica, helping herself to a steak and coleslaw and a tiny top-off of wine. It was her turn to have an hour drive back to her house.

"That is true," said Saunders.

"And she decided not to get out of the Air Force because she had been accepted into the Air Force Academy and she felt she had to go because of those who believed in her and supported her. She couldn't let them down."

"Also true," said Saunders, excusing himself to get a beer from the cooler next to Roscoe's chair. "Nice prayer, Roscoe," he said as he leaned over between Roscoe and Magda.

"Your daughter is a sweetie, and she is such a fan of yours!" Magda beamed.

Saunders thanked her and returned to his chair, stopping behind Kristina.

"Now about this 'Father' business, Roscoe… We finally gonna have only one chat about all that," insisted Magda.

"You mean a chat between you and me, and me and the church?" said Roscoe.

"It's either or, baby, either or…" Magda punched him in the arm. He feigned a grievous injury.

Leaning over Kristina, Saunders said, "Amazing how much territory you covered with Veronica getting lunch ready," referring to their romantic history.

"Not so amazing really; we can communicate very, very efficiently when required… Now move along; Nathan and I have much to talk about. He's a restorer too," said Kristina, pushing Saunders back toward his chair.

Veronica asked her father, "And are you still in love with her?"

"Much to your mother's unhappiness, I'm sure, I've never stopped being in love with Kristina, and I will never stop being in love with her. Kristina graduated from the Academy and married another pilot I know," he revealed.

"A friend of yours, Dad?" asked Veronica, again stunned by the afternoon's revelations. Saunders cut another slice of steak and chewed on it for some time. "What did you think about him—the other pilot, I mean." Veronica was now aware how quickly she had devoured her steak.

"I didn't and I don't," lied Saunders.

Now Kristina broke out in raucous laughter in her conversation with Nathan, who stopped pretending not to be enjoying himself.

"I mean, Dad, she changed her name to Huguette. What kind of name is Huguette anyway?" said Veronica, playing with her coleslaw, so far resisting the urge to finish it off and go for another helping of potato salad.

"An old name to be sure. And a name of a mysterious heiress whom she was just dying to meet because she was so sure that she and the original Huguette would get along fabulously." He imitated Kristina, not in a mocking way. "But the heiress died and Kristina never had the chance. I have little doubt she would have succeeded in getting to meet the most reclusive Huguette. She is a master in working to get what she wants."

"But that's odd though, don't you think—to want to change her name—why? To pretend to be someone else?" asked Veronica, fidgeting and fighting to resist another helping of everything. Her father was very aware of his daughter's urge. "I can tell you that Mom would not like Kristina—at all—whichever name she goes by," said Veronica, abandoning all resistance and going for a breast of chicken.

"True enough," said Saunders.

"Unrequited?"

"No. Fully requited."

"Carrying a torch all this time?" The shocking new revelations about her father spurred a confidence to press him, but only to answer questions she asked herself about love. Veronica had begged to be in love, and novels steeped in romance she had read with complete absorption, creating a false emotional nostalgia for a lost love she never had in the first place. She finally abandoned those novels and approaching twenty-four had already formed a hardened belief that no love was to come her way, and therefore any hint of nostalgic sentiment for a lover, whether in a novel or not, raised only a low-burning ire.

"Stuck in adolescent nostalgia, Dad?" she asked, slicing through the chicken breast as if to slay the animal for a second time.

Saunders sensed his daughter's frustration and sought to give her relief and perhaps too, an admission to himself.

"You may be right, Veronica. I never believed that to be so, but you may be right on the money." Saunders stopped eating and looked at his daughter. "You're a very pretty woman, Veronica, full of life, and you seem to be a natural in making people feel like you care about them."

"I'm a hundred and fifty pounds overweight, Dad. I can't control my eating, and I can't see any future with anyone," said Veronica in a voice of detachment, without any self-pity.

"And why do you think you're a hundred and fifty pounds overweight?"

"Because I confused myself on the notion of the pursuit of happiness by letting myself believe I could find happiness by making others happy. That was a big, big mistake, Dad."

"I'll make you a promise, Veronica," said Saunders, now watching Nathan and Kristina get up from the table, still laughing; together they picked up their plates and glasses and took them into the house. "I'll team with you to get you one hundred and fifty pounds lighter," he said.

Veronica spit a piece of chicken onto her plate, causing Roscoe and Magda to stop their conversation. "What a grand gesture," she said, loud enough for all to hear. "What a grand gesture!" she shouted as she struggled to get up from the table to clear her place setting. Streams of sweat flowed from her temples.

"You nostalgic ass," said Veronica. "You made all that beautiful furniture in a fit of resurrected sentiment—for what? Is that the only thing that can inspire you? Cheap, lousy sentiment? What is it now, cheap, lousy sentiment taking over you again in your new delusion that you can help me lose one hundred and fifty goddamn pounds?"

Roscoe stood up and said, "No, it's not cheap or lousy sentiment; it's a willingness to do something, to be that which you want to be. And you can believe me, young lady, very few people got the guts to be willing to do something, especially when that something's hard and offerin' no goddamn guarantee of success."

"Spare me your self-help crap, whoever you are—oh, I know, the man who roams around pretending to be a Catholic priest. You're a fake!" screamed Veronica, who now slapped away her father's arm attempting to console her.

Magda had had enough, rising quickly and walking over to Veronica, motioning to Saunders to back off and go sit back down. He did so, this time sitting next to Roscoe, who then sat back down. Veronica resisted Magda's first attempt to get close to her and talk. Then Magda grabbed Veronica's forearm with a strength that gave Veronica pause. With still a firm grip of Veronica's thick forearm, Magda led Veronica away from the table and over toward Veronica's car. Their backs turned to the house and the table where they had lunch, and as Veronica leaned against her car, Magda began to talk to her in a soft, quiet voice.

"Can you believe it?" said Roscoe, shaking his head, smiling.

Watching Veronica and Magda talk, Saunders believed his daughter might be doomed to find any happiness.

"I mean, seriously, can you believe it? Nathan, talking, laughin' with a woman. And a white woman!" That Roscoe wasn't thinking about Veronica and Magda but instead his own brother gave Saunders unexpected relief, and he became grateful for the relief.

"Now they're out on your kitchen deck smokin' a joint no doubt, but, I will say, I am happy to see Nathan smile. Yes sir, I am very happy to see that. Never saw that comin'. Not for all the world did I see that comin'," said Roscoe, slouching into his chair, putting his hands behind his head.

"See how long it took Nathan to get to where he could smile? All those years with that yoke of anger around his neck? And your old flame, that woman Huguette you told me you loved your whole life, just like I loved Magda my whole life, that woman makes Nathan smile and laugh."

"Her name's Kristina," reminded Saunders.

"I know her by Huguette—that's how I met her. So to me, she's who she introduced herself as," said Roscoe, with tired but beaming eyes. He was capturing another flash of happiness, because that's how happiness comes, only in a flash, *and soon it will be gone*, he thought.

Saunders heard Kristina's distinctive laugh, full of life, as if she was ever trapped by youth. He could see the smoke from their joint float from around the corner of the house, and soon a high yip of a laugh came from Nathan. Roscoe pulled the last two beers from the cooler, twisted off both caps, and handed one to Saunders. They toasted and both took healthy swigs from their long necks. Neither Saunders nor Roscoe noticed the sedan coming down the long driveway, but Magda did, and after whispering something to Veronica, left her and walked up the drive toward the sedan.

Roscoe could not help but notice the intensity of labor Veronica displayed striding over to him and Saunders. She probably rarely exerted that much effort, thought Roscoe, now noticing the redness of her fat cheeks expressing genuine fear. As Roscoe told Saunders his daughter was running toward him, Roscoe now noticed the sedan, coming to a stop just up ahead of Veronica's parked car, with Magda standing in the middle of the dirt driveway, blocking any further advance. Out of the driver's side came Jeanette, and as she slammed her door she stood still, staring down her mother. With much more caution, a man with a shaved scalp of noticeable girth soon exited the passenger's side, closing his door with restraint, and stood by their sedan, alternating pensive looks at his wife and then his mother-in-law.

"Magda told me she's coming for you and to be ready for the worst," said Veronica to Roscoe with great effort, gasping for more air, fully flushed and already dripping in perspiration. "And for you to get your pistol," she sputtered as she collapsed onto her chair, only for it to crumple under her weight. Losing any semblance of balance, Veronica fell to the ground, causing the beer bottles to bounce up from the table. Stoned laughter exploded from both Kristina and Nathan at the sight of Veronica's fall. The pair were now on the front porch, high as the golden arches above a McDonald's restaurant, and without cause to care about anything. Saunders, until a moment ago without care of anything himself, knelt down and assisted Veronica—with no small amount of effort, back on her feet and asked if she was hurt. Her embarrassment did hurt, but the hurt was subsumed into self-loathing, which no longer could be hidden from view, for she heard the laughter from the porch. With self-control she would beg to have with regards to her caloric consumption, Veronica allowed her father to help her to stand, and she allowed him to hug her, without any outward anger toward him, because none was deserved, nor toward the laughing duo on the porch, to whom much was deserved.

As Magda was pointing at Jeanette's husband to remain where he stood, Jeanette pointed toward Roscoe, accusing him in an acid tone mixed with harsh profanity that Roscoe had kidnapped her mother, cementing in both Magda's and Roscoe's minds that Jeanette's blind and dangerous rage was never again to be tolerated.

Now Kristina and Nathan stood silent, their marijuana mood squelched. Roscoe wasted no time walking to his pickup and Nathan noticed him retrieve the pistol and place it in his waistband and un-tuck his priest's shirt to hide it. Saunders also heard Kristina and Nathan laughing at Veronica's fall. He looked at Kristina, who now appeared uncomfortable on the porch next to Nathan. Kristina only wanted to be with Saunders, and wanted everyone else to disappear. She could not look at Veronica now. She began crying. Magda and Jeanette were now face-to-face, the mother taller and much prettier than the daughter. Only Spanish was being spoken between them, and Jeanette was unwilling to control her volume of speech, while Magda was inaudible. Listening, Jeanette's husband leaned against the roof of their sedan, arms outstretched wide against the roof, shaking his bowed-down head at the words being said. Kristina stepped off the front porch and ran to Saunders, mustering the courage she knew she must in order to convey her apology to Veronica. The afternoon was marching onward with no known direction, the breeze stopped, and dust seemed reluctant to settle back to earth once disturbed underfoot.

"I'm a complete, careless idiot, Veronica. Please forgive me. Please," said Kristina, catching her breath.

For now, Veronica's nodded acknowledgment and tight smile were the best either of them could hope for or expect.

"Saunders, I am so sorry," said Kristina. Saunders kissed her. He continued to hold her hand, and she could not stop squeezing his, in constant need to affirm she was present with him, at this moment.

Roscoe kept watching Magda and Jeanette as he walked toward the front porch and joined Nathan. The two brothers entered into conversation, neither expressing outward emotion, both watching Magda and Jeanette. Then Veronica left Saunders and Kristina and walked back to her car. Retrieving her shoulder bag, Veronica went inside the house, saying nothing to Roscoe or Nathan as she passed. Nathan turned to say something to her as she opened the screen door but said nothing.

Saunders introduced himself.

"Two very hot-tempered Puerto Rican women saying what they're gonna say," said Reyes Ramon Medina, husband of Jeanette. Magda and Jeanette paid no attention to anyone other than their grievances. In that they were now simpatico. Saunders motioned for Reyes to join him over at the lunch table, and reached into the second cooler and popped off the cap and handed Reyes a beer. Without hesitation he accepted, swallowing half the bottle in two swigs.

"You're the one who makes the furniture, right?" asked Reyes.

"Right," said Saunders, not wanting to know how Reyes knew. He introduced Reyes to Kristina, and together they watched Jeanette unleash her carefully nurtured resentments onto her mother. Magda's placidness only served to fuel her daughter's venomous accusations of not getting her share of the money Magda received from her mother's passing.

"I've only been with Jeanette a few years, and I can tell you, she always is about the money she believes she deserves. And she believes one hundred percent or more that her mother is holding out on her," said Reyes to Saunders and Kristina. Magda and Jeanette had not moved from the driveway since Jeanette began her tirade against all the wrongs committed against her.

"And Jeanette had me convinced at one point that Roscoe had kidnapped her mother in order for her not to get her fair share of money," said Reyes, sipping his beer. "But my mind was changed halfway through the drive down here. And I'm sorry to be here now, bothering everybody. But Jeanette doesn't let go. All this supposed money's got her all obsessed. She won't let it go. She even called the cops to see if they would arrest Roscoe for kidnapping. And that's how we found out about your place in Arizona," said Reyes, looking at Saunders.

"Victoria, the lady who owns the RV park you stayed at for a while—we talked to her about where Roscoe may have gone next. She's the one who told us you made furniture. The cops asked about you and Roscoe. They couldn't find out where Roscoe lived but they found out about your place here." Reyes emptied his beer and looked for a place to leave the empty bottle. "Mind if I have another?" he asked. Saunders told him to help himself.

"Did you know that people that bought your furniture have gotten it stolen out of their house? That's what the cops told Victoria. I got that from her. Just your furniture—and the thief leaves cash in an envelope. That is strange, don't you think?" said Reyes.

"My god, Saunders, hadn't you heard about that?" asked Kristina, pretending to be shocked and now staring at Saunders—her suspicions confirmed about what was in the building across from his house. Saunders remained silent and returned Kristina's stare. At that moment Jeanette slapped her mother. Without hesitation, Magda slapped her daughter in return.

"They got a lot of things to say to one another. She's got a lot of anger under her skin, that Jeanette. I don't know what I got myself into marrying her. For a tiny woman—she's got a lot of anger she carries around," said Reyes, more to himself than anyone in particular.

Then Roscoe stepped off the porch and approached Magda and Jeanette. Veronica finally reappeared from the house and replaced Roscoe on the porch clutching her shoulder bag, standing apart from Nathan, who now decided to sit on one of the porch chairs. Looking refreshed, Veronica said something to Nathan with a nervous smile and stood there standing in front of the screen door.

"From what I'm observing watching her and her mother go at it, I certainly hope you didn't marry that woman for money—because it looks to me that unless Magda's left it in her will or is carrying the money on her right now, your wife Jeanette isn't going to get a dime," said Kristina, chortling, the effects of the marijuana just now starting to dissipate. Saunders elbowed Kristina and stared at her out of the corner of his eyes, not impressed with the wisecrack.

"Get your ass away from me this minute!" screamed Jeanette to Roscoe. From then on Jeanette changed to English, but Magda continued in Spanish, and Roscoe was failing from his first words to mollify Jeanette. She was in no mood to be mollified; she was only in the mood to be justified.

"The police are coming to arrest your ass for stealing my mother away!" screamed Jeanette.

"Now that most likely is not true at all," said Reyes to Saunders, enjoying his beer. "The police didn't seem all that anxious to go out looking for Roscoe, mainly because most people in town know that Jeanette is one angry woman, the way she'll carry on at times about her being wronged. She pretty much pisses everybody off."

"I agree, she's pissing me off right now and I don't know the woman," said Kristina, now grabbing Saunders's elbow to prevent him from jabbing her again. "Maybe Nathan will get along with her just fine!" she said, chortling again.

"Who's Nathan?" asked Reyes.

"Roscoe's brother—the man sitting in the chair on the porch," said Kristina.

Reyes looked over and saw Nathan sitting in the chair, rocking gently, and Veronica standing on the porch, staring at the trio in the driveway.

"Jeanette does not like black men at all," said Reyes, finishing his second beer, and after standing the empty next to the first beer, reached down and opened beer number three. Now Roscoe wrapped his arm around Magda's waist, and she moved in close to him, appearing grateful for his presence, and wrapped her arm around his waist.

"Half a million dollars—if what she claims is true—a half a million dollars is what Jeanette claims she's got comin' to her from her mother. I should say her mother's mother," said Reyes. "But the money's dirty, Magdalena told Jeanette."

"Dirty?" said Kristina.

"Yeah, dirty, from the way Magdalena's family got the money," said Reyes.

"How did they get the money?" asked Kristina, now completely hooked on the unraveling story of Magdalena, Jeanette, and Roscoe.

Saunders's mind was elsewhere, thinking about the possibility of the police visiting him, asking him if he knew anything about why the furniture he made was being stolen from the homes of those who bought it.

"Magdalena's family are fortune-tellers and channelers, and they swindled a lotta people for their cash. It's the family business, or was until Magdalena's mother died. Magdalena's father got run out of the family a long time ago, so it was just Magdalena and her sisters that was in the business," said Reyes, unconcerned he was finishing his third beer and reaching for a fourth. "All Magdalena's aunts are dead too—so that leaves just Magdalena—and she won't touch the money because she says it's dirty."

"What kind of fortune-tellers? Is Magda a fortune-teller too?" asked Kristina.

"Some kind of sophisticated astrology, Zodiac signs and everything. And—those women convinced everyone they were channeling some mysterious wise group or Council of Beyond or somethin' like that. This Council of Beyond would give them knowledge about the future or somethin' like that," said Reyes. "Jeanette told me her mother refused to be an astrologer anymore, or channeler or whatever they call themselves—she ran off and joined the Air Force."

Reyes continued, “So Jeanette says that if her mother won’t spend the money, then give it to her and she’ll have no problem spending the money of suckers. Money’s money to Jeanette.

“Excuse me, you have any leftovers I could snack on? I’m starvin’—and could I use the bathroom too? Jeanette wouldn’t let us stop to eat, she was so obsessed about coming down here and wanting to ask you questions about where Roscoe was. Her instinct told her he’d be here at your place. I can’t believe it but she was dead right about that, for sure,” said Reyes, shaking his head.

Kristina grabbed his arm and began to lead Reyes to the house, then quickly let go of his arm lest Jeanette see her and start screaming something about taking her man. In fact, Kristina was dying to know more about the astrologers and why Magda thought they were all fakes. Her mood became somber when Reyes called them fakes. *They can’t be fakes! They helped me with my crazy life! I need their wisdom to guide me!* She must talk more with Magda once all this money business settled itself out, she promised herself.

For the first time since she began arguing with her mother, Jeanette paused—to watch Kristina lead her husband Reyes into the house. “Where in the hell are you going, *pendejo*!” she screamed. Reyes flinched as he quickened his pace up the porch steps. Veronica stepped aside to let Reyes and Kristina enter. Now Saunders walked over to the trio arguing in the driveway.

“My name is Saunders Ravel.”

"You're part of this too, *pendejo*," said Jeanette.

Up close Saunders noticed that her anger contorted her unwelcome face into ugliness, like a tattoo to show all the world her rage. Around her waist was a tight-fitting holster holding a small-caliber pistol under the holster strap. "Magda, your daughter is not welcome here at my place." Addressing Jeanette he said, "Mrs. Medina, once your husband is finished in my house, you will leave."

"The police are coming for you too, *pendejo*, for helping this asshole kidnap my mother," said Jeanette, now resting her tiny right hand on her holstered pistol. Saunders slapped her hand away from the holster and unsnapped the holster strap and withdrew the pistol. He checked the safety back to the "on" position and slipped the pistol into his front pocket.

"Certainly being a full-time asshole yourself must be tiring, and especially so after your long drive. We have plenty of food left over from our lunch. Have something to eat before you leave," said Saunders, now stepping in between Jeanette and Roscoe and Magda, who was clearly worn from her daughter's withering tirade. They had been at each other for almost an hour. The day was coming to a close, and as the sun approached the higher, faraway hills, it was evident that a pleasant dusk and evening was to be, complete with bright burnt orange streaks of distant striated clouds, the prime ingredient for a gorgeous desert sunset.

Then from behind them came Nathan's roaring clarion, "Roscoe!" Down the driveway a Cadillac Escalade kicked no dust, with tinting as dark as the black paint. The crunch of loose packed dirt underneath the wide tires was heard over the engine. Roscoe recognized a Louisiana license plate. Magda wrapped her arm around Roscoe's waist and felt his pistol stuffed in his waistband. She withdrew the pistol and held it behind her back as she grabbed her daughter and led her in retreat toward the house. Roscoe made no move to retrieve his pistol from Magda and instructed Saunders to go to the house. Reyes had little intention of hanging around the lunch table by himself and hustled to join the rest on the porch. Upon noticing the pistol in Magda's hand, Veronica withdrew a .32 caliber from her shoulder bag and held it behind her. Joining everyone on the porch, Magda said to Saunders, "Give Jeanette her pistol back now. You don't need to be holding a small pistol when these guys decide to start to do their job."

Saunders didn't want the pistol, but he didn't want Jeanette to go full stupid and start threatening to shoot either.

"Tell your daughter to hide her pistol—see if she can control herself," he said. Although Jeanette swore in Spanish, everyone on the porch knew what she said. Saunders pitied Jeanette, and her mother. Whatever Magda whispered in her daughter's ear appeared to succeed in returning Jeanette to some level of calm. Rage was her favorite emotion, but something stronger than rage overtook her after Magda's whispering.

Out of the Cadillac came a black man dressed in a matching deep blue silk shirt and trousers, wrinkled beyond Roscoe's tolerance of wrinkles, but then he knew they'd been on the road for some time. Still, thought Roscoe, the wrinkles made Clemons Tercel less intimidating, less mean. Roscoe recognized his old high school friend immediately; they were once close as buttons on his silk shirt. And like almost all his high school friends, Clemons Tercel never left Louisiana, for he had little care to see the world other than what he wanted in New Orleans. And when riverboat gambling started back up, Clemons Tercel was there to take it all in. Never quite intelligent enough to run the whole show, he settled in as a debt collector and enforcer, eventually succeeding in finding younger toughs and managing them effectively. He'd been an excellent chief master sergeant, thought Roscoe, knowing that behind the wheel of the Escalade, and yet to show himself, was a much younger tough, waiting for a signal from Tercel to emerge.

"I talked The Man into lettin' me come along and talk to you, seein' how we don't believe your lame-ass brother has nothin' left to pay up. His debts ain't square, Roscoe. And I intend to make his debts square—and you're gonna do your part." No small talk about how long it had been since Clemons and Roscoe had seen each other. No catch-up about their families and kids, since neither had any. No smart-ass remark about Roscoe looking like a fool dressed as a priest, since Clemons had known Roscoe dressed as one of God's main men for some time, and had no issue with Roscoe siding for the Good Lord. They were of equal height, but Clemons carried much more weight on his gut. The untucked shirt didn't help his appearance. Nor did the wrinkles in silk.

"Nathan says his debts are square, Tercel, and you or one of your toughs almost killed him. He'd have died if I hadn't come along, and since it sure seems pure chance I came along,

I've built up some anger towards your savagery. You've sunk pretty damn low, Tercel, to be employed as a savage." Roscoe was calm, but his anger was hurting his heart, he knew it, and tried to let the anger seep out of him. "You cleaned out the garage, took all the cars, and emptied the house my father built."

"Maybe so, but Nathan's debts ain't square, Roscoe. Perhaps you sign over that property and house and The Man will call the debt square," said Tercel.

Now both men were close to each other. Both studied the other's face, and neither showed any fear. Although Roscoe looked ten years younger, his heart was ten years older than the both of them.

"No, you are not gettin' our land or our house."

Now Saunders walked off the porch to join the two men. As Saunders neared Roscoe and Tercel, a younger man, shorter than Tercel but muscled, opened the driver's door and got out to intercept Saunders. He carried a short, steel black rod.

"Roscoe, I'll need these two to leave my property—now," said Saunders, looking at the shorter man approach.

"Not gonna happen, cowboy," said the shorter man. He struck Saunders on the side of the knee with his steel rod, and Saunders collapsed to the ground. Kristina's marijuana high was cut down to earth and she had to kneel in order not to faint. Nathan remained frozen; the sight of the black steel rod nauseated him.

Veronica launched from the porch and began to run toward her father, squeezing her .32 caliber. The sight of an enormous woman running, all of her massiveness lurching up and down with each stride, initially generated a mocking laugh from the short man. But she wasn't stopping and the scream coming from her bright pink red face now caused him to stop laughing. When she raised her pistol the short man felt panic surge through him, knowing his gun was in the Cadillac. Veronica fired once, missing the short man by a wide distance, and fired again, missing him narrowly. He was unable to move because of his disbelief in what he saw, and Veronica ran him over and crushed him with her massiveness. She then got up and rolled onto the short man, who was on the ground, struggling to get to his knees. Veronica sat on his chest and shoved her pistol into his eye. The short man screamed and Veronica's bladder released. Veronica struggled to avoid fainting as she began to hyperventilate. Perspiration was released all over her body, and her body odor was particularly pungent. The short man still gripped the black steel rod, but was unable to wield it. He labored to breathe under her massive weight, fearing suffocation.

Then Nathan leapt off the porch and ran toward Roscoe and Clemons Tercel. Roscoe watched Tercel's eyes widen at seeing Nathan coming toward them, and Roscoe turned around to catch Nathan before he reached Tercel. Saunders got up from the ground, forgetting the pain building in his knee, and went over to his daughter. He could see both she and the short man were panicking, Veronica due to hyperventilating, and the short man due to being suffocated and a pistol barrel plunged into his right eye socket.

“Veronica, get off of him,” directed Saunders in a low voice. He put his arms around her wide, sweat-soaked shoulders and slowly maneuvered her off the short man. He lay there gasping for breath, the black steel rod lying in the dirt, freed from his grip. Saunders picked up the rod and then pried the .32 caliber pistol from his daughter’s hands. He placed the pistol barrel against the short man’s cheek.

“Attempt to move and I will give my daughter back her pistol and she will crush you first and then shoot your balls,” said Saunders.

Roscoe wrestled with Nathan as Nathan struggled to be freed from Roscoe’s grip. Nathan just wanted to hit somebody, anybody. Tercel didn’t move. Sweat stains appeared on his wrinkled silk shirt. Magda and Jeanette stepped off the porch and went over to check on Veronica. Jeanette went and aimed her pistol at the short man, still lying on the ground.

Magda joined Roscoe and pointed her pistol at Clemons Tercel, screaming, “I know what you’re here for. How much you tryin’ to get from Nathan this time?”

Nathan weakened his struggle against Roscoe—in truth, he could easily escape his brother’s hold, but something in him caused him not to escalate his anger and free himself. Roscoe eventually released his brother, not because he wanted to, but because his strength was not enough. His breath shortened and he collapsed to his knees. Kristina watched all the happenings in tears—tears of a fool, she thought. She finally got off her knees and went to Saunders. Reyes, now alone on the porch and still sipping a beer, felt it necessary to go stand by Jeanette. He was still hungry, hoping there were more leftovers. The day was ending, and the desert sky did not disappoint as the setting sun illuminated the streaking high clouds once again in orange and fading pink.

"The debt is between The Man and Nathan Armstrong—got nothin' to do with you," said Tercel, failing to maintain any semblance of a position of intimidation.

"How much?" said Roscoe, slowly standing, attempting to regulate his breathing.

"Fifty thousand," said Tercel.

"That is bullshit!" screamed Nathan.

"With all you took, we are more than square," said Roscoe.

"The Man prefers cash money," said Tercel.

"Then tell The Man to sell the tools and cars and get his goddamned cash money," said Nathan.

Kristina began to take pictures with her cell phone of the short man on the ground soaked in urine holding his eye, and Clemons Tercel, blob stains of sweat dotting his wrinkled silk shirt.

"I don't believe that's gonna work for The Man," said Tercel.

"Oh, I do believe it's gonna work for The Man," said Magda. She raised Roscoe's pistol and shot out the windshield of the Escalade. "And I do believe that I believe Roscoe, who told me he thinks you stole all those expensive tools and cars and didn't tell The Man. I do believe you're tryin' to keep all that for yourself. That's what I believe."

"Clemons, do you think I don't know who The Man is? I know exactly who The Man is. And I'm gettin' hold of him tomorrow to see if he knows you ripped us off and then lied to him you couldn't get the debt from Nathan," said Roscoe, standing not so firm, now holding onto Magda's arm.

"You just gonna continue to piss off The Man, shootin' up his Escalade, not squarin' Nathan's debt," bluffed Tercel, walking over to the short man, kicking him to get up off his ass and back into the Cadillac. "You're not gonna wanna return to your place anymore. We'll know," he said, closing his door.

Roscoe let go of Magda's arm and went over to Tercel and whispered to him. Tercel failed in his attempt to give no reaction to what Roscoe whispered. Tercel then instructed the short man to start up the Cadillac. He did so with born-again enthusiasm. Soon they were gone—as was the day.

Chapter 16

"Are you sure this afternoon was really a total shemozzle, or just part of a much grander shemozzle?" asked Saunders. He had limped over to Roscoe to check on him. Roscoe gave a weak smile. With the help of Nathan they got him to the left porch chair.

"Maybe this afternoon was the location of multiple shemozzles—all colliding," said Roscoe.

Kristina appeared from the kitchen with a tall glass of cold water. "Rapped you pretty good, didn't he? Going to be one helluva bump and bruise on that knee, yes sir," said Roscoe, adding, "Nothing that four aspirin and a few beers can't overcome—for a while anyway." Roscoe accepted the cold water and blew Kristina a kiss. She turned back around and reentered the house to find aspirin and fetch some beers.

"What the hell is a shemozzle?" asked Nathan, the pit of his stomach still holding the nausea induced from this afternoon. Back in Louisiana, both Clemons Tercel and the short man had beaten him.

"You mean schlimazel? God, I hope no one here has schlimazel! I was told it's contagious," said Kristina. Her impish impulse was more often delightfully frivolous than mischievous.

"What the hell kind of language y'all talkin' for Christ sake?" asked Nathan.

"It's Yiddish, and I do believe Christ did not speak Yiddish, or probably cared one way or the other about speaking Yiddish," replied Roscoe, sipping his cold water and staring out in the distance as the vivid sunset passed into a slow approaching dusk.

"Yiddish? I thought that's what Jews speak. You convertin' to a Jew now?" said Nathan, sitting on the step, turning around to face everyone on the porch. At the end of the porch stood Reyes, leaning against the railing and eating a thick sandwich prepared for him by Kristina. In between bites he sipped his sixth beer. He was back to enjoying himself.

"Shemozzle means a big-ass mess of things—confusion and chaos in worst cases," said Roscoe. "And no, I am not convertin' over to be a Jew. I'm stuck with being a Catholic until the end of days."

Saunders had no idea what shemozzle meant. Not so with Kristina, who piped up, "Thank God it's shemozzle and not schlimazel. I most certainly do not need to be anywhere near anyone with a case of schlimazel."

Nathan and Saunders looked to Roscoe for help.

"A persistent streak of bad luck," translated Roscoe. Nathan promptly turned around, his back now to everyone.

"Go check on your daughter, Saunders," reminded Kristina. Magda and Jeanette had taken her inside to clean up and wash and dry her dress and undergarments. When Saunders entered the house he passed Jeanette strutting on her way out—all set to bark commands at Reyes to finish stuffing his mouth and get in the car.

"Polyester does have its moments—fast clean and quick dry," said Magda, indicating

Veronica was finishing dressing in the guest room. Saunders spoke through the guest room door, asking if Veronica needed anything. She replied no, and said she would be out in a minute and then on her way home. She wanted more than anything to be home. Saunders offered to drive her. She thanked him earnestly, and insisted she was fine and wanted to return alone.

Veronica opened the door, her face still flushed but not nearly so as earlier, her breath back to normal, her demeanor touched by sadness.

"Show her your furniture, Dad. If you're going to be a fool, you might as well be a complete fool. Show her your furniture." She offered a weak smile, opened the door wider, and kissed her father. Afterward, Saunders and Veronica went out to the porch. Veronica gave a short wave to everyone and said good-bye. Nathan felt the porch step sag under her weight and watched in silence as Saunders walked Veronica to her car. There would be another time to talk about her actions, or maybe there would never be an inclination to talk about her fierce, pistol-firing charge and crushing of the short man from Louisiana. Regardless, Nathan, along with the others, would never forget the sight.

As Veronica turned her car around and left, Reyes appeared and stood next to Saunders. He waited until Veronica turned onto the main road and then said, "Sir, need to let you know that I'm a deputy sheriff in my town, and after Jeanette stirred everything up about her mother being kidnapped and all, they started checking up on you—since Roscoe was staying with you for a while. In the course of their investigation it appears they came across information that someone was breaking into homes in a couple states besides Nebraska and stealing furniture, but leaving an envelope full of cash to apparently cover the cost of the furniture. Damn strange behavior, as I said earlier—ask anyone—damn strange behavior to be sure. They think it's your furniture, furniture that you built. Just thought you should know. Someone may come around asking questions about the whole matter.

"…And thanks for the beers. Jeanette didn't want me to say anything and I'm sure I'll hear about it all the way home. That's the way that shit goes, I guess." Reyes handed Saunders his last empty beer bottle. "Don't worry; she'll be driving the first leg," he said. "Pretty exciting life you lead here in Arizona, Mr. Ravel." Reyes smiled, envious of more such diversions.

"Tell Roscoe that nobody in my town thinks for a minute Jeanette's mother was kidnapped."

Jeanette had been waiting in the car, occasionally revving the engine. Reyes got in and they turned around in haste and departed. Saunders smelled oil from their car. It needed prompt attention, he thought.

Back on the porch, Kristina was telling everyone her version of how she and Saunders met. How she fell madly in love with him on the flight line long before he could be bothered at all to even say hello, and how someone, unknown for sure to this day—but she had a few good leads—felt the need to inform leadership of an intimate relationship between a lieutenant and an enlisted crew chief, how leadership threatened them both, Saunders with an Article 15 that would end his career before it started, and taking away her appointment to the Air Force Academy, which, by the way, she admitted to never telling Saunders about the appointment until after the whole shemozzle.

"Honey, there surely is more to your story than that. Don't for a second think I believe otherwise," said Magda, standing behind Roscoe's chair, arms around his shoulders. Kristina pretended to be unfazed by Magda calling her out. That's all she was prepared to say about Saunders.

"It's really about that time, Saunders, you know, in fact, it's past that time for you to take Kristina over to that building and show her what you need to show her," said Roscoe, pointing to the building where all the furniture was hidden. That morning, Saunders had made up his mind about the furniture.

"I've got to lie down, baby. I'm not all that well," said Roscoe, reaching up and holding Magda's arms wrapped around him.

"Nathan, help me take your brother to the RV," said Magda. Nathan bounced up off the porch step and together he and Magda assisted Nathan to the RV.

"And Nathan, after you take care of your brother, I need a favor from you," said Saunders.

"Your knee must hurt like hell," said Kristina.

"You make me forget that pain exists."

Saunders embraced her, standing on the bottom step as Kristina stood on the porch, now equal in stature. He then held her hand and led her to the building where the ex-handyman kept his larcened gifts. Kristina let go of his hand and ran back into the house. Saunders waited, unconcerned of the sureness of her return. Minutes later she popped the front screen door open, a bottle of wine and glasses in her hands, and rejoined Saunders as he unlocked the storage building door and turned on the lights. Only the room lights could be seen leaking through the blinded windows. Saunders wasted no time pulling off the tarps and piling them in the corner. He had rearranged all the pieces the night before, in the order in which they were made. Saunders became very much aware of his age at that moment—in relation to the purpose of his creations, and the acts of larceny to retrieve them—all for this occasion. An opportunity, no, it was *the* opportunity to take himself and Kristina from the past and imprint the present—in order to find a place in the future that held the both of them in the same place, at the same time, for the rest of their time. The pinnacle of foolishness, thought Saunders, now with a wide smile and a dominant air of supreme contentment. His daughter was absolutely right, to give her great credit. But, in truth, Saunders had already thought through the entire foolish, yes, he admitted, ridiculous scenario. A few months back, in his tiny RV kitchen Saunders dropped to his knees when he discovered Kristina was leading the theater restoration in the same Nebraska town. The serendipity brought him to tears. It then became an easy and welcome task of nudging Kristina down to Arizona. She always let him nudge her toward some unexpected excitement, just as he always allowed her equal rights to do the same. And now they were here, under the high fluorescent lights of his storage room, not ideal for an actual showcasing of his works, but, in this bright room, the lighting more suited to a hospital waiting room, Saunders presented Kristina the efforts of his best abilities.

"I'm a terrible letter writer," said Saunders, standing next to the first piece of furniture, a hutch of such overwhelming thickness of dark woods, a strong and noble safe house for all that is kept, all that is precious to one's identity—to one's being.

"No you're not! I loved your letters. I kept every one. To this day I have them—as part of my treasure," said Kristina, overwhelmed with the presence of all the pieces of furniture created by Saunders, and stolen back by Saunders.

"No, I don't have it in me to write what I feel. I'm not okay with that, but I know what I know," replied Saunders. He accepted a glass of red wine from Kristina. "The time I invested in bringing these pieces to life was my willing labor of love—love of creating with wood, for a love that I could never shake, or fly away from, or bury so deep I'd forget. I have a memory of you as long as eternity. You are inside most waking thoughts, whether I want you present or not, not always causing my mind mischief like you so love to do, but doing your damnedest to try. I'm okay with that—that is who you are, and that is one of many stars in the constellation of my galaxy of love for you.

"So, displayed before you are my love letters to you. Letters I can't write, but I can make."

With the sweeping gesture of a grand master of the grandest ceremony, Saunders announced, "I present to you my climactically foolish collection, my sentimental pursuit of telling you once again that no woman has ever altered my being to the intoxicatingly vibrant extent as you. I love how you alter the prism in which I view life, I mean—I don't know if I could view life in another way that I'd find joy in being so unsettled. Or should I say, I don't want to view life in any other way. And after realizing what this collection actually signified to me, I had no choice but to commit the three acts of larceny to reclaim them—in order to present them to you.

"I didn't think I could go through with the final theft—and only until I knew you were the last was I able to go through with it. So, in total, I present my love letters to you—only mine are carved in wood." And then Saunders weaved in slow motion in and around each piece, caressing them with a light, sweeping touch.

"Call me off-kilter, call me a nostalgic old fool—that's what my daughter believes me to be—I care little what I'm called."

Kristina only took one small sip of wine. She put her glass down next to the bottle she brought. She was fearful of dropping them both, for her trembling felt impossible to control. Saunders approached her and in his arms he felt her body in motion.

"I request you get to know these pieces now—because in a short while they'll have to go," whispered Saunders, kissing her forehead. And he left her alone amongst the creations he spent nine months making—working uncountable hours—as long as necessary to complete them, because all the pieces were in him and had to be released.

Saunders left Kristina and went outside and met Nathan halfway between the big garage where the RV was parked and the building holding his pieces of furniture.

"They all have to go. I need your help getting all my pieces out and placed right here," said Saunders, pointing down to the ground beneath them. Nathan looked at his hands and flexing his fingers brought pain. He agreed to help.

Upon entering the storage building, they found Kristina lying on the dining room table, slowly moving her hand across the surface. Saunders wanted to watch her until dawn. With no hesitation, Saunders and Nathan started with the heaviest piece—the hutch—and ten or so feet at a time, pausing to rest and rub their backs, they lifted it outside. It was built as three interlocking pieces; otherwise, Saunders could never have stolen it by himself. More time was spent carefully emptying its contents than stealing it on that early morning of the theft.

Darkness was now with them and the stars were in divine adornment in their cosmic arrangement across the endless vastness of the sky. The sound of crickets raged. During the move Saunders asked Nathan about how his brother was faring.

"Hangin'…real tired but hangin'. He's got a good woman in Magda, for sure," said Nathan.

Inside, Kristina was sitting in every chair, talking to each one as if it were her children, telling them the secrets to a happy life and kissing the high back and then settling in on the next one.

As they entered, Kristina pleaded, "Take the table last!" She was lying back down on it. She did not question where the pieces were going. All that remained was the table. Kristina had poured another glass of wine and held the long stem in her hand next to her cheek. Saunders motioned to Nathan to step back outside.

"I want to touch and smell the beautiful woods you use, and to sense the strength of your work," said Kristina. She was still, her eyes closed.

"I wanted you to have all the pieces—and keep them until you no longer felt you wanted them," said Saunders, kneeling down, facing Kristina.

Her eyes now open and looking at Saunders, she replied, "I would never want to ever part with them. Thank you, Saunders. Thank you." Saunders kissed Kristina's cheek and left her and went to find Nathan and check up on Roscoe.

Nathan emerged from the big garage where the RV was parked and said to Nathan, "Magda says Roscoe is all set to die, but that don't seem to be happenin' just quite yet. They're havin' a conversation—I guess that's what you'd call it—a lot of things goin' back and forth between them right now."

"Thanks for the hint, Nathan," said Saunders. He asked Nathan if he would arrange the furniture pieces tightly together, and afterward to get the other materials from the garage storage cabinets that he mentioned to him earlier and bring them outside.

"You got a real good eye for makin' furniture. And I can surely tell you care about the smallest details. That I can relate to and that I can appreciate," said Nathan, adding, "and I appreciate how you may feel inside your gut at having to do what you think you gotta do."

Nathan and Saunders exchanged small head nods, and Saunders went and knocked on the RV door and entered.

"Is she still lyin' on the table?"

Walking away from Nathan, Saunders nodded again, saying, "She'll fall asleep. And that's just fine."

As he entered, Magda announced to Roscoe in a soft voice, "It's Saunders." Roscoe was lying down on the bed, his black shirt and priest collar removed, lying down against two propped-up pillows in his white tank top T-shirt, still with his trousers and shoes on. Roscoe lifted his hand to caress Magda's fingers as she positioned the cold compress on Roscoe's forehead.

"I've been trying to tell her, Saunders—trying to tell her that who wants to die a death stretched long and laid out for strangers to see, because I know in the end it's going to be my mind wrestling with being no longer, and it's a wrestling match where I know the outcome, even though I don't—you know? I know I don't know really what the outcome is going to be like, but I know the outcome is I'm no longer *here*," said Roscoe, slapping the bed.

"I'm ready to try to grasp the impact of that moment at death. I know death most certainly is not an illusion but a bona fide fact so much different than living—and that excites me now. You know—we believe we can masquerade until the end of days, and then death rips off your mask and throws it so far you can never get it back…and you can't ever rip off the mask that death wears."

Magda had heard Roscoe go on about death earlier before Saunders walked in. "In case you hadn't noticed, death is on his mind," she said to Saunders with a small smile. "The problem is death ain't ready to pay him a permanent visit, and he's getting frustrated he can't go out on a funeral pyre that evidently you're building for him.

"And he says he loves me to death. Well—I'm tellin' him he's going to have to love me for as long as we got together in this life—so I don't know if he's not ready to accept that and maybe that's why he's talkin' about funeral pyres and such," said Magda, now holding Roscoe's hand in hers. Beneath the cold compress Roscoe was smiling and nodding to himself.

Watching Magda and Roscoe, Saunders knew he was witnessing the best that love could be, as if he had been presented an insight through witness. Saunders was filled with nervous but joyous excitement, knowing the feeling would soon flee, but the residual effect upon him would remain—and that was the knowledge and memory of a manifestation of joy.

"Right now I don't need to pray to God. I think I'm doin' all right by dying now," said Roscoe, removing the cold compress and tossing it at Saunders.

"But you're not dying now—according to Magda, and I am learning to believe what Magda says," said Saunders, taking the compress and tossing it into the kitchen sink. Small wonder Magda's family got into the fortune-telling and channeling business, he thought. An ability to persuade, that combination of delivering a look, conveying body English, the perfect tone, just the right words, listening to and observing responses from those who want to hear what they want to hear. *Easy to see, if you can make money off that ability, why not? But the "why not" answered itself in a moment,* he thought, *obviously.*

"The furniture is being prepped now, and I'm not waiting. That means you're going to have to wait for another time to die," said Saunders. He grabbed Roscoe's right foot and shook it briefly.

In Kristina's mind, prior to dozing off on the fine dining room table—of appealing aspect and rectangular shape, with an intricate parquetry of three different types of mahogany, and thick gate legs inspired by the English furniture makers of the seventeenth century—she finally dismissed the competing notion that she was almost as attracted to his acts of larceny as his furniture. She thought that the planning of the larcenies and the acts themselves, especially with scant forethought of consequence, served as a trigger for an intense emotion that in turn validated her pursuit of emotional experiences as the fundamental essence of defining what it meant to live a true life. She was entranced with the idea of deliberate denial of rational consideration in decisions in order to be led to unexpected outcomes that further generated other intense emotional experiences, building upon themselves to create a truer self. And her self-creation would be held up as testament to a life lived second by second—not as experiences came to her but as she came to them. She thought of herself as an offering to circumstance to affect consequence. That was to be her legacy upon the world. Regardless of her legacy, she thought, she absolutely *loved* the idea of lovely furniture serving as love letters.

Before Saunders woke her, he watched her sleep. She had curled up tight, her sleeveless summer dress failing to keep her warm. The blanket in his arms was from the foot of his guest bed. As much as he wanted to cover her and let her sleep, he instead woke her in a soft voice, whispering into her ear only what he could ever say to Kristina, and no other. Saunders released the glass stem from her fingers, half a glass still remaining, and two tiny flies zigzagged away, the mysterious kind that can always find an unattended wineglass and can never resist a sip. He wrapped her in the blanket and assisted her outside and onto one of his porch chairs and returned to help Nathan move the table outside. From the big garage came Magda and Roscoe, and they joined Kristina on the porch, now with two added chairs from the side kitchen deck Nathan had helped to move. Onto four dining room chairs Saunders and Nathan lifted and set the four legs of the dining room table. All the other pieces, except the Mission-style armoire that had the same intricate mahogany parquetry on its doors as the dining room table, were placed on top of the table or under the lifted table.

Saunders was only focused on what he committed to doing next, nothing else. Not why he built all the beautiful pieces, not why he sold all his pieces, not why he stole back all his pieces. He had reflected on all those *whys* many, many times over. The air was desert still, complete with cricket cacophony.

Five billion galaxies valiantly tried to light the blackness of night. With three long kitchen matches aflame, Saunders filled their infinitesimally small piece of the universe with the brilliant and soon to be crying flames of his love letters set in wood. And at the time the flames peaked nearly four stories high, all the furniture raging in fire, Kristina dropped from her chair and collapsed on the porch in screaming tears. Saunders remained standing near the pyre, now dangerously hot, a cathartic sweat pouring from him. He could not hear Kristina cry, but her cries joined the crying of the wood burning to ash. Nathan bent down to try to console Kristina, but she would have none of it.

"I know you wanted this to be your funeral pyre, and don't you for a second tell me otherwise," whispered Magda to Roscoe. "That's too damn easy, baby, too damn easy. You're going to live with an old woman, just as I'm going to live with you—and you will see a damned doctor, and you will marry me, and we will make a go of it, for better and worse, until God is done with us living on this Earth. Consider your priestly days over. I demand some damned lovin' from a man of this world—not the next."

Roscoe laughed out loud, got up out of his chair, kissed Magda hard, and went to join Saunders. He was looking too damn pathetic standing there by himself, thought Roscoe. Nathan followed. The porch had become suddenly a lonely place that he wanted no part of.

Picking Kristina up from the porch, Magda whispered, "Now, honey, you two have got to get yourselves squared away on what you're gonna do about each other. You know—it's in my blood that I have a prediction for you and that damned handsome tall man out there standin' like a big fool—way too close to those flames. But fortune-tellin' is pure bullshit that smells like milk and honey—and please don't go gravitating around any huckster who claims they're channeling some spirit from the *other* world. My God, woman, my family did that for a living. This *is* the only world. And whatever lies next nobody has ever seen, and those who claim they know otherwise are liars of the worst kind.

"And if you're gonna change your name to Huguette, or whatever name I heard you call yourself, then commit—and quit namby-pambyin' around about whatcha gonna do. I do hate to see a woman with all you got be mesmerized by some fantasy of who you think you are. Let a little humility into your windows, honey—just a bit now and then. Before you know it, you'll open up all the windows in your soul. This is from one cocky woman who finally let the windows open.

"Sorry if I sound so damned preachy, honey—but get on with it—and soon. That's the fortune-teller in me—*tellin'* you." Magda smiled, hugging Kristina, who became stiff in her acceptance of embrace, and she left Kristina alone on the porch to join Saunders, Roscoe, and Nathan next to the funeral pyre that Roscoe believed he wanted to be his. Magda thought, *If only I could have said all those words to my own daughter once again.* She had done so, for a few years, until she gave up, and at that point Magda believed she stopped being a mother to her daughter. But she never did stop being a mother—as Roscoe had told her many times. Jeanette stopped being a daughter.

His mind far from still, Saunders felt ensconced in the heat of the pyre, and within the heat, he felt his dreams of what he would do next were being forged. After his military service, he set out to determine whatever paths he traveled by his own choosing, not to be bound by any hierarchical restraint—for he had spent enough years within a hierarchy. Being a handyman offered him plenty of options, and in the beginning Saunders was a handyman. He performed handyman work in the small town where his wife grew up and wanted to return; not only to care for her mother, but to reacquaint herself with her town and her brother and sister and cousins and friends of her youth she left behind who either remained or returned much earlier in their lives. Saunders's wife liked her hometown, and always did. But that was not Saunders's life. And his wife told him the military life was not hers. The bond of marriage seemed to be weaker than the bond to a way of life that formed both of them, two very different ways of life that entailed seemingly incompatible approaches and perspectives toward one way of life or the other. Saunders's wife told him he never gave himself a chance to live in her small town, unlike her, who worked very hard to adapt to the three-year assignments in one location and then off to another location, each assignment equally foreign as the previous. At first his wife encouraged him to set up a woodworking shop and build furniture in her town, but he refused. Saunders believed her small town was attractive to *them*, but he felt no attraction to their way of life. He perceived their town as a hierarchical structure of its own that necessitated conformance, and an acceptable level of obedience to their way of how things were and were going to remain. Saunders admitted to himself later he built his perception of the small town as a hierarchical entrapment so he could justify his decision to accept the job in Nebraska servicing the fast-food restaurants his old buddy from the Air Force owned in partnership with two others. The job was for two months but extended to six, in part because the partners underestimated the work to be done, and in part because Saunders did not want to return to his wife's hometown. And the longer he stayed away, the clearer his dream became on what he believed he needed to do. The clearer his realization was that whatever kind of love bound him decades ago to his wife—that love was barely recognizable anymore, and the depth to which love was supposed to grow never occurred, perhaps by the accumulated fatigue of knowing his love for her could only go so deep, and then would hit an impenetrable layer—of what? The human certainty that some beliefs wither the innateness of desire? Desire of what? Saunders would not admit to himself what the "what" might be. He had spent too many waking hours over the many years thinking about his marriage, and thinking about why he spent so much time questioning his marriage. The years and years of questioning had always been worrisome. And for some years it troubled Saunders to think that he was just another selfish asshole in a life where selfish assholes seemed commonplace. And now, in the confessional heat of the pyre of his own creation, built upon his own creations, Saunders realized he had at least as much disdain for feeling so commonplace—as Roscoe disdained the same, and Kristina likewise. And as the pyre raged on Saunders thought about obligations and duties that hierarchical institutions he had been part of and that which he willingly remained to be part of had instilled in him, and were permanent precepts of his being. He was now drenched in piteous sweat, and he questioned himself whether it was his duty and obligation to even dream at all.

Chapter 17

Losing one hundred and fifty pounds meant that Veronica's skin had stretched to such an extreme that its draping folds, free of the constraints of clothing, were grotesque. The infections after Veronica's second surgery to remove the additional fifty pounds of excess skin were still worrisome and painful, but she was undeterred. Her grotesqueness was cut away, and she cried many nights, realizing that some of her physical beauty had returned.

"I *am* going with you," she told her father as he finished packing his RV for the trip. She no longer labored in walking. Her knees and ankles no longer ached under weight. Prior to starting her weight loss regimen, Veronica's medical leave of absence had been approved. But as she began to organize herself during the summer before the new school year, the new school administration released her.

Over the past year and a half since the furniture burning, Saunders had prayed his daughter would not make an enemy of him. He had decided that his first duty and obligation was to support the promise she had finally made to herself. There were a few occasions of such overwhelming self-doubt as to continuing on with her weight loss program, which resulted in enraged screaming bouts and tears poured for fear of failing. For some of the time, Veronica's mother stayed with her to keep her company and offer support. But Veronica's grandmother on her mother's side needed full-time care, and Veronica's mother seemed torn between the two. On the third trip out to Arizona,

Veronica's mother expressed deep relief in Veronica's adamant decision that she return home and care for her own mother. Although Veronica and her mother loved each other, there was mutual relief both could return to the lives they inhabited. Rather than give them all away, and at the same location where Saunders set his furniture ablaze, Veronica chose to burn all her old clothes. The burning brassieres gave them both hysterical fits.

No one recognized Veronica anymore, and she could not be more pleased. The housing market had finally recovered from the terrible crash, and Veronica sold her house in Chandler and moved in with her father. Over the course of her weight loss regimen, she reinvigorated his online furniture store (again under the name Pascal Bonaventure) and became her father's wood supply purchaser.

As Saunders and Veronica drove down the long dirt driveway toward the highway, Veronica recalled the day the woman came to ask her father questions about the pieces of furniture stolen from two homes in Texas and Oklahoma. She was younger than her father, medium height and slim as a long distance runner. Veronica also recalled with clarity that the woman was attractive—her father called her handsome. If Veronica had not been such an addictive reader, she might have taken his description as pejorative. It was the woman's lean face and square jawline. The woman investigator asked for a tour around the place, and Saunders offered no hesitation, and together they visited both the big garage where the RV was parked and where the wood studio was housed as well as the storage room where Saunders kept the built furniture. The place of the furniture burning one month prior to the investigator's visit lay underneath the investigator's car, all the ashes having been removed and scattered into the Verde River the morning after the pyre raged.

"You evidently have a strange, secret admirer of your furniture, Mr. Ravel," said the investigator. Saunders nodded, saying nothing. "A very strange thing," she said as the two of them stood next to her big red SUV. "You know a woman who goes by Huguette Sands?" She placed her reflective aviator sunglasses back on, and Saunders worked to keep his unruffled demeanor intact, allowing himself only a moment's glimpse of relief that the investigator was winding up her questioning. All her previous questions about online customers and inquiries of prospective customers were answered by Veronica, who had handled the original transactions. She had told the investigator all those old email and phone inquiries had been deleted.

"I do know her," said Saunders.

"You know her real name?" asked the investigator.

"Kristina."

"Well, Huguette, or Kristina—you have to admit she's tuned to a wavelength all her own, and proud of it, too," said the investigator. "She wouldn't let me see the furniture of yours she bought off a real nice homey couple in Nebraska. But she tells me she still has her pieces in some storage garage. Evidently the thief either was satisfied with what he had or may still be looking to steal again—or maybe didn't want to bother with Huguette because she might be the type to sit up at night naked with a shotgun, waiting for someone to try to steal from her. That name—Huguette—odd, but sure seems to fit her."

The investigator laughed in reminiscence of her encounter, and Saunders suspected she had perhaps fallen under Huguette's spell, if only briefly. What the investigator did not say was how Huguette reacted when talking about Saunders. *Talk about being all over the wavelength frequency spectrum*, she recalled after her visit with Huguette. She knew she had to meet the man who affected Huguette in such a visible way. For a brief period she suspected Huguette to be the larcenist. "Don't you think it's strange to break into a house, steal only certain pieces of furniture, and leave an envelope of cash—more than enough to cover the cost of the purchase?" asked the investigator, opening the door to her SUV.

"I do," said Saunders, repeating, "I do indeed."

Out of habit, she gave Saunders her card, never expecting or hoping to hear from him again. *More to this whole story.* Just like so many of her investigations, she thought. *But this story I want to leave a mystery, and let it go at that.* She drove away. She loved mysteries, especially those that remained so, and this one in particular ranked very high on her list of preserved mysteries.

Upon seeing the investigator drive off, Veronica stepped off the porch and joined her father, the midday sun overhead. As ridiculous as all that had been, it was also ridiculous to be outside in this heat, recalled Veronica.

Now, smiling while looking out the RV passenger window, she shook her head, remembering what she said to her father on that ridiculously hot afternoon.

"Dad, next time you become overcome with such notions, write letters instead—and know once you send them you're not supposed to see them anymore, because they're no longer yours, but someone else's."

They were now off to Louisiana, again.

Chapter 18

Unlike Roscoe, who believed some government or industrial agency was monitoring everything and so chose to keep only disposable cell phones to communicate—and only when he thought absolutely necessary, Saunders, on the other hand, couldn't care less what agency was monitoring him. He had left a message the day prior on Abbot William Mercer's office phone that he and Veronica were arriving the next afternoon. And as a fellow career military man would expect, Saunders found Abbot Mercer, Colonel, MD, US Army retired, standing outside the main building, waiting for them, with Magda by his side. Had Saunders known the Abbot's religious order, he'd have also added that to his title.

The afternoon was hazy and hot. The sticky humidity was an unwelcome shock to the skin compared to Arizona's bone-dry days. Abbot Mercer gave a gracious welcome to them both while Magda went to embrace Veronica, giving her a look of high praise for her radically changed appearance. Saunders hugged Magda in silence. Magda led Veronica inside the main building and then on to her guest room. Abbot Mercer assisted Saunders with their luggage and after dropping off Veronica's bags, Saunders followed the Abbot to a guest room. Saunders again smelled the mustiness inside, not overwhelming as when he first detected it the previous year, but noticeable in the absence of such an odor in Verde Valley. The transition from the Arizona desert to the Texas plains and into the piney green forests of East Texas and Louisiana never failed to capture

Saunders's attention. To get his fill of green he diverted north of Houston and through Davy Crockett, Angelina, and Sabine National Forests before joining Interstate 49 south, to Interstate 10, and on into Wharton, Louisiana. Veronica didn't mind at all. She had not been out of Arizona since the last time they went to Louisiana, a little over a year ago. Last year, for Roscoe and Magda's wedding, they flew into New Orleans and rented a car. This time, her father told her they were taking a road trip in the RV.

Her father had to go for an hour run after they completed the hookup at each RV park. Then the pushups and sit-ups that seemed to never end. Veronica was not ready to begin running, although in the mornings her father would accompany her for a half-hour brisk walk around. Veronica never found any enjoyment in exercise, but she began to enjoy walking, not because of the benefits of physical exertion, but because walking gave her mind an excuse to wonder about experiences she never would have dreamed of—as obese as she had been.

Late that evening, after Saunders and Veronica retired for the night, Jeanette arrived, without Reyes, who was wisely now her ex-husband. And though Magda was very tired, she wanted very much to stay up awhile longer to visit with Jeanette, who refused to attend the wedding the year prior but decided to come for Roscoe's funeral. Her daughter just wanted to go to her room, unpack, and take a cool shower. Jeanette missed everything, thought Magda, as she went to her room for the night. She missed the wedding celebration and the hours of dancing—every resident of the abbey was out on the dance floor (the abbey's cafeteria was transformed to host the wedding reception—a first and last wedding reception location according to Abbot Mercer, who enjoyed himself late into the evening). She missed all the stories about Roscoe and Nathan's upbringing (Magda told a few select stories of her past, mostly true, but thoroughly sanitized for even the best of friends). Jeanette missed the story Magda told about why she selected the assisted living home near her daughter—her daughter from a man she thought she knew. He was an insecure man, a man whose facade was so convincing, even to Magda, with her natural ability, as well as being taught by her own family to read a person to their depths. She let herself be blinded, admitted Magda, because he was so damned handsome and seemed so sure of himself. At her age! She knew better! And in a champagne-filled moment, with Magda and Roscoe's special wedding guests all at the same table, she confessed the story of how she convinced the assisted living administrators and doctors on staff that she was dying. So easy to convince those who want to hear what they want to hear, she thought. She would have told Jeanette—again—in front of all their friends that she moved to Nebraska to give them another chance to reconcile. But Magda could not find the words her daughter wanted to hear because there were no words that would ever satisfy Jeanette. And Jeannette missed the story of Magda finally admitting to Roscoe she was not dying. Everyone believed Magda when she said Roscoe was humbled rather than angered because he knew immediately that her admission meant Roscoe passed her test and she had chosen him for life.

Magda terminated the assisted living contract and gave the remainder of the money, seventy-five thousand dollars, to Jeanette. Jeanette wanted what she believed she was owed, reparation for a life that not only was unfulfilled, but was hollowed out by hate, so that only a brittle shell remained. And she was not yet thirty years old. Magda knew the money wouldn't satisfy her, and she was right. She wanted more, and Magda knew that what her daughter thought she wanted was nothing more than a false want, a numbing agent to diminish her pain of rage. Magda knew Jeanette came to celebrate the death of Roscoe, not mourn. The celebration of a step further toward the satisfaction of being witness to her mother's suffering. If Jeanette was going to lose out, then so must everyone else.

Turning out her lamp, Magda lay in her bed and stared out the window, praying her prayers for her daughter and Nathan, and then for those she very much loved. She talked to Roscoe as she would always do in the years ahead—and she fell asleep while waiting to see the brilliant full moon appear from the towering clouds of night.

Nathan too was waiting for the full moon to reappear as he sat in his pickup next to the concrete slab that was to serve as Roscoe's and Magda's new home foundation. Since Roscoe's death Nathan liked to come out to this spot next to a lazy stream on their property, a quarter mile past the house where Nathan lived, on the border of the abbey's property. He also talked to Roscoe, reciting the promise he made that day he died. It was as if that was what Roscoe was waiting for—waiting for Nathan to promise him he'd set himself on a new path and not look back, because there was little that looking back would accomplish anymore. *Besides*, thought Nathan, *I'm carrying every bit of my life with me as I go on anyway.*

Nathan was in the grease pit in his garage draining the oil from a faded sky-blue '56 Mercury Montclair hardtop that they'd found one week earlier over in Natchez. The Abbot had to go fetch the car and pay for them because the old widow who kept it enshrined in her single-car garage said her late husband would never sell it to a black man, no matter how much he offered. Roscoe and Nathan rented and drove the flatbed to transport the car, pretending to work for the Abbot. The car had not been driven since the day the owner died, twenty-five years ago.

That day Roscoe was helping Nathan change the oil. They had worked for the past week going over every inch of the Montclair to get her drive-worthy. All that was required was replacing the battery, one headlight that they had put on order, and all the hoses and fluids. It only required five minutes of inspection to see that the owner from Natchez had maintained the Mercury Montclair as if it was part of his family. Then they were going for a long ride to see what the Montclair could still do.

The oil can slipped from Roscoe's hands and rolled into the grease pit, oil gurgling out in spurts. Nathan yelled at his brother but he never heard him, as Roscoe fell to the floor dead of a heart attack. He lay on the floor, his face level with Nathan's as he stood in the grease pit. Roscoe's eyes were still open and his apparent gaze froze Nathan in place. The garage radio was off and the only sound was the gurgling oil from the dropped can onto Nathan's boots. What no one would ever know was how long Nathan lay curled up against his brother, releasing all the tears he never had the courage to release, and singing aloud the three hymns he could still recall from his early childhood, the hymns of lonesome longing for forgiveness and redemption and better days ahead in the footsteps of Jesus.

Magda, in her depth of grief three nights after Roscoe died, lay awake, and suddenly she became thankful that Roscoe had died in the presence of his brother instead of herself. It was Nathan who needed Roscoe's last moments in life, far more than Magda, who was fully secure in her love for the man who finally had the courage to marry her. It was that night that Magda was finally able to sleep.

Nathan wasn't sure how long he'd continue to come out to the place where his brother and wife were to build their house, but he was pretty sure after tomorrow evening he wouldn't be visiting as much. He got out of his pickup and began unloading the wood, a ladder, and a toolbox from the flatbed. Within the beams of his headlights, Nathan constructed a high pyre, hammering into the night and singing the only hymns he could remember from childhood.

On this same night Saunders lay awake, his head turned to the window, watching the clouds take their ever-loving sweet time transiting the sky, the full moon illuminating their billowy passing, and then in clear skies, the moon reflecting the brilliant sun in bright evening fashion over the abbey and surrounding land. He could not make up his mind whether he believed

Kristina would return for Roscoe's funeral, regardless if it was to be a party of celebration. She had replied to Magda's email of Roscoe's death, sending her tears and deepest condolences. She did attend the wedding the year prior, driving all night from Georgia, together with two whippets that she loved but equally loved to complain about. She adored the fact they were sight hounds rather than led by their nose. Visual was paramount to Kristina, she proclaimed aloud at midnight of the wedding reception. She wore a canary yellow short dress and was adorned in silver bracelets, threatening to look as beautiful as Magda, who was indeed stunning—dancing with Roscoe under the disco ball next to Kristina—who was in the mutually grateful arms of Saunders. On the dance floor Kristina announced in a champagne flourish that her loss of sight would be her demise.

As much as they wanted to spend all their time together, Kristina and Saunders had not seen each other since her visit to Arizona, when the convergence of all related happenings arced. She left Arizona in a cloud of soft drama, threatening not to think about Saunders and his maddening, evasive ways. Rolling down her window as she drove away, she called him a coward for not deciding on certain things. Kristina kept up appearances by claiming she was deceived. Both knew that was bunk. They kept in touch via smart aleck texts, snippets of email to exchange calendar events of their lives, and voice messages that either begged a response or attempted to be the beginning of a threatening finality. As Saunders recalled it all once again, he smiled, knowing Roscoe would want it to be at his funeral where they come together to get what Roscoe described as their "sweet-ass, honky, uptight shit together."

The next morning Kristina arrived at noon—with her whippets. That evening Roscoe's ashes were scattered in two places—at the site of Percy Standing, the man who steered him onto the path that Roscoe felt suited for and loved, and atop the funeral pyre built by Nathan. Considering the magnitude of her loss, Magda was in the best company she could imagine; Abbot Mercer being the funeral presider and evening companion. Atop the funeral pyre Nathan placed a portion of Roscoe's ashes, and the pyre illuminated the overcast sky so it appeared like a soft gray blanket that invited those who needed comfort and warmth.

At his wedding, Roscoe confided to Saunders that he wanted crepuscular rays beaming in a wide fan array at his funeral as if to announce his future place of residence, but even he admitted that was a bit over the top. Not so, said Kristina, overhearing the story told by Saunders that night at the funeral pyre. She believed it should be fitting for all humanity; as absolute was each person's dignity, so should their sendoffs be absolutely over the top.

After the pyre was extinguished, the five returned to the abbey, where they joined Veronica and Jeanette. Both decided not to attend the funeral for different reasons, but felt the same reason to be together and talk. Jeanette wasn't sure she liked Veronica, but she had almost reverential respect for her taking down that asshole short man in Arizona who thought he was a tough guy. She'd never forget that sight.

They all gathered in Abbot Mercer's large private study, in a sphere safe from all distress, within candlelight and the music of the great Al Green, Roscoe's all-time favorite singer, and they drank Courvoisier with an ice cube, in honor of Roscoe's favorite drink of sophistication and pontification. Veronica had Jeanette smiling, and although Jeanette never would approach her mother that evening, she did give thought to saying something respectful to Magda the next morning, before she returned to Nebraska. Nathan smelled of burnt pine and could not be happier, standing near a table lamp, wholly immersed in his own world, and promising Roscoe to drive the '56 Mercury Montclair straight to the Gulf Shores tomorrow morning and have a dip in the hot salt water.

Kristina, after talking with everyone that evening, and especially Nathan—the two had an explicable bond—they both loved marijuana—finally decided to stop ignoring Saunders and joined him as he looked out the grand window and admired the stunning full moon. He knew she would come.

"I need a very, very skilled carpenter, capable of creating some delicate pieces and finery of past ages. Just the kind of work you so love. It's at least a three-month project in Fargo. In the middle of winter. Are you interested? I can be very demanding."

"And you do know I take your eighth chair with me wherever I go." Saunders wondered how long that habit would last.

Unconcerned the Abbot was near, Kristina said, "And now it's time to tell you that it was Roscoe who told me you were going to take your furniture back. I didn't know why, but I just had to be part of the conspiracy!" She laughed, stomping her foot in approval of her actions. Saunders knew this, because Roscoe told him later. He smiled and stomped his foot and joined in her laughter and approval.

Abbot Mercer looked about his study at all present. He felt he was inside an infinite sphere of a limited life and then laughed to himself at the comforting paradox—and swore to himself he intended to fill it with gratitude, knowing it could never be filled in this life. But he gave thanks all the same.

Made in United States
North Haven, CT
01 December 2022